GHOSTS OF THE BIG SANDY RIVER

Ghosts of the Big Sandy River

Edward C. Hartshorn

Ghosts of the Big Sandy River
©2020
All rights reserved.

ISBN: 978-1-953198-00-6 (paperback)
ISBN: 978-1-953198-01-3 (eBook)

Editors: Dennis Doty. Kelly Sohner.
Formatting: Kari Holloway
Cover Design: John F. Green
CrazyFiction.com

Dedicated to my son, Scct Eric Hartshorn
November 03, 1972—April 25, 2018

Author's Note

Ghosts of the Big Sandy River is a story that takes place in Louisa, Kentucky, and Fort Gay, West Virginia. Both are real towns that I love to visit. In January of 2018, the tale came to me. I turned to my second eldest son, Scot, for input and research since he lived in Louisa and Fort Gay for several years. Scot was a substantial contributor to my information. On April 25, 2018, a mere 100 days into the manuscript, Scot died of a heart attack at the age of forty-five. He is buried outside of Fort Gay near Tolsia Highway on Cyrus Mountain. It took me over a year to get back to working on our project. But I knew that I had to finish it. Scot would have expected me to.

The story follows brothers Clayton and Scot and their cousin Jaylynn on ghost hunting ventures with a twist of local history mixed in. The kids soon discover that not all demons are spectral when it comes to haunting humans.

Sometimes death has nothing to do with dying.

I hope you enjoy the adventures—both real and imagined.

Have a safe and fun journey!
Eddie

"Burning bridges behind you is understandable. It's the bridges before us that we burn, not realizing we may need to cross, that brings regret." — Anthony Liccione

"Monsters are real, and ghosts are real too. They live inside us, and sometimes they win." — Stephen King

I

Something wasn't right. It was too quiet. Birds had been chirping throughout the woods as if they were engaged in a singing contest.

Now, complete silence.

What was he doing in the woods anyway? How stupid could he be? It was because of the two rabbits that were chasing after each other like puppies. He had been mesmerized by their playfulness and followed them from his back yard to where he now stood.

Alone, in the middle of the forest, just like in the horror movie, *Wrong Turn*.

Oh, yeah, he was beyond stupid. His new home was barely over a mile from West Virginia, the very state where the setting was for the slasher flick. Never mind if it might have been filmed elsewhere. A forest was a forest where anyone or anything could hide.

What was that smell? Rotten eggs? He pinched his nose and spat on the ground. If the stench was visible, he imagined it was in the process of turning into a dense fog. He spat again. Both rabbits rose on their hind legs and sniffed the air, then bolted into the thick cover of undergrowth.

A high-pitched scream broke the silence, and he nearly peed himself. What the heck was that? No human could produce such a screech. It sounded like it came from the pits of hell! He scanned the trees. Nothing moved, and another heavy silence fell over the forest. The urgency to run filled every fiber in his body, but in which direction? He had been following the rabbits in a straight line, as much as the assorted trees allowed, right up to when the screech caused him to turn 360 degrees. Or, had he stopped halfway in his frantic spin to look back in search of what had made the shriek? That was the crazy thing about sound. It was hard to pinpoint where it had come from.

Why hadn't he paid attention to the trees? He could use them as a signpost to find his way back. The ground flourished with growth, saplings, greenery, dead and broken branches scattered here and there, but no sign of his footprints.

A yelp, much like that of a dog, echoed through the woods, followed by another ear-piercing scream. The shriek sounded wicked as if on a bender to kill, bouncing off trees and slamming into Scot's ears, sending his heart pounding against his ribcage like an out of control jackhammer.

Pick a direction and run like hell!

Sprinting for his life, twigs, and brush crunched under his tennis shoes. Beads of sweat trickled down his brow and into the corners of his eyes, blurring his vision. He wiped his forehead with the inside of his wrist and repeatedly blinked. Trees passed in a blur.

Adrenaline pumped, saliva thickened in his throat. Hairs on the nape of his neck bristled. What if he had made a wrong turn?

Run! Faster! Don't look back.

He hurdled over a dead log and then another. Had he walked around them earlier? If he had, he couldn't recall.

"Damn!"

Where had that low hanging tree branch come from? The collision knocked him to the ground on his backside. A liquid trickled down his forehead and into the corner of his mouth. He dabbed a fingertip into the substance.

Blood!

He panted like a racehorse down the backstretch, his lungs crying for air. Another eerie silence filled the woods. He tried to stand, but his head throbbed, little, bright, flashing spots danced before his eyes. His knees buckled, and he slumped back to the ground on his butt. He buried his head in his palms and closed his eyes to clear his vision while his ears stood on high alert, listening for any sound other than his lungs working overtime.

Suddenly, the ground shook, and with it, the crunching of brush, disrupting the soundless space that surrounded him. Whatever had made that scream earlier was getting closer. Eleven was much too young to die.

Stand up and run!

Can't stay here!

He stood and jumped over a small bush.

Another high-pitched scream!

His eyes scanned the woods as he ran, not daring to look back. There were too many trees. One collision was enough. The forest seemed to be closing in around him, darkening sky pressing down. Behind him, snapping twigs told Scot that whatever was chasing him was getting closer. If the trees could speak, they would be laughing at the petrified human.

Finally, a slight lightening in the forest ahead alerted him to the presence of the clearing. He crashed to a halt just outside the tree line and fell to his knees, head bent down, heaving for air.

"Scot Eric Hall!" his mother shouted. It was never good when Mom spoke all three of his names. "What were you doing in there?"

Really? There was no way that he was about to tell her he heard a scream like a banshee and ran like a chicken. His brother, Clayton, would love to hear that. Clayton was a year older and braver, sure to make fun of Scot. Clayton was determined to become a Marine. Scot was destined to be a...

"Scot Eric Hall!"

Scot's head snapped up. Mom was growing impatient. She stood on the porch with her arms across her chest. He forced a smile and rose to his feet. "Just checking out the woods, Mom."

Mom rushed toward him. "Are you bleeding?"

"Bumped into a branch."

"Looks like the tree won," yelled Clayton exiting the house.

"Get a bandage, Clayton." Mom inspected the wound. "It's not a deep cut."

"Where are they?" Clayton stopped near the top step and threw his arms up in the air.

"In the glove box of my van. And bring a sterile wipe." Mom raised Scot's head back. "You shouldn't wander into the woods alone, Scotty."

Scot turned his attention to one of the movers who had stopped carrying furniture into the house to watch the nursing his mother was giving him. The man's face held a smirk as if to say, *Kid, you haven't seen anything yet.*

"Did you hear me about the woods, Scotty?"

"Yes, Mom." His mother was right and he was certain not to do it again. Heck, he was ready to move back to Columbus, Ohio. The sounds of the big city were easier to deal with compared to the shriek in the woods. It had sounded like a mixture of Rodan and Godzilla. It was strange that his mom and brother had not mentioned hearing the squeal. "I was watching rabbits." That was one reason. The other, he saw no cause to mention.

Clayton came running over to Mom and handed her the bandage. She swabbed the cut and applied the patch. Scot looked over to the delivery van at the sound of the engine starting. The driver backed the truck out of the driveway, tooted the horn, and drove off.

"I'm going inside to unpack." Mom walked toward the house. "Don't you boys wander off," she said over her shoulder.

"I can't believe you went into the woods alone." Clayton's eyebrows arched.

Scot shrugged and said nothing. There was no need to explain. It had been a stupid move on his part.

"Well?" Clayton looked from Scot to the woods and back to Scot.

"What?"

"What scared you? A squirrel fight?" Clayton grinned.

"Funny." Scot shoved his brother's shoulder and took a step toward the porch.

"Scotty!" Clayton's voice came as a whisper but carried a tone of urgency.

Scot turned to his brother. Clayton was pointing in the direction of the woods.

"Whoa! Is that..." Scot stopped short of finishing his question. The way the animal held one rear foot slightly off the ground explained the yelp he had heard. But what caused the injury? The remnants of the screech still rang in his memory. The cry must have been from a beast more massive and fiercer than a wolf.

"Yeah. I'm pretty sure."

"What if it's a dog? Like the ones that pull sleds in Alaska."

"That isn't a dog, Scotty. No matter how much you want it to be." Clayton raised an arm out in front of his brother. "Let's get inside." Clayton tugged on Scot's shirt. "Walk slowly."

Clayton was right. Scot wanted a dog more than anything. He needed a best friend who would accept him without judgment. What was wrong with that?

The brothers took three steps, and the animal did the same. When they halted, it halted. Its nostrils twitched as it caught and studied the scent of the humans. Then, as if the wolf had heard something that Scot had not, it took a step back and gazed toward the street.

Both boys looked to see what had drawn the animal's attention.

A pickup rolled down the street and pulled into the driveway. Grandpa Boyd stepped out, slamming the door shut. "Hey, boys." He spread his arms wide. "Give the old man a hug!"

Scot turned back to the canine, but it was no longer there.

"You boys look like you've seen a ghost."

Scot faced his grandfather. "Are there wolves around here?" Maybe Clayton was wrong, and it was a dog after all.

"Oh, yes. It's part of life here in Louisa. There are wolves all over Kentucky." Grandpa gave a quick wink. "Did you see one?"

Before Scot could answer, the passenger door of Grandpa's pickup swung open, drawing Scot's attention. "Jaylynn!" He and Clayton hadn't seen their cousin and her three brothers since last Christmas. "I didn't see you in the truck."

"She insisted on coming with me." Grandpa pulled his smoking pipe partially out of his shirt pocket then dropped it back in.

"I wasn't about to wait for my brothers." Jaylynn walked over to where the others stood near the porch. "They take forever."

"Me and Clayton saw a Siberian husky near the woods." Scot elbowed his brother.

"It was a wolf." Clayton lightly smacked Scot's forearm.

"Was it white and had yellow eyes?" Grandpa rubbed his chin.

Clayton's head wobbled like a bobblehead. "White as snow."

"I'd have to see it to know for sure." Grandpa met Scot's stare. "But it sounds like the one I've seen roaming the hillside near the cemetery, not far from here."

"There's a graveyard near our house?" Scot exhaled a soft moan. Great! Their new house was close to a burial ground!

"Yep. Pine Hill Cemetery." Jaylynn slapped her palms together. It sounded to Scot like his cousin was a fan of the dead. "Just on the other side of the woods. Right, Grandpa?"

"Yep. We all need a place to go when the time arrives." Grandpa opened the door and entered the house.

Scot, Clayton, and Jaylynn climbed the stairs to the porch and plopped down on metal chairs. Scot couldn't keep his gaze off the woods. Ghosts didn't roam during daylight, did they?

***

Clayton held his gaze on Scot, sensing his brother's nervousness. Scot must have seen something in the woods or *thought* he did. He would have never figured his brother to venture into the woods by himself. Scot wouldn't do anything alone. Yet, he did. Why? What caused him to burst from the woods like he was performing a long jump at the Olympics?

"You're joking that the cemetery is close to our house." Scot inched out to the edge of his seat.

"Nope." Jaylynn leaned forward. "Your street, Town Hill Road, connects with Cemetery Road at the top of the hill. Or…" She twisted in her seat and pointed. "You can walk straight through those trees."

"A cemetery has…" Scot gulped, lowered his head, and smoothed a leg of his jeans.

"You won't see any ghosts, unless…" Jaylynn's eyes narrowed.

"Unless what?" Scot raised his head and sat upright.

"Remember the bridge you cross to get to our house?" Jaylynn pointed to the east.

"Yeah. It's downtown." Clayton was about to get up and go inside, but now, curiosity drove him back into the chair. Where was Jaylynn going with her story? How much more did she want to scare Scotty?

"That's the one." Jaylynn tossed her hair.

Clayton eyed Jaylynn. She must do that a thousand times a day.

"Anyways," she said, with grit in her voice, "people say that an old man from the 1800s drowned near where the bridge is. He was searching for a kid who'd gone missing. The man was caught in the river current and never seen again." Jaylynn cleared her throat before continuing. "They say, if you stand under the bridge and announce your wish to see ghosts, your wish will come true." She wiggled her eyebrows.

"Yeah, right." Clayton twiddled his fingers at her. He couldn't let Scot fall for her nonsense. "She's messing with us, Scotty."

"Then, you'll meet me at the bridge tomorrow at one o'clock." Jaylynn leaned back and pursed her mouth in a self-satisfied smirk. "My brothers will probably come along."

Clayton started to speak, telling her to forget it, but he clamped his mouth shut. He would like to see her brothers and explore the town on bikes. Her brothers were triplets, a year older than him and Jaylynn, and no doubt knew the best spots in Louisa.

"What if…" Scot's eyes went round as softballs.

Clayton choked back a chuckle. Scotty's eyes held a hint of fear. He needed to come to his little brother's rescue. "We have to get permission to ride our bikes that far."

"Yeah." Scot tapped Clayton on the knee. "We have a lot of work to do."

"Tomorrow. One o'clock." Jaylynn's grin deepened.

"Scotty's right. We have to help Mom unpack."

"Uh-huh, sure. Don't worry, boys. I'll protect you." She broke into a full-blown laugh.

The back door swung open, and Grandpa stepped out onto the porch. "What's so funny?" He took a seat on the porch swing and leaned back, tilting his chin upward.

"I told them about making a wish under the bridge."

Grandpa shook his head. "They just moved in, and you're trying to scare them."

"I'm not scared," blurted Clayton, holding his gaze on his brother. "It's just a fairytale."

"She didn't scare me," said Scot. Clayton watched his brother scan the woods.

"That story goes back to when I was a kid." Grandpa removed his smoking pipe from his shirt pocket. "Hard to say when it started."

"I'd say in the 1800s." Jaylynn chortled and slapped her knee.

Grandpa rolled his eyes. "Girl, sometimes you're too much."

Clayton silently agreed with him.

"I try to be." Jaylynn slapped her knee again.

"Well, you're good at it." Grandpa leaned out and faced his grandsons. "The first bridge wasn't completed until 1906, not the 1800s." He glanced over to Jaylynn, and she stuck out her tongue. "The specter, if there's one, is called the Tributary Ghost."

"Trib what?" Scot's head snapped back.

Clayton watched his brother's face scrunch into a dozen creases. Here we go. Scot would be sleeping in Clayton's room tonight.

"Trib-u-tary." Grandpa pulled out a pouch of pipe tobacco from his back pocket. "Tributary is a waterway that flows into a larger river. In our case, we have two tributaries." He jutted out his chin. "The bridge spans Tug Fork River and the Levisa Fork River. Both rivers flow into the Big Sandy River. If you stand on the bridge and look north, you can see where the three rivers come together."

"Really?" If Louisa were to be his new home, Clayton would need to see the rivers.

"Yep." Grandpa packed tobacco into the bowl of his pipe with his fingertip. "That ghost story is a folktale. Nothing more. No one in my day has ever shown proof of seeing a ghost. Sure, several folks have claimed such, but no solid proof."

"Like a video or photo?" The sudden excitement in Scot's voice surprised Clayton.

"Well, son." Grandpa winked. "We didn't have cell phones back then."

"Wow." Clayton leaned forward. Time to have some fun where he called the shots. "If we can capture a ghost on video, we'll be famous, Scotty."

Scot shook his head. "A lot of people didn't become famous until after they died."

Clayton grinned.

Grandpa broke into a hearty laugh.

"Now, for other myths and legends." Jaylynn raised her hands and wiggled her fingers as a sly grin twitched at the corners of her lips. Clayton had expected her to keep going. She had Scot on the hook and wasn't about to let go. No doubt Jaylynn was trying to hook him too. "There's the one about the floating lantern," she said, now grinning from ear to ear.

"Yeah, that's another folktale." Grandpa flipped the top of his Zippo lighter with his thumb and placed the flame to his pipe. He took a couple of deep draws and smoke billowed from the bowl. "Folks have stated that, on rainy nights near midnight, a lighted lantern floats above the water until it passes under the bridge. No one has ever observed the lamp emerge from the other side. Nor has anyone claimed to set eyes on a person holding the light. It floats above the waterway on its own."

"My pa saw the lantern last Halloween while driving over the bridge." Jaylynn leaned back with arms folded, and from her expression, she was genuinely enjoying the story.

"Re-re-really?" Scot's mouth dropped open like a catfish going for the worm.

"Honest?" Clayton sat upright. Was Jaylynn using her dad for bait, or had Uncle Brian really made such a claim?

"Yep." Jaylynn crossed her ankles in front of her. "Pa watched the light float above the water, just like in the legend, until it passed under the bridge."

"Your daddy told me that story." Grandpa blew two smoke rings out his mouth. "It was a downpour, raining like he imagined Noah saw for forty days and nights. When your pa reached the midway point on the overpass, he saw the light coming down the river from the north and watched it pass under the bridge. He crossed over to the railing on the south side, but the light never came out."

Clayton sat in silence on the edge of his seat. Grandpa was good at telling stories and adding a special touch to them. Maybe Uncle Brian also stretched the truth. How could someone see a lantern during a downpour like what Noah saw for forty days and nights? It just didn't sound right, but it did make for a great Halloween story.

"Louisa is full of history and ghost stories." Grandpa took a deep draw on his pipe and blew a long stream of smoke from his mouth.

"Yeah," said Jaylynn. "Like the Screaming Thing on Paddle Creek."

"The Screaming Thing?" Scot's lips trembled.

Clayton grinned. Here we go again. Jaylynn was about to reel Scot in.

"There's a road and a creek over by our house. Both are called Paddle Creek." Jaylynn pumped a thumb over her shoulder. "The folks over there claim to hear a horrifying scream coming from the woods every day. Mark McGee told the sheriff he saw a killer clown running through the woods near his barn."

Clayton choked back a snicker. The way Jaylynn had inspected her nails while telling her story, she either didn't believe much in it herself, or she made it up. She should go into acting.

"A killer clown?" Again, Scot's voice wavered. Keep this up, and Clayton's little brother wouldn't sleep for a week.

Grandpa took a deep draw on his pipe and raised his chin. "Don't forget the hatchet."

"Hatchet?" gasped Scot. Clayton nearly spoke to calm his brother but figured it best to be quiet and listen. His cousin and grandfather had a good thing going, feeding off each other.

"I grew up with McGee." Grandpa leaned back. "He's always been a storyteller. But this time, McGee looked me dead in the eye and swore he saw that clown swinging a hatchet over his head and screaming something fierce."

"I've been listening." Clayton and Scot's dad walked onto the porch carrying three cans of root beer. He handed one to each kid. "Other stories include voices of children, a woman sobbing, and the patter of footsteps. The sounds are all from invisible spirits. Various citizens of Louisa and Fort Gay have claimed to witness these sounds."

Clayton choked back a giggle. Now, his dad was getting in on the action. Funny, Dad had never shared those claims with him and Scot. Sure, Dad grew up in Louisa, but not one word about ghosts or invisible spirits.

"Let's not forget the Hairy Man." Grandpa blew smoke out the side of his mouth.

"Hair-hair-hairy Man?" Scot's face twisted in such a knot that Clayton had trouble choking back a scream to further mess with his brother. To do so would guarantee an extra body in his bed tonight.

"He's like Big Foot, or Sasquatch, a creature some folks claim to have seen running between trees on mountainsides in both states." Jaylynn raised her palms to the air in a spooky gesture. "If you could see your face, Scotty." She laughed.

Scot took a deep breath and released it slowly. "You're just trying to scare us."

Clayton nodded. Bingo, little brother. Now, you're catching on!

Jaylynn said nothing as her lips formed another sly grin.

"Here, Gary." Mom opened the door and handed Dad a tray of hamburgers and hot dogs. Dad took the platter and made his way over to the grill, giggling like a toddler at Christmas.

Clayton caught sight of movement near the edge of the woods. A shadow darted from behind one tree to another and stayed there. It was too tall to be a wolf. It was more the size of a man. "Does anyone live in the woods?"

"You'll have to make your wish under the bridge to know that." Jaylynn again displayed that stupid grin of hers.

Someone was there, hiding behind a tree, watching his family. Clayton was sure, but not positive enough to call attention to the creeper. How would he appear to the others if no one were there? Or worse, how would Scot take the news? Then, there was the other possibility—someone was indeed watching them and that someone had chased his little brother through the woods.

2

The following morning, Scot and Clayton washed and towel-dried their bikes.

"Are you really going to the bridge?" Scot tossed his towel into a bucket.

"Come on, Scotty." Clayton eyed his brother. "Surely, you don't think the Tributary Ghost is real."

Scot shrugged. Anything was possible. More than once, Grandpa had said not to tempt fate. Wasn't standing under a bridge and inviting a ghost to appear doing exactly that?

"What were you doing in the woods yesterday? Alone."

Sure! Like Scot was going to admit that Clayton was the reason. Clayton always poked fun at him for being scared of his own shadow. Scot had to prove to himself that he wasn't afraid. He saw how that turned out. "I was watching a rabbit."

"And?"

Scot's gaze dropped to the driveway. He had nothing more to say about it.

"You looked scared. What happened?"

"I scratched my head on a branch." Scot yanked the bandage from his head and tossed it in a garbage can.

Clayton's lips formed a smirk, and he nodded once. "Whatever you say, little brother."

Scot had never yearned to slap a smile from his brother's face more than at that moment.

"Hey, if nothing else, we get to ride our bikes downtown and explore the city."

"But what if..." Scot's stomach churned. His heart picked up speed. He liked to believe that ghosts weren't real. Whenever he and Dad watched a spooky movie on TV, Dad would always remind him it was only a movie.

"But what if…" Scot repeated. Why couldn't he tell his brother that hunting ghosts wasn't how he pictured spending his summer? Deep down, he knew why. His brother would make fun of him or worse—think of him as being a coward.

Clayton walked over to Scot. "We can even skip stones across the river." He held out his pinky finger. "We stay together, no matter what. Like the Marines, we leave no man behind."

Several times, Scot had heard his brother declare his love for the military. There was nothing more significant to Clayton. Their dad was a Marine, served four years fresh out of high school. It was Clayton's goal in life to do the same, except Clayton was thinking more about making the military a career. Scot nodded once, interlocked pinky fingers with his brother and sealed the commitment by yelling along with Clayton, "Oorah!"

A horn beeped, and Dad pulled his pickup into the driveway. He opened the door and climbed out.

"Hey, Dad, can I ask a favor?" Clayton held open the truck door while his father leaned inside the cab.

Scot shifted his weight from one leg to the other. Dang! Clayton was about to seek permission to hunt for ghosts. Riding bikes through town would be cool, but he drew the line with specters. Grandpa and Jaylynn had sounded convincing. What if…

"Sure, Son." Dad grabbed a bag off the seat.

"Can me and Scot ride our bikes to the bridge?"

Another horn sounded, drawing everyone's attention to a second pickup as it entered the driveway and parked alongside Dad's vehicle.

"Grandpa!" Scot allowed himself to relax a little. Maybe Grandpa would take him for a milkshake, away from hunting dead people.

Grandpa stepped out and embraced Scotty. "What are you boys up to today?"

"They want to ride their bikes to the bridge," Dad said.

"The Tributary Ghost, eh?" Grandpa patted Scotty on top of the head. "You boys don't believe in that legend, do you?"

Scot forced a smile. Now was not the time to be ribbed by Grandpa. He had no real plan to hunt ghosts, now or ever. If Clayton saw it as he did, hunting spirits was nothing more than an excuse to ride bikes through town. He and Clayton were never allowed to do such a thing in the big city. Usually, skipping stones across the river would be cool, but it required standing near the underside of the bridge. What if…

Grandpa looked over to Dad. "Gary, if I remember right, when you were a boy, you searched under that bridge many a time."

"And the only thing I found under there were fish on the end of my pole." Dad went through the motion of casting a fishing pole.

"Whew!" Scot wiped the sweat from his forehead.

"Then, you should let them go." Grandpa pulled out his pipe from a shirt pocket. "They need to explore their new town."

Louisa wasn't exactly new to Scot and Clayton. Grandpa was born in Louisa almost seventy years ago and had lived there all his life. Mom and Dad brought their sons to visit with Grandpa two or three times a year, but they had never seen the town from the seat of a bicycle.

Dad leaned his backside against the front fender of the truck and crossed his arms over his chest. He cocked his head from one side to the other.

"Jaylynn and her brothers are to meet us there at one o'clock," said Clayton.

Dad glanced at his watch and entered the house.

"While you're under that bridge, be sure to look for the floating lantern." Grandpa squeezed Scot's shoulder. "Search good under the support beams for a rope or pulley."

Of course, a rope and a pulley can easily pull a lantern! Why hadn't Scot thought of that? His heart raced. He and Clayton could be the ones to uncover the mystery. Let's get this show on the road!

Dad reentered the garage, smiling. "Don't get too close to the river. And don't cross the bridge."

"Yes, sir!" Scot shouted simultaneously with his brother.

"And be back by the time I get home. I'm planning on being here by four."

"Don't forget, boys, Louisa is full of history." Grandpa placed his smoking pipe between his lips. "And history is full of ghosts."

Or trickery, Scot suppressed a chuckle.

"Boyd, please don't smoke in here." Mom stood in the doorway, glaring at her father-in-law.

"There's no tobacco in it, Lola." Grandpa took a draw on the pipe and pretended to blow smoke her way. "See?"

Scot choked back laughter. Grandpa Boyd was funny like that, always joking. Sometimes it wasn't easy for Scot to determine if his grandfather was fibbing or telling the truth.

Upon saying their goodbyes, both boys guided their bikes out of the garage.

"Look!" Clayton pointed.

"It's back." Scot's breath caught in his throat. What were the odds of seeing the canine in their yard a second time? What was it up to? It didn't seem to be aggressive for a wild animal, even with its yellow eyes locked on Scot. "Dad! Grandpa!"

Dad exited the garage. "A Siberian husky. I'm sure he lives nearby."

"What if he's lost?" Scot spun toward his father. It would be great to have a dog to love.

"That old wolf isn't lost," said Grandpa, walking outside to have a look. "I have seen it at all times of the day, but mostly at night."

"So, it is a wolf. Cool." A part of Scot wanted it to be a wolf from the wild, while a bigger part of him yearned for it to be a dog.

"I think it's a husky like they use in Alaska to pull a sled," Dad repeated. Scot glanced from the animal to his father and back to the creature. Whatever it was, it was beautiful.

"I disagree, Gary." Grandpa loaded tobacco in his pipe. "It's a wolf. Mark my word." He placed the pipe stem in his mouth. "It stands close to two and a half feet at the shoulders. I bet it's not far from five feet long."

Scot watched the animal disappear into the cover of the woods. "It's gone." Who was right? If Dad was, maybe Scot could tame him. If Grandpa was, maybe...

"Some say that wolf resides in the cemetery." Grandpa's eyes went round as fat, homemade biscuits. "The graveyard is—"

"Enough, Boyd," snapped Mom, exiting the garage.

"Aw, Mom." Clayton spread his arms wide. "It's not like Scot and I are little kids. We know what's in a graveyard."

We sure do! Scot silently agreed, and we're not going anywhere near one!

"I don't care. I know what your grandfather was going to say." Mom glared over to Grandpa. "If you boys are going to meet your cousins, you better get moving...and stay away from stray dogs."

Scot rode off like he was going to the races with Clayton alongside him. He had a myth to bust!

***

"Which ghost do you think we'll find first?" Clayton asked, bringing his bike to a stop near the bridge. "Well," Clayton added. "Which ghosts do you—"

"I think we'll find a rope and a pulley under the bridge." Scot put his kickstand down. Discovering trickery was not tempting fate.

"What if we do find a ghost, Scotty? We'll be famous."

"I don't want to see a ghost."

"Don't chicken out now." Clayton winked. "Besides, here comes Jaylynn."

Scot grunted. Jaylynn's brothers were nowhere in sight. Scot had planned to follow Roger, the largest of the triplets, stick to the big guy like a mouse on a glue trap. This adventure was quickly turning into something that he didn't want to do. A person didn't have the lives of a cat.

Jaylynn applied her brakes hard. The rear tire skidded in a half-circle and came to a stop alongside the boys. "Hey, cousins. Let's do this." She grinned from ear to ear.

Scot released a heavy sigh. It wasn't like a girl was really going to hunt for ghosts.

"Where are your brothers?" A hint of disappointment crept into Clayton's question, and Scot felt it.

"They're helping Pa work on the fence." Jaylynn tossed her hair back. "So, which ghost do we track down and kill first?"

"Funny." Clayton chuckled.

Scot sighed. Joking about hunting ghosts was something he could do, as long as it stayed as a joke.

"I brought Pa's binoculars along with sandwiches, stick matches, bottles of water, snack cakes, candy, gum, bandages, five bandanas, a sweat towel, a pair of jersey gloves, a twenty-foot rope, rubber boots, socks, five dollars, a nail file, fingernail clippers, a hairbrush, my purse, a long-sleeved shirt, and a Bowie knife. The knife is in here." She patted a zippered pouch and then cocked her head back and closed her eyes like she had forgotten something.

Girls! Scot gave thanks that he wasn't one.

"What?" Clayton's mouth dropped open. "You didn't bring your laptop or ice cream?"

"Don't have a laptop, but I nearly brought ice cream bars."

Scot rolled his eyes at the expression on her face. She was serious.

"Oh, yes," she said, patting her fingertips to her shirt pocket. "And my cell phone. It can record video."

Don't they all? Scot bit his tongue. Besides, he and Clayton had cell phones as well.

"Let's go." Clayton positioned his bike to head west on Madison Street.

"Wait!" yelled Jaylynn. "Let's search under the bridge first. We might find a lantern hidden somewhere."

Scot forced a grin. It had sounded great when Grandpa had mentioned that there might be evidence of rigging of some type, but he suddenly realized that someone should have discovered it by now.

"There's a path leading down to the water where people fish." Jaylynn dropped her bike to the ground and walked down the embankment.

Under the bridge, Scot halted and took a step back. A shadow on the ground, shaped like wings, moved out in front of him. Scot forced himself not to look up. It hadn't been that long ago he and Dad had watched a movie titled *The Mothman Prophecies*, about a creature with a massive wingspan. It was a piece of West Virginia folklore. The monster often visited the city of Point Pleasant. How far was Louisa from that town?

Jaylynn gasped and pointed upward at a metal beam on the bridge. "Wow," she called out. "A falcon. Awesome!" The bird took flight, dipping and swaying across the river and out of sight.

"Let's go to the park." Scot sighed and allowed his shoulders to relax. He took a step as if to leave. Searching for a rope or pulley could wait another twenty or thirty years.

Clayton took hold of Scot's forearm. "We're hunting ghosts."

Scot looked up at the steel beams and cement pillars supporting the bridge. "There's nothing here."

"Let's eat first." Jaylynn set her backpack on the embankment and opened it. "Bologna and mayonnaise."

Scot thanked her. His stomach did feel empty. Maybe that was due to the possibility that he was born without guts.

"I have extra water too."

"Me and Clayton saw the dog again." Scot faced Jaylynn. "It was standing in our backyard a few minutes ago."

"Grandpa said it was a wolf." Clayton narrowed his eyes.

"Dad said it was a husky." Scot tossed his head back, not about to cave. He had more to gain if it was a dog.

"I wish I'd seen it yesterday. I can tell the difference. We have both running around here, more wolves than dogs. Of course, it could be..." Jaylynn's eyes rolled upward.

"Could be what?" Scot stiffened and silently scolded himself. The way she had stopped in mid-sentence told him that she was up to something.

"A ghost." Jaylynn raised her arms above her head and clapped her hands with a noise like a minor explosion. "Boo!"

Scot flinched and glared over at Jaylynn and Clayton, who had broken into laughter. Scot's entire head felt as if his neck was attached to a potbelly stove with a full-blown fire inside it. He needed to change the subject before he exploded. "Why does the river look green?" There was only one place for him to go, should they keep ribbing him.

"Looks like emeralds." Jaylynn scratched her nose. "It's beautiful like this all summer. During the winter, the water looks muddy."

"Why?" Scot knew it was because of the reflection of leaves on the water. He was stealing time from the hunting expedition. Playing dumb was better than being dumb.

"Reflection of the trees." Clayton thrust his chest out like he was proud of his answer. "No green leaves during the winter."

Scot loved snow, but not the cold. Summer was the best time to ride a bike, not to mention school wasn't in session. Sitting under the bridge wasn't too bad, after all. A gentle breeze swept through his hair. His eyes searched the treetops, hoping a hungry falcon didn't return...or a Mothman.

"We need to find that lantern," Jaylynn broke the silence. Scot forced his tongue to stay still. At least she wasn't asking him to make a wish.

Clayton cocked his head up like his eyes were scanning the rafters under the roadway of the bridge.

Scot scrunched his nose. Clayton was wasting time that they could be spending cruising through town. Scot locked his eyes on an area of land accessed by roadway connected at the bridge's halfway point. Tree branches swayed in the wind. Wait! What was that darting from one tree to another? "Did you guys see that?"

"What?" Jaylynn stood and faced the river. "I see it!"

"You do?" Scot squinted. It had disappeared from his view.

"Where?" Clayton walked to the edge of the water. "I don't see anything."

"It's gone now." Jaylynn grinned.

"I wasn't joking! I saw something move." Scot jerked his head in the direction of his cousin. That potbelly stove was about to blow its stack!

"Describe it." Jaylynn grabbed a bottle of water from the backpack and handed it to Scot.

Scot blew out his cheeks to let off steam. "Thanks." He took a sip of water. "I couldn't tell what it was. It was dark, like a shadow."

"Wolf or dog?" Clayton peered across the river.

"It was much taller. Like a person." Scot took a long swallow of water.

A massive cloud moved in front of the sun and darkened the area.

"Uh-oh!" Jaylynn blurted. "What if it turns dark this very minute, and we can't find our way out of here without a lantern?"

There she was, stirring up the coals again, filling Scot's cheeks with blazing heat. He could get to his bike in seconds and leave the two jokers behind to play their stupid game. His cousin and brother had no idea that they were down to their last wisecrack.

"Not funny, Jaylynn." Clayton wrapped an arm around Scot's shoulder.

Scot appreciated his brother's gesture, but knowing Clayton as he did, it was probably a prelude to another joke.

"This area has some serious history," Jaylynn said. "I bet neither one of you know that back in 1789, Louisa was a settlement called Balclutha." Scot shook his head. Clayton did likewise. "And near the same time," she continued, now pointing east across the rivers, "Fort Gay was called Cassville. The name didn't officially change until 1932, long after the first bridge was built here."

"So, when did Bal-Bal, whatever name you called it, become Louisa?" Scot smiled. Keeping Miss Wikipedia off the subject of ghosts was easy.

"Bal-clu-tha," Jaylynn said. "The name changed to Louisa in 1823."

"Wow." Clayton's eyes widened. "Long before us."

"That mass of land where Scot saw something is called the Point Section, a neighborhood of Louisa. George Washington surveyed the area in 1767."

"President Washington?" Scot had no idea that Washington had been in this area.

"He wasn't President yet, but yes, him." said Jaylynn.

"I wouldn't mind seeing the ghost of George Washington," Scot spoke the truth.

"George's probably haunting Virginia or Philadelphia." Jaylynn smiled as if she knew it to be factual.

"Aw." All the stories Scot read on Washington were good ones. The spirit of the first President had to be friendly.

"Grandpa was right. It was in 1906 when the original bridge was built. Even way back then, people claimed that the bridge heard your whispers and knew your secrets."

"Yeah, right." There went his goal of avoiding the myth of making a wish. Scot waved his hand at her. He didn't want to believe her, but something told him that maybe he should.

"You're sticking to that story." Clayton slapped his thigh.

Scot stared over at his brother. Shut up, Clayton. Don't egg her on.

"I'm serious." She raised her eyebrows. "Try it. Tell the bridge you wish to see a ghost. I dare you."

Silence. Scot stood stock-still and clamped his jaws shut. Clayton was doing the same. Jaylynn grinned from ear to ear, clearly enjoying the moment.

"Well?" she finally said. "Who's the brave one?"

There's that warning again, hairs on Scot's arms dancing like they were contestants on *Dancing with the Stars*. "You mean if we whisper that we want to find a ghost, we…" Why had he opened his mouth? It wasn't like she was going to say she was joking.

"Yep, that's what I believe." She grabbed her backpack off the ground. "I guess I'll head home. You guys aren't serious."

Great! Scot silently screamed. Hit the road, girl.

"I want to find a ghost!" Clayton thrust his chest out and pumped a fist in the air. Scot shook his head. Clayton had a big mouth.

At that exact moment, the wheels of a large truck met the pavement of the bridge and sent a loud groan through the steel trusses. Jaylynn shrieked. Clayton ducked. Scot jumped and staggered backward and fell on his butt, where he determined the timing to have been freaky!

"If…you…guys…could…see…your…faces," Jaylynn forced out between giggles.

"Not funny." Scot got to his feet and brushed off his jeans. "I wasn't scared." He needed to convince his knees of the fact, but they weren't listening.

"Me, either." Clayton tossed back his head.

"Then tell the bridge what you want to find, Scotty." Jaylynn wiggled her eyebrows.

It was clear to Scot that she was pushing his buttons, making him look chicken. Scot glanced up at the bridge and then over to his brother, finally fixing his eyes on his cousin. "I'm not afraid." Ghosts don't appear during the daytime, do they?

"Prove it." Jaylynn dropped her hand out in front of her, palm up, and moved it forward in a "go ahead" gesture.

Scot started to tell her to back off. He wasn't playing her goofy game. But he knew that, if he did, it would confirm his fear to her and Clayton. He thought long and hard. She wasn't about to let him get out of saying the words. His brother was going to be a Marine. What was Scot going to be, the joke of their new town? "I want to find a ghost!" Scot yelled. "Bring them on. I'm ready." He pumped a fist over his head, bringing hearty laughter to his brother and cousin. Scot pretended to laugh along with them. Those hairs on his arms had yet to stop dancing.

Once the laughter subsided, a long silence ensued, during which Scot drew in a slow breath. "Now it's your turn, Jaylynn."

"Wh-wh-what?"

"Make your wish." Scot snickered. This game played both ways.

Jaylynn widened her stance and planted a hand on her hip. "I'm not scared."

Scot detected a lack of conviction in her voice. He wasn't about to let it go. What was that phrase Grandpa often said, "What's good for the goose is good for the…boy," or something like that? "We're waiting."

A slight smile played at the corners of Jaylynn's lips. "Show me a ghost!"

Scot relaxed his stance. She said it. Now, they were all three in this together; however it should turn out. Jaylynn and Clayton shared a fist bump and laughed again. Scot pretended to join in while watching for a massive shadow to appear overhead.

Scot looked back across the river out to the Point Section. Was someone or something standing between the leafy branches of two white oaks watching them? Another large vehicle made contact with the surface of the bridge. Deep resounding thuds and clangs reverberated in the air. Scot cocked his head in response to a high-pitched squeak that followed. "What was that?" It hadn't come from a vehicle, he was sure of it. The sound wasn't anything near what he had heard in the woods, but it was still spooky.

Clayton shrugged. "I think it came from the other side of the river."

"Yeah," said Jaylynn. "Might have been a spectral snicker."

"Not funny." Scot glared over to his cousin. She seemed to love shoveling fuel into his firebox. "I'm out of here."

Jaylynn took hold of Scot's elbow. "I was joking. Sorry."

Scot blew out his cheeks. "I doubt it."

Jaylynn tugged on Scot's shirt. "Do you really think I would hunt ghosts if I thought it was possible to find any?"

Scot glared down at the ground. Face it. He was the only one of the three who showed fear of seeing a ghost. But the impossible happened all the time. You just had to believe it could.

3

"Something moved." Clayton walked over to a thicket where he picked up a stick and stabbed at the underbrush. "Snake!"

"Let me see." Scot leaned down. Snakes were nothing to mess with, but this was his first opportunity to see one up close. "Cool." It had to be three feet long or more. "Is it a copperhead?" It had distinctive light-yellow spots on the top of the head and a yellow stripe down its back to the tip of its tail. Unique black bars marked its lip.

"No, it's a garter snake." Jaylynn leaned over. "It's not dangerous."

"How do you know?" Scot figured it might be useful hanging out with her after all.

"Down here, you learn quickly about snakes, or…BOO!"

Scot jumped back and rose on his toes. He blinked rapidly. Just when the fire was about to go out, she tossed in another log! "Stop doing that!" Scot kicked the toe of his shoe across the pavement. Had he lost his mind hanging out with these two jokers?

Clayton flipped the snake over onto its back, revealing its gray-green belly with small dark spots along the edges. It released a pungent, musky smell and opened its mouth as if to attack.

Scot grabbed his brother by the back of the shirt. "Don't kill it."

"I'm not." Clayton flipped the snake further into the thicket and tossed the stick to the ground. Scot mounted his bike to leave. It was either that or his brother and cousin could deal with an exploding smokestack. Clayton must have been watching him because his next words were, "Let's go to the cemetery, Jaylynn."

"Which one? A lot of families down here have their own." She slipped her arms through the straps on the backpack and pulled it tight against her body.

"The one near our house," said Clayton. Scot felt his brother's eyes on him, probably expecting Scot to complain. But going to the graveyard meant that they would be closer to home.

"Pine Hill is up there." Jaylynn pointed to the west.

"Wow." Scot found himself hesitating. It looked as if the cemetery was located high on a mountain. Jaylynn and Grandpa had said that it was near their house. But riding to town hadn't involved a great descent. Something didn't seem right.

"I know an easy way to get there." Jaylynn pedaled away.

Scot found himself alternating his attention between the road and the tires of Clayton and Jaylynn's bikes. Now would be an excellent time for one of them to get a flat. He needed an excuse to return home. None came to mind that his brother would accept.

Not far from Scot and Clayton's home, Jaylynn stopped where the road branched to the right and ascended further up the mountainside.

"This is Pine Hill Road." Jaylynn pointed at a street sign. "The locals call it Cemetery Road. We want to go to the top of the hill."

We? Scot felt his face twist in a knot. He knew where he was now. Home was just down the road, not more than a couple of minutes away. He could probably be home before they noticed him gone.

"The other side of Cemetery Road twists and turns like a snake on its way down and comes out on Old U.S. 23." Jaylynn pointed toward town.

"Maybe we should—"

"Don't be a wuss, Scotty." Clayton squinted. "We can make it. But it may be a heck of a ride coming down." He giggled and slapped his thigh.

Scot dropped his bike to the ground. "I'm walking. I'm not flying downhill. And I'm not going to be in there when it gets dark."

"There's plenty of daylight left." Jaylynn grinned. "This should be exciting."

Scot glared at his cousin. She was crazy. Did she think that her comment about daylight made him feel better? "What if we get in trouble for trespassing?" Scot raised his chin and gazed over to his brother. Why can't Clayton read eyes?

"Simple," said Jaylynn. "We stand at a headstone and pretend the person is family."

"Yep," mumbled Scot. "Crazy."

"Do what?" Jaylynn cocked her head sideways.

"Nothing." Scot refused to answer further. No need to take a stand against a lunatic.

Jaylynn grabbed her binoculars. "Looks clear to me. I don't see anyone."

"You can't see if anyone is in there." Scot wasn't about to fall for her tricks. "Too many trees." Did she really think he didn't know what she was up to?

"We won't go down the other side, Scotty. We'll come back out this way." Clayton jumped out in the lead.

Scot glanced back at the road before following Clayton and Jaylynn to the top of the rise. He hoped that he wouldn't come to regret not listening to the voice in his head. At the entrance of the graveyard, Scot's eyes scanned the area. Faded, crooked headstones and tall gray concrete monuments littered the cemetery. Nothing seemed to be out of the ordinary...yet.

Scot followed Clayton as his brother pedaled his way down a slight hill, passing hundreds of grave markers. Clayton stopped where the road began its descent toward town. He dismounted his bike and walked over to the nearest headstone.

Scot stayed on his bike. "How soon will it be dark?"

"Stop whining. Damn." Clayton weaved his way through the cemetery over to another grave marker.

Scot looked up at an American flag gently flapping in the wind from where it hung atop a metal flagpole. A second flag did the same off in the distance attached to a taller pole and a higher hill. That had to sound spooky at night.

"See, nothing to worry about." Jaylynn walked over and stood alongside Scot.

"I'll wait here." Scot turned his front wheel in the direction from where they came.

"Which way is our house?" asked Clayton.

"It's beyond those trees behind the church." Jaylynn aimed a finger to the west.

Scot etched the route into his mind. He wasn't about to be confused as to which way to travel.

Clayton moved over to another headstone. "This one goes back to 1918. Wow. That was over a hundred years ago."

"It's probably a kid," Jaylynn said. "There was an influenza outbreak that year, and many children died. Several were buried with no marker."

"Not good." Clayton made the sign of the cross against his chest.

Scot cocked his head back at that remark. Was Clayton trying to sound like a great thinker? "I don't like it here."

"Imagine how these poor souls feel." Clayton laughed.

"Now, I have to admit that's funny," Jaylynn said, and then she broke into laughter.

Why were they making fun of the dead? Scot scanned the fence line. Don't they know ghosts have ears? Idiots must come in a pair nowadays. He spotted a movement out of the corner of his eye. "Something moved in the bu-bu-bushes!" He pointed to a thick clump of shrubs.

"Probably a squirrel." Clayton imitated a chicken clucking while he flapped his arms at his side and rotated in a circle.

"Is it the size of a man and hairy?" Jaylynn walked like a gorilla.

"I'm going home!" Scot's foot kicked up the kickstand on his bike. Now, they were adding lumps of coal to the fire.

Clayton ran up to his brother and grabbed Scot's forearm. "Okay, sorry. We'll leave in a few minutes. Dad will have a fit if you ride home alone."

Scot looked from his brother back to the bushes. Dealing with Dad would be Clayton's problem, not his. Vast streams of heat had to be escaping out his ears. Why had he made that stupid announcement under the bridge? Certainly, someone was watching him, or worse yet, something. It was just a matter of time before…

"Come on, Scotty." Clayton released Scot's arm and walked away.

Scot had run out of time to linger. His brother and cousin were making their way further from him. He wasn't about to be caught alone in a graveyard. With a grunt, he followed them on his bike.

"Do you know how many are buried here?" Clayton turned to Jaylynn.

"All of them," Scot cracked before Jaylynn could reply.

"Whoa! My little brother has finally come alive." Clayton gave his brother a fist bump. Scot grinned. Everything would be okay, Scot told himself.

Snap!

Scot's breath caught in his throat. Where had that come from?

"Who's there?" Jaylynn wheeled on her heels.

"I told you." Scot's hands tightened on his handlebars. He adjusted his pedals for a quick take off. Idiots didn't come in threes, not this day!

"Shhh," said Clayton, and he pointed. Scot looked over at a bush. Its stems moved without the benefit of wind. Something was indeed hiding within its cover. Clayton walked over to the shrub, picked up a stick, and poked it into the underbrush. Then he smacked the lower tree branches. Nothing stirred.

"There!" Scot glanced over at the sound of Jaylynn's voice. "Something's hiding behind that pine tree," she added, also pointing.

"I don't see anything." Clayton leaned on the stick in his hand. "And I'm not trudging through briars to go see."

Scot wanted to say, *I thought you were the brave one*, but he didn't.

"Looks like a buck deer," she added. Scot failed to see anything. It could be Jaylynn stirring up the stove again. "Doesn't matter now. It's gone." Jaylynn gave a half shrug.

Something moved in the grass across the way. "What the heck is that?" Scot hopped off his bike and chased after it.

Jaylynn bolted after him screaming, "Don't touch it!" She tackled him inches from it.

"Ow," Scot wheezed. Maybe his cousin should try out for football.

"That's a blue-tailed skink. It's poisonous." Jaylynn jumped to her feet and pulled Scot up by the forearm. "Some scientists claim it's not lethal, but I put my believing in my Pa, and I think you guys better too."

"Not going to argue with you on that." Clayton nodded.

"How do you know all of this stuff?" Scot bent down and brushed loose grass and dirt from his jeans. His friends back in Columbus would have a grand time ribbing him over that tackle. He could hear them laughing, "You let a girl take you to the ground."

"I'm a country girl." Jaylynn shuffled her feet. "I can milk a cow, pluck a chicken, slop hogs, chop firewood, start a fire by rubbing two sticks together, follow the north star, read moss on a tree, throw a hatchet and make it stick in a tree ten yards away, and hunt for food. My Pa taught me how to live off the land. Hunting requires a certain mindset. Stick with me, and you'll get an education for sure."

Scot grinned. She wasn't short on bragging. He stood over the lizard. "It's pretty. Black body with stripes on its back and a shiny blue tail."

"Pretty can be misleading." Jaylynn tossed her light blonde hair from her ears and started walking, swaying her hips as if she were on a catwalk. Scot and Clayton laughed.

"We need to come here after dark." Clayton took hold of Scot's arm. "Not going to find a ghost in the daylight."

"No way." Scot twisted out of Clayton's grasp. Had his brother lost his mind? Clayton's face proudly displayed the answer to that stupid question.

"We'll see." Clayton winked.

"I can't unless Pa will allow me to spend the night." Jaylynn frowned.

Scot looked up to the sky. Here's to the power of prayer.

Clayton climbed onto his bike. "The last one down the hill is a blue-tailed skink."

Scot hesitated. "You said we would go out the way we came." Why had he allowed himself to get in this mess?

"Come on. It'll be fun." Clayton rode away.

Scot released a heavy sigh and shrugged. He wasn't about to stay there.

As Scot caught up to Clayton and Jaylynn near the first bend in the road, an ear-piercing squeal came from somewhere in the graveyard.

4

Scot slammed on his brakes and looked over at his brother and cousin. They both were staring back at the cemetery with their mouths wide open.

"What the heck was that?" Scot gulped. His heart was pounding so hard he thought it might tear through his chest.

"Nothing I ever heard before." Jaylynn blinked repeatedly. "It sounded like a monkey caught in a bear trap."

"Or…a…jackass," Clayton barely got the words out of his mouth from laughing.

Jaylynn giggled and held her gut.

Scot snorted like a pig to mask the fear that had to be clearly dancing all over his face. That scream was like the one he had heard in the woods. He kept his eyes peeled up the hillside, and his feet pressed against the bike pedals.

"Are you thinking what I'm thinking?" Jaylynn said once she had regained her composure. She was staring over at Clayton with her idea shining through her eyes.

"Heck yeah," said Clayton. Scot looked over to his brother. Clayton had that same gleam in his eyes and all over his face.

Scot ran his hand through his hair. Odd, how Clayton could read Jaylynn's eyes but not his. Or, didn't his brother care what Scot felt? Clayton was brave and a little stupid, a dangerous combination. Maybe one day, Scot would be as daring, but today wasn't that day. "I'm going home."

"If you do, we'll be grounded." Clayton motioned for Jaylynn to follow him.

"Wait." Scot couldn't keep quiet any longer. "I heard that same scream in the woods." Clayton's eyebrows raised, but he said nothing. "When I cut my head."

Clayton grinned. "Then, we need to see what it was." Again, he motioned for Jaylynn to follow him. The two rode their bikes midway up the hill and stopped.

Scot stood near the entrance of the cemetery. He peered to his left and then to his right and sniffed the air. Everything seemed peaceful. The graveyard covered the grassy knoll, its paths wound up the mound and back down in different directions. A light breeze blew through the treetops. Both flags flapped in the wind while a squirrel raced across several gravesites. A rustling of bushes came from somewhere behind him. He peddled as fast as he could and brought his bike to a halt between his brother and cousin. "Can we go now?"

"At the top of the hill. Do you see it?" Jaylynn glanced over to Clayton.

Clayton narrowed his eyes. "Antlers."

"Yep. No doubt, a buck." Jaylynn looked over to Scot.

Frustration churned in Scot's stomach, along with a trace of fear. The wicked screech from minutes earlier was not typical in a graveyard at any time of day. Heat from Scot's chest erupted upwards, his face on fire. "Big deal. You can't even see the deer's body. I want to go home." Again, Scot's grip tightened on the handlebars.

"It's grazing on the other side of the slope. We need to go further up." Jaylynn stepped ahead.

A rustling of branches caught Scot's attention. "The wolf."

"The same one from your house?"

"Yes." Clayton nodded.

The animal walked over to where the antlers continued to raise and lower.

"I agree with Grandpa," said Jaylynn. "It could be a dog, but it looks like a wolf."

Surprisingly, both creatures vanished. Before Scot could turn away, a man came into view in the same location where they had spotted the animals. He wore denim bib overalls, ragged and dirty like they had seen better days years ago. Propped on his shoulder was a wooden-handled metal rake.

"Must be the caretaker." Jaylynn raised a hand in greeting.

"Here he comes. We're going to jail." Scot steadied his bike. Dying in a graveyard or doing time in prison was not on his things-to-do list.

Clayton and Jaylynn grabbed hold of Scot's handlebars.

"Howdy!" The man's voice was loud and rough, and there was an odd edge to it. He stood tall and thin, dark-skinned, like a Latino or Indian, and leaned on the rake like it was a cane. "I'm Rand Dockery. My friends call me Rand-Dock." He raised a brow. "From the expression on your faces, you kids look like you've been caught reaching in a cookie jar." He slowly rotated the rake like a witch churning a pot. "You kids need help in finding a marker?"

A shiver coursed up Scot's spine, and he found himself rubbing the back of his neck. The man stared as if he had an empty plot to fill, and a kid would do just fine. Scot firmly placed a foot against a pedal. Graveyards hide more than what they reveal. A scar extended from the man's left eye across his weathered face down to his lip. But it was more than the man's face. His eyes were cold and dark like they had a headstone of their own.

"Did you see a deer and a wolf at the top of the hill?" asked Jaylynn.

Scot watched her balance the backpack on the handlebars as she unzipped the pouch containing the Bowie knife. Dying in a graveyard or doing twenty-five to life crept back into his thoughts.

"A deer?" Rand-Dock glanced back at the mound. "And a wolf? No, can't say I did or do. Where are they, exactly?"

"They were standing in the same spot you came from," said Clayton.

"You don't say?" Once more, the man glanced up the hill. "One is liable to see anything in this land of the dead. And when I say anything, I mean exactly that...anything." He spat tobacco juice to the ground.

"You mean like..." Scot sucked in a deep breath.

"No better place to find ghosts than right here." The man stomped the metal prongs of the rake twice on the ground. "I believe we have several spirits roaming this graveyard nearly every night. The first soul to enter this place was in 1839."

"Wow." Clayton's head snapped back.

"It's right over there." The caretaker aimed the rake toward a headstone a few feet from where they stood. "There are over twelve acres here. Do you know how many folks are buried in this graveyard?"

Scot bit his tongue. He wasn't about to repeat his answer to his brother's joke.

"I would say over twenty-two hundred souls lie here, give or take a few. After all, there are several unmarked graves and thus unknown." Rand-Dock spat a wad of tobacco to the ground. "Granted, most of these souls sleep deep or take no interest in the night-to-night affairs of this place. But the rumors claim that some do mosey about now and then." He pulled out a pouch of Red Man chewing tobacco. "Funny thing is, few adults talk about experiences they can't explain. Might make them appear unstable. This hallowed ground is not the place for the squeamish. According to the tittle-tattle of small-town gossips, there's several roaming spirits of soldiers from the Civil War, both North and South. I would think that the letters of their names engraved on the headstones would hold them down. Keep them beneath the surface. I guess it's not always the case." He opened the pouch and stuffed a fresh wad of tobacco into his mouth. "Now, I haven't seen these specters myself, but many a folk in Louisa swear they have." He chewed on the wad for a moment. "Long before white men invaded this land, it belonged to Native Americans…Indians.

"Along with them were many folktales and powerful beliefs. Never underestimate those legends. According to some stories, Indians turn into towering creatures. They're hideous looking." Rand-Dock cocked his head back and rubbed his chin. "Best time to find a spirit, I'd say, is after the darkness sweeps over this place. That's when it seems madness comes with it."

"You're joking, right?" Scot forced a grin. The man's words were spooky, and he looked spooky, big bushy eyebrows, hairless arms, and that scar on his face. He could pass for a hundred years old. A ragged John Deere ball cap covered his shaggy gray hair. Rand-Dock's penetrating stare seemed to be dissecting Scot, secretly cutting him into a billion little pieces in the dark depths of the man's mind. His body or clothes, or both, reeked with an odor of sulfur.

"I wish I were kidding, young man." The caretaker narrowed his eyes. "But I don't joke about the dead…out of respect. And the spirits here are no different than you and me. They yearn to be remembered. And even more, they want to protect what was once theirs." The man turned as if he were about to leave only to turn back and face Scot. After a moment of hesitation, he leaned in close to Scot, far too close, and looked him in the eye. "If you're fixing on coming back after dark, be sure to have your last will and testament in order." He spat again. The juice landed near Scot's shoe.

Scot flinched. "What's a last will and—"

"Nothing important to us." Clayton winked at Scot.

"How long have you cared for this place?" Jaylynn asked.

The man cocked his head back and closed his eyes. "I reckon it's been over forty years now, give or take." He opened his eyes and grinned at her. "Why do you ask?"

"Have you ever seen the Hairy Man?" Jaylynn released the zipper from the grip of her fingers while continuing to balance the backpack with her other hand.

The man's eyebrows shot upward like fuzzy caterpillars on a chin-up bar. "Ha, the Hairy Man! Now that's a demon I tell you. He's a boogieman. That's for sure." The man squinted then opened his eyes wide. "He's for real. I know that. Ain't no one can convince me he's not."

"What do you mean?" Jaylynn cocked her head to the side.

"Well, I'm the one who cleans up this place." Rand-Dock swept his free hand from the right to the left like he was swatting at a fly. "Several times, I've found a stack of dung too big for a cow, let alone a buck deer."

"What's dung?" Scot hadn't heard that one before.

"Poop." Clayton elbowed Scot's ribs.

"Ewww!" Scot wailed, pinching his nose. He would have used a different word to describe it. The same word that Grandpa uses when talking about it hitting the fan.

"No, I haven't seen the Sasquatch with my own eyes," the caretaker continued. "I reckon that's because the beast is fast on its feet...a swift runner. But I've felt being watched from afar. And if it's not the Hairy Man, then it's one of these poor souls." Again, he stomped the metal prongs of the rake twice on the ground like he was trying to stir one up for Scot to witness.

Scot wanted to believe the man was joking. "Aw, you're fibbing." The words came out of Scot's mouth before he had considered how the man might react.

"Kid." The man's dark eyes narrowed, making his eyebrows appear to be an unbroken line of hair. "I told you, out of respect, I don't joke about such things." There was nothing in the man's voice but pure ice.

Scot swallowed the lump in his throat. Had the others heard it go down? It sure was loud to his ears. "Does the creature roam the woods?"

Rand-Dock stared at Scot for a long second before speaking. "Are you going to tell the monster where it *can't* go?"

"No way." A twinge of nervousness struck Scot's stomach. The man was watching him with an amused grin.

"Regardless of what or who the creature is, take care not to show fear. I've got a feeling it thrives on such." Rand-Dock peered over his shoulder like he was checking on someone. "You know, come to think about it, there's an old woman in Louisa who claims to have seen a beast back when she was a teenager. She must be in her sixties now. Her name is Wanda Kitts. She lives on South Main Cross Street, not far from the bridge."

"Was it the Hairy Man?" Jaylynn asked.

"Can't rightly say." Rand-Dock rubbed his chin again. "I was a lad when the story circulated through town that Wanda had seen something. After gossip, jokes, name-calling, and nursery rhymes sung about her, the ruckus finally settled down, and folks left her in peace."

"How's an old woman going to help us?" Clayton asked.

"I don't know, kid. She may or she may not." Rand-Dock's voice came down as a rumbly whisper that sounded like distant rolling thunder. "The only thing I can be sure of in life is death." He transferred the rake from one hand to the other. "Wanda seemed of sound mind when I saw her sitting on her porch the other day. I can tell you she's the only living soul who ever sounded convincing. She may tell you a description of what you're searching for. But if I were you kids, I'd leave it alone." He paused for a few seconds before he spoke again. "Time for me to get back to work. Whatever you do, don't forget that one word I've been telling you about. Respect. Don't forget it, and don't neglect it." He strolled away, passing over the top of the hill and out of sight.

"Look!" cried Clayton. "At the crest of the mound."

"Antlers," said Jaylynn. "No way the caretaker missed seeing them. That's exactly the spot where he traveled."

"We need to go. Now." Scot aimed his bike to the west.

"Wait." Clayton held a finger to his lips.

In the heavy silence, Jaylynn's cell phone rang. The ring tone sounded like an exploding atomic bomb. Clayton flinched and jerked his handlebars. Jaylynn jumped and exhaled a pained breath. Scot screeched like a primate about to attack. Another act he wouldn't live down back in Columbus.

"Hello, Pa," Jaylynn spoke with the cell phone wedged between her cheek and shoulder. "Yeah, we're heading back now." She went silent for a moment and then said, "Is it okay if I spend the night with Clayton and Scot? We want to explore more of the town." Another pause. Scot stared up at the sky, hoping God was listening. "Okay, Pa. I'm coming." She shoved the phone in her pocket and shook her head. "Not tonight. But hopefully, this weekend."

Scot followed his brother and cousin down the hill, applying his brakes all the way. At the bridge, he and Clayton waved goodbye to Jaylynn before riding home.

5

The week passed without hunting for ghosts. Jaylynn had chores to do at home. More than once, Clayton asked Scot to return to the cemetery with him, and each time his brother refused.

"It gives me the creeps." Scot made a face. "Everything about it, the caretaker, the bushes, dead people, everything."

"Nothing happened."

"So!" Scot's voice rose, and his face tightened. "Doesn't mean something won't happen."

"We might find a friendly spirit." Sometimes, Clayton wished Scotty wasn't easy to scare. He would never let anything happen to Scot.

"Really? If I was dead, I wouldn't be happy."

"But you're not dead, Scotty."

"Exactly. And I want to stay that way."

"Did you really hear a scream in the woods?"

Scot looked from Clayton to the window but said nothing.

"Well?"

Scot walked over to the window and stared out. "There's something out there."

"Then why didn't I hear it?"

Scot whirled to face his brother. "You tell me."

"Sometimes squirrels screech."

"It wasn't a squirrel." Scot stormed from Clayton's room.

Clayton cackled like a chicken.

"I'd rather be a live chicken than a dead duck!" Scot yelled back.

Clayton didn't know what to think. Had Scotty heard a scream in the woods like the one at the cemetery? And if he had, was it from someone playing a joke? It was possible that Rand-Dock, the caretaker, was somehow behind it. There didn't seem to be any other explanation. Regardless, he wasn't about to leave Scot at home and search alone. Where was the fun in that? They were in this together. There was nothing for Clayton to do but wait for Jaylynn to find the time.

Clayton had considered paying a visit with Miss Kitts, the lady that the graveyard keeper had mentioned. But what would he say to her? Would she even speak with him? He had to come up with a better reason to visit the woman. Informing her of his meeting with Rand-Dock wouldn't do. He could visualize himself walking up to her door and knocking. "Hey, I heard that, when you were a teenager, you saw a monster and became the joke of the town. Can you describe the creature to me?" Sure, that would go over nicely. Ridiculous. Utterly a crazy idea!

It was Saturday night. Clayton and Scot's parents had promised an evening of fun at the local roller rink. It was a special night. Skate Palace had gone out of business. Tonight, was a trial run to see if the citizens would offer enough support for the rink to reopen weekly. Jaylynn and her brothers were to meet Clayton and his family there.

As Clayton tied his shoe, a light tapping came from his bedroom window. He walked over to it. Rain splattered beads of water against the glass. The treetops swayed back and forth. A rumble of thunder sounded, and the rainfall exploded into a downpour. Within seconds the gutter at the edge of the roof flooded and overflowed rainwater to the ground. A horrifying howl rose above the pounding storm. It had to be the wind. Clayton's eyes scanned the tree line. The water pummeling the glass made it difficult to see. What did the Hairy Man do on a night like this?

"Whatever he wants," he answered himself.

A flash of lightning filled the sky, and with it, the rain downgraded to a splatter. According to the clock on his nightstand, it was time to leave. Turning back to the window, a movement caught his eye. A white blur streaked across the yard, headed for the trees. Clayton pressed his forehead against the glass. The wolf stood at the tree line and stared up at the house, watching Clayton as much as he was it. Its drenched hair gave it the appearance of being deathly skinny. The wolf ran into the woods. "Gee," Clayton whispered. "It must be starving." Did the animal live nearby?

Pushing from the window, more flashes of lightning lit up the night sky, illuminating Clayton's bedroom like a short-circuited disco light. It was too bad that the skating rink didn't stay open until midnight. Maybe he could talk his parents into driving over the bridge in search of the floating lantern. Yeah, what was the likelihood of achieving that? There was no way Mom or Dad would wait two hours to help him lock for proof of a spirit. He left his room and checked on his brother. Scot was getting dressed.

"Don't you knock first?"

"Sorry." Clayton nodded toward the window. "I saw the wolf in our backyard."

"Really? When?"

"A few minutes ago. It ran into the woods."

Scot pressed his forehead to the glass. "I don't see a thing. Has anyone ever tamed a wolf?"

"Don't get any ideas." Clayton walked out to the hallway. "Let's go."

At the bottom of the steps, Mom handed Clayton a duffle bag. "What's this?"

"A few books that your Aunt Lucille wants to borrow," said Mom. "Put it in the van. I'll give it to her when she picks up the kids at the rink."

Clayton and Scot climbed in and buckled up. Mom instructed Dad to drive. She had a few text messages on her phone to answer.

Dad guided the van down the main thoroughfare into town. He usually had the car radio tuned to WFGH, the local station. But tonight, the only sounds to reach Clayton's ears were that of rain pelting the roof like hail and the tires splashing through puddle after puddle. The wipers were unable to keep up with the rainfall. It was evident that Dad was concentrating on driving.

"Maybe you should pull over and wait it out." Mom placed her phone on her lap.

"I'm driving careful." Dad leaned closer to the steering wheel.

Clayton glared out the side window. It was difficult to see much through the blurred glass. It was like riding through an automated carwash. No one would be walking in this storm. An umbrella would be pointless. Dad brought the van to a stop at a traffic light in front of a gas station. Once more, the rain slackened. A bearded man with a potbelly stood at the side of the roadway, staring at Clayton. The man wore denim bib overalls and a hardhat with a headlamp attached above the bill. The man and his clothes appeared to be dry. "How can that guy not be soaked?" Clayton said.

"What man?" Dad peered out his window. "I don't see anyone."

"Me, either." Mom leaned over the console.

The man was most certainly there, pointing a finger directly at Clayton. Clayton nudged his brother's arm. "Do you see him?"

Scot pressed his head against the glass. "Nope."

That didn't make sense. Was Clayton losing his mind? With some anxiety, Clayton looked back across the street. The man was gone. What's going on in this town? Here one second and gone the next. Was the man a warning of things to come? Forget it. Tonight was for fun, not hunting ghosts.

Wham!

Something slammed against the side of the van. Mom shrieked. Clayton twitched. Scot panted. Dad barked like a dog. Mom slapped him upside the head, and he laughed.

Dad opened his car door. "Tree branch," he said, closing the door. The light changed green, and Dad drove onward to the parking lot of the roller rink.

Once inside, Clayton observed a group of women gathered at a table, inspecting and admiring lady's garments. A placard sat on the tabletop reading, Ladies Bazaar Sale. The rink was of moderate size with a maple wood skating area. Black tube lights and multicolored spotlights hung near the ceiling. Red carpet with colorful neon triangles covered the floor of the concession stand. Several tables and sitting benches sat nearby. The familiar smell of piping-hot pizza and a faint musty scent, like gym shoes after P.E., filled the air. A stainless-steel railing encircled the rink. His parents chose traditional roller skates while he and Scot preferred inline skates.

"Clayton!" came a voice from near the front of the rink. Clayton looked over to see his three cousins, Roger, Jimbo, and Johnny, exiting the restroom.

"Where's Jaylynn?" Clayton spread his arms wide.

"She's in front of the concession stand with her friends." Roger nodded.

Clayton spotted Jaylynn sitting on a bench, hunched down, tying the laces on her skates, and flanked by four girls. "Who are her friends?"

"From left to right, Annette, Connie, little Karen Merie, and Mae Bug." Roger grinned.

"Mae Bug?" Clayton choked back a chuckle. Was Roger joking?

"Yep." Jimbo smacked Clayton on the back. "Welcome to the country way of life. My brothers and I have nicknames too."

"Really?" Clayton cocked back his head and waited for the punch line.

"Yeah, *son*," Johnny added. "Stud-muffin, Sweetie-pie, and Hot-stuff." He and Jimbo roared with laughter.

Clayton had to admit it was funny, especially the way Johnny had a habit of using the word 'son' when he spoke, with an emphasis on the word. He rolled his eyes. "Does the rink have a flea market?"

"Nah," Roger replied. "It's women from the PTA selling clothes and baked goods to help the school. Sometimes they raise money for military veterans too."

"The management allows that?" Clayton had never seen such in the big city.

"Louisa is a tight-knit town. Management is family-oriented," Jaylynn answered, rolling to a stop alongside Clayton. "I hope they decide to stay open. I love skating."

Despite the three brothers being triplets, they didn't look much alike. There was a resemblance in their faces but a considerable difference in their build. Roger was tall and stout, a good head taller than his brothers and Clayton. Jimbo was thin. Johnny stood near the same build as Clayton.

The triplets slipped on their skates and took to the floor, each wobbling back and forth.

"Is that the best you guys can do?" Clayton said, forcing himself not to bust out laughing.

"I bet I can out milk you." Roger raised his hands out in front of him, closing and opening his fingers repeatedly into fists.

"What?" Clayton felt his face crumple into what had to be a dumbfounded expression.

"Milk a cow." Jimbo chuckled. Johnny began to laugh, but he fell to the floor, landing on his back in a spread eagle.

After pushing from the wall, Clayton was free as a bird, holding his arms out and grinning from ear to ear. His body broke into a slight bounce, crossing his right leg over the left. He navigated his way down the length of the rink and rounded the corner. Now, rolling down another straight stretch, he folded his arms across his chest and gazed over to his dad. His dad pumped a thumb to the air. The triplets rolled into Clayton's sight, still wobbling, and smacking each other with their arms. A second later, the brothers crashed to the floor, stacked three high. Clayton laughed hard enough to hold his gut. Jaylynn sped past him, waving her arms to the air. He sighed. She was good at everything.

Clayton stared over to his dad and watched him break free of the crowd, pumping a fist in the air while holding the other flat against his stomach. He wiggled his hips in front of an imaginary dance partner. Dad was a skilled skater in navigating a floor packed like a swarm of bees. Dad flipped around to skate backward and swayed to the left and then to the right, like a pro. Raising one skate high above the floor, he balanced himself on the other, making the sport look easy. Clayton saw his mom smile as Dad sped by her. There was no way his mother was going to try and stay up with Dad's speed and maneuvers. She skated alongside Scot, who was trying to get the hang of it. As Scot moved away from the railing, his arms flapped like an airplane propeller.

***

Three hours quickly passed. The overhead lights came on, lighting the rink like it was daylight. A voice announced over the speaker that it was closing time. Clayton skated to a stop near the concession stand, where he waited for Dad and Scot. Upon Dad's approach, Scot wandered into his father's path. Dad's body twisted one way and then the other in a desperate attempt to steer clear. Clayton couldn't swallow the lump in his throat, as he stood unblinking, rattled by the obvious. Dad raised his heels to brake, but there wasn't enough distance. He bent his knees and placed his arms out in front of him like he was attempting to grab Scot before the collision. At that precise moment, Scot fell. Dashing past his son, Dad entered the concession area and collided with a metal trashcan. He went sprawling through the air and landed on top of a table, belly first, scattering cups of pop, pizza, and women's garments to the floor. His momentum carried him off the table and onto the lap of a burly man sitting on a bench. The bearded man dressed in a plaid shirt, resembled Paul Bunyan, the lumberjack in American folklore.

Dad's head shot up, with a pair of women's panties covering his hair, and groaned a wordless sound. The burly man sat silent and motionless, staring at Dad. The man wasn't smiling. "Did I hit a wall?" Dad moaned. The big man's lips formed into a sly grin. "Sorry," Dad whispered and stood, balancing himself on his skates. He removed the garment and held it out to a group of ladies standing nearby. The women giggled. It was evident to Clayton that not a single woman was willing to claim the panties.

The manager hurried over to the area and began picking up trash strewn about the floor. Dad reached down as if to help and lost his balance, tumbling headfirst, and landing on the trashcan. The entire crowd roared with gut-wrenching laughter.

Aunt Lucille arrived and helped Mom pull Dad to his feet, where he skated over to a bench to remove his skates.

Mom brushed her fingers across Clayton's hand. "Please bring the duffle bag in for your aunt."

Clayton hurried out to the parking lot alone. The rain had stopped, but everything was still dripping. As he neared Mom's van, he stepped around a puddle and a growl, like that of a dog, came from somewhere nearby. He stopped and listened. The cry came again, this time louder, and it had come from behind the building. Was it the wolf? A figure materialized in his peripheral vision. One part of his brain registered the fact that it was smaller than a man, more dog size, and that it stood in the shadows as if it were watching him. Another part, the part that ruled common sense, told him to run for his life. Turning to face it, Clayton expected the wolf to step out into the light. But the figure had moved elsewhere, out of his view. His eyes scanned the darkness beyond the direct limit of the lighting in the parking lot. Trees, bushes, and a trash dumpster lined the area.

Bang!

Clayton's heart slammed against his chest. What was that? Of course! It sounded as if someone had struck the dumpster with an aluminum bat. This was a prank.

"Who's there?" Clayton stepped toward the rear of the building. Wait! Two red orbs rose from behind the dumpster and lingered for a couple of seconds before dropping back out of sight. A loud screech broke the silence, much like the wicked cry at the cemetery a week ago. Jumping back, Clayton tripped over his own feet and landed on the ground in a sitting position.

He didn't dare take his gaze off the dumpster. A louder shriek followed, and Clayton cupped his ears with his hands. A massive form, ten feet or more, rose from behind the dumpster, wicked in its shape. Its head, big as a buffalo, supported a rack much like a deer. Its mouth opened wide and revealed a long tongue. If this was a prank, it had Hollywood written all over it.

"What are you doing back here?" Scotty asked from behind.

Clayton twisted on his rump and stared up at his brother and Jaylynn.

"Are you okay?" Jaylynn took hold of Clayton's arm and pulled him to his feet.

"Your pants are soaked," said Scot.

"Did you guys see it?" Clayton wheeled on his toes. Whatever it had been, had vanished. His heart banged against his chest at rocket speed, and his stomach muscles stiffened. He took a deep breath and let the air out slowly. What he saw had to be a prank, the best joke that he had ever seen.

"See what?" said Jaylynn.

"Dad! Mom!" Clayton yelled as his parents, Aunt Lucille, and the triplets came walking up. "I saw something back there." He pointed at the dumpster.

Dad aimed the light from his phone out in front of him. "Nothing there."

"Not now," said Clayton. "It was huge, like a monster. And it screamed so loud I had to cover my ears."

The triplets broke into laughter.

"Probably some kids playing a joke on the new kids." Aunt Lucille rubbed Clayton's back.

"If you would have seen it or heard it…" Clayton stepped aside. What was the use in trying to convince anyone of what he had seen? He had his own doubt to deal with.

"It's the brakes of a train," Dad replied. "Get in. We're going home."

Mom handed Aunt Lucille the duffle bag. "Enjoy. Take as long as you need."

Clayton shook his head. The train tracks were at the east end of the bridge on the West Virginia side. Trains passed by at all times of the night. But that was not the sound of the brakes on a train. And whatever was running in the darkness was not a teenager. No need to argue with his father. Dad had his mind made up.

Clayton blew out his cheeks. This was maddening. First, was the man with a hardhat standing in the rain, and now this. Was there actual truth to the myth of making a wish under the bridge or…of course not! It was nothing more than a silly prank, but he couldn't deny the fear it stirred within him. The act was definitely first class. Still, why was he the only one to see both? Scot and Jaylynn had also stood under the bridge and made that stupid announcement. Maybe his brother and cousin were involved in the joke?

6

The rain returned that evening, waking Scot from his sleep. A flash of lightning brought shadows to life for a second in his room, and he gulped. He was confident that his brother was sound asleep. Clayton could sleep through anything. He never stirred from the deep rumbles of thunder. Clayton wouldn't know if they had a tornado or a military invasion. It was crazy and unfair. Scot woke at the slightest noise.

Scot hated the storms. He always had, even though he was older now and positive that nothing severe was going to happen. Scot hated nearly everything about them, the wind, the rain, and the thunder. The lightning wasn't too bad when it flashed across a dark sky, except when it lit up a tree in a ghostly manner. Mom said that, when he was a newborn, he would bawl all night during a storm. Well, he was halfway to manhood and still hated them, but they no longer scared him. He pulled the blanket up over his head and peeked out. Another flash of light filled his room, along with a loud crack. Was that a tree splitting in two? The rain pounded against the roof. It sounded like someone dumping a truckload of marbles on the shingles over and over again.

Scot kicked the covers down to his knees and sat up in bed. His heart banged against his chest like it was trying to escape his body and run for the closet. He exhaled a heavy sigh and climbed out of bed. A gust of wind slammed against his bedroom window. He wheeled on his toes and stared over at the glass. Raindrops splattered against the windowpane. A bolt of lightning flashed, followed by a volley of flashes, and the sky went black. Where was the thunder? Instead of a boom came a howl. Or was it a scream? Whatever it was, a quiver reached his chin.

Once more, a cry rose above the sound of rain pelting the roof and windowpane. "Wow," Scot whispered. "That shriek sounded half-human, half-beast." He took one step toward the window. No, don't be stupid. He took two steps back. Whatever the cry was, it wasn't thunder or the wind. Scot exited his bedroom and crept along the dark hallway. On a night like this, it was best to have company. His parents had forgotten to turn on the nightlight. He inched along, feeling the wall for guidance. Usually, the creaks and groans of the house's wooden floorboards would have been audible, but the rain and storm drowned out his footsteps.

As Scot suspected, his brother was sound asleep. He climbed in bed alongside Clayton and curled up beside him. Scot loved his big brother, didn't know what he would do without him. Clayton included him in his adventures, never left him behind, and always protected him. Still, his brother needed to give up the notion of ghost hunting. It wasn't long before Scot dropped into a deep sleep.

***

Clayton pulled his hand over his face. Bright sunlight streamed through the window, and the room glowed in the early morning light. He sat up and found Scot sprawled alongside him, sleeping. "You asleep?"

"Yes."

Clayton swept his hand through Scot's hair. "Get up."

Scot pulled the covers over his head. "Check with me tomorrow."

Clayton snatched hold of the covers and yanked them across the foot of the bed and onto the floor. "It must have rained hard last night."

"You wouldn't wake up if a train ran through the front room."

"Hurry up and get dressed." Clayton slipped into his jeans and laced up his tennis shoes.

"I'm staying home." Scot covered his face with a pillow.

"We'll see." Clayton walked over to the bedroom door. "I'm going to cross the bridge today and visit our cousins on the bike." He walked to the doorway and waited, choking back a chuckle.

"Really?" Scot flipped the pillow onto the mattress and sat up. "Wait for me!" He dressed in record time. "Dad said riding a bike was the best years of his life. I don't want to miss my best years."

***

At the intersection of South Main Cross and Madison Streets, Clayton brought his bike to a halt. Could he go through with walking up to a woman's door, knocking, and informing her that he saw what she saw fifty years ago? A big part of him still believed what he had seen was a prank with an awesome costume. No doubt by local actors, in an attempt to bring back the legend of Miss Kitts' sighting. Then, there was that small part of him that kept thinking that the creature might be real, and that worried him. Could Miss Kitts guide him to the truth?

"Why are you stopping here?" Scot pulled alongside his brother.

"The caretaker at the graveyard said Miss Kitts lives down this street."

"So?"

"After what I saw last night at the skating rink, I need to talk to her." Clayton rose on his toes as if to take off.

"Jaylynn is waiting for us."

"We left an hour early, Scotty."

"I want to see our cousins, not some old woman."

Clayton leaned over his handlebars. "Nothing's going to happen. We're going to look under the bridge and visit Miss Kitts. Which one do you want to do first?"

"The bridge."

Clayton nodded and rode off with Scot close behind. They brought their bikes to a halt at the bridge and dismounted. "Wouldn't it be cool if we found the lantern?"

"There's nothing down there."

"It'll only take a couple of minutes." Clayton dropped his kickstand and walked to the riverbank. He turned back and watched Scot scrape the sole of his tennis shoe against the ground before making his way down the sloped embankment.

"Whoa! The current is high, Scotty." The tide splashed three feet higher than last week. A powerful undercurrent pushed the water northward in a rush, carrying small tree branches and debris with it. Waves slapped against the bank, making a loud and repetitive sound. A smoldering cigarette butt lay on the ground. "Someone has been here recently."

Scot snuffed out the butt with the toe of his shoe. "Cigarettes stink."

"Look." Clayton pointed at a dark stain on the cement embankment. "Blood."

"How do you know?"

"I know blood when I see it." Clayton crouched down for a better inspection.

"Don't touch it!"

"I'm not." Clayton stood, facing upriver. "I suppose it could be from someone gutting a fish, or…"

"Or what?"

"Or that falcon we saw ate a meal here."

"Yeah, it makes sense to me." Scot began walking up the embankment. "We better get going." Halfway up, he bent down and picked up a couple of rocks and stuffed them in his pants pocket.

"What's up with the rocks?"

"Going to toss them into the river, make a splash and watch the ripples."

"You won't see any ripples. The river is moving too fast, Scotty."

"I'm doing it anyway."

Clayton picked up a couple of stones from the ground.

"Hey, boys," came a man's voice from behind the brothers.

Clayton formed a fist around the rocks in his hand. Dad and Mom had taught him and his brother to be wary of strangers. Keep their distance. A person often gave small hints of what they were thinking through body movements or facial expressions. Clayton paid close attention to the man. He was soaking wet, head to black leather boots, and looked to be in his late twenties, nearly six-foot-tall, with a fair complexion but needing a shave and haircut. His long brown hair dropped over the tips of his ears. The man's faded jeans were dirty, with a large hole across one knee, exposing his pale white skin. His water-soaked crew neck T-shirt clung to his chest. The shirt had several stains, dark, like dried blood. Had the guy been swimming in the river? The stench of fish and rotting seaweed swirled around the man.

"There you are," said the man.

Clayton took a step back as he made a mental connection with the rocks in his hand. Was the man speaking to him? He had never seen this man before. It could be a trick to get him and Scot to lower their guard. Clayton repositioned himself to stand in front of Scot.

"Come here, boy." The man raised his arms out in front of him.

Clayton spun on his toes and found a mix-breed dog standing at the riverbank. Its fur was dripping wet, giving the canine the appearance it had died a hundred times over.

The man crouched down and hugged the dog. "I've been searching for you all night. Where have you been?" Turning toward Clayton, he added,

"This is my wingman." He patted the dog's head. "Guess I should say my wing-dog. His name is Parliament. He's a good ol' boy." The man scratched behind the dog's ears. "Part terrier, part mutt, part this and that, but smart as the dickens." He pulled a pair of sunglasses from his back pocket and placed them over his dark eyes. "Old Parliament and I had been tugging along in my canoe last night when a storm hit, and we capsized. I've been looking for him ever since."

The dog leaped on Clayton's thigh and panted. Clayton rubbed the dog's chest.

"Well, that's a first." The man grinned from ear to ear. "Usually, old Parliament is shy with strangers." The man looked at the river. "Guess that old boat of mine is gone forever."

"Were you carrying a lantern?" Clayton had to ask. If this guy was playing a joke, it was a good one.

"Why yes, I was. It was a bull's-eye lantern, over a hundred years old. It belonged to my great-grandpa dating back to the Revolutionary War. I guess it's gone too." He fanned a hand out in front of himself. "Well, boys, me and Parliament will make our parting from you now. My advice…stay away from the water." The man and his dog walked upriver and out of sight.

"Do you think he was a…"

Clayton laughed and slapped his knee. "Right. About as much as I am. But I admit it was a good try at scaring us."

"He mentioned the Revolutionary War a hundred years ago. It's been a lot longer than that."

"Correct. That would mean he was from a time near the Civil War. Do you think they had sunglasses back then, Scotty?"

Scot shrugged. "It did storm last night. And Jaylynn said the floating lantern appears during—"

"Don't be silly." Clayton raised his arms above his head. "We're from a big city. What better way for a small town to welcome us?"

"The whole town?"

Clayton nodded. "We don't have time to visit Miss Kitts. Maybe tomorrow. Let's go."

Near the middle of the bridge, the brothers tossed the rocks down to the raging river into oblivion.

As the brothers stepped back from the railing, Scot gasped and pointed across the river. "How did they get over to the Point Section so quickly?"

Clayton shrugged. The stranger and his dog, Parliament, stood near a tall oak tree with their eyes fixed on him and Scot. "Weird. They walked away to the north. The opposite direction." It was strange, indeed. "The folks here in Louisa are pretty good actors."

"But what if…"

"Don't be silly, Scotty." Clayton began walking his bike toward the West Virginia side of the bridge.

Scot fell in behind his brother. "Is there a way to take back a wish?"

7

To reach the home of Jaylynn and her brothers, Scot followed Clayton on U.S. 52, a two-lane road that was also known as Tolsia Highway. It was only a three-mile journey from their home to their cousins'. The traffic wasn't heavy, unlike the big city he and Clayton had left behind. Occasionally, Scot took a quick look beyond the roadway, to his left and right. A man and his dog could be anywhere.

As Scot and Clayton entered the driveway of their cousins' house, Jaylynn swung open the screen door, came to a halt at the edge of the porch and waved. She slipped on her backpack and jumped to the ground, where she skipped over to the boys and their bikes. "I see you guys made it."

Jimbo and Johnny came strolling into view from the barn with Old Blue, their coonhound.

Scot hopped off his bike and hugged the dog.

"Where's Roger?" Clayton asked.

"He's helping Pa," said Jimbo.

"Mending a fence in the far pasture," Johnny added. "Here, Scot." He handed Scot a pack of dog treats. "Old Blue loves them."

Scot scooped a handful of the treats and handed the pack back to Johnny.

"Have any trouble getting here?" Jaylynn aimed her question at Clayton.

Clayton shrugged. "Not really."

"Yes, we did!" Scot squared his shoulders. His brother wasn't telling the whole story. "We found the gho…" he caught the word before it rolled off his tongue. "The guy who carries the lantern under the bridge."

Jaylynn and her brothers cocked their heads to the side. Their eyebrows raised, and mouths dropped open.

Clayton shared the event with the man and dog under the bridge.

"Wow." Jaylynn sucked in a deep breath. "Did the guy evaporate?"

Clayton shook his head. "No."

"Could have been somebody playing a prank," said Jaylynn.

"I told you." Clayton gave his brother a friendly shove.

"Well, I believe the guy was a ghost. We can stop looking." Scot gave Old Blue another treat.

"We were going to visit Miss Kitts but ran short on time." Clayton thrust his chest out.

"Maybe tomorrow," Jaylynn said.

"Who's Miss Kitts?" Johnny stepped closer.

Jaylynn shared the event with the caretaker at the graveyard.

"That's freaky, *son*, but today we investigate a West Virginia ghost." Johnny pumped a fist to the air.

"Yeah. Time to hunt for the Screaming Thing. It's about twenty minutes away by bike." Jimbo shuffled his feet and grinned.

"The killer clown?" Clayton cocked his head and raised one eyebrow.

"What if it's real? What if it catches us? Do we have to wait until dark?" A drop of sweat trailed down Scot's face, but he resisted the urge to wipe it away. His cousins were wacky.

"Whoa!" Jimbo held up an index finger. "One question at a time."

"I haven't heard the Screaming Thing," Jaylynn admitted. "I don't think the legend's real. As Grandpa said, old man McCord's a storyteller."

And it better stay that way, Scot nearly said.

"Because we've never been there," Johnny said defensively. "But that's changing today, *son*. The people on Paddle Creek claim the beastly screams can be heard daily at thirteen-thirteen." Scot felt his face twist in a knot. "One p.m. is the thirteenth hour of the day. And 1:13 is thirteen-thirteen."

"I could have told you that," said Clayton, staring over at Scot.

It wasn't Scot's fault that he didn't give a hoot about military time. All he knew was that it hadn't sounded reasonable. Scot ran a hand through his hair while his other hand tightened on the dog treats. Thirteen and ghosts definitely didn't mix. Yep, wacky was a good description for his cousins, and Clayton fit right in with them.

Jimbo rolled his eyes. "I have to see it for myself, before I believe it."

Jaylynn checked the time on her cell phone. "We have forty-five minutes."

"I'll wait here with Old Blue for you guys." Scot wasn't about to tag along. "There's no way I want to see a killer clown."

"You're going with us." Clayton squinted. "Now get on. We're running out of time unless you want to ride home in the dark."

Scot bit his tongue. Why couldn't his brother read his eyes? Maybe Clayton didn't care how Scot felt about clown hunting? The bridge was one left turn from where they were. If he left now, he would be home long before dark. Let Clayton deal with Dad later. But if Scot were to do that, it would be against their promise to each other. With a grunt, he kicked a pebble with the toe of his tennis shoe.

Johnny bent down and rubbed the dog on the neck. "Go inside, Blue." The dog whimpered and walked over to the porch.

Shoving the remaining dog biscuit into his pants pocket, Scot hurried over to his bike and mounted it. He filled his lungs and blew out his cheeks. Clayton was right. His brother would be in deep trouble if Scot rode home alone. Leave no man behind.

"Hey, guys, wait for me!" Roger stood in the doorway of the barn, waving his arms. "Give me a couple minutes." He ducked back inside the barn and out of view.

Scot relaxed his grip on the handlebars. It was great that Roger was coming with them. It would take a large clown to be bigger than Roger.

The front screen door of the house opened, and Aunt Lucille stepped onto the porch. "Have you boys had your breakfast?"

"Yes, Aunt Lucille." Clayton raised a thumb.

Scot nodded reluctantly. Eating required going inside the house, away from clown hunting, but he couldn't eat more.

"You kids be careful on those bikes." Aunt Lucille waved and went back inside the house, taking Old Blue with her.

Roger came scampering from the backyard.

"Were not done yet, Roger!" Uncle Brian yelled from the doorway of the barn.

Roger threw his arms up over his head and scuffed a heel of his work boots in the dirt. Without a word, he gestured for the others to proceed without him, and he walked back to his father. Just Scot's luck! There went the guy he planned on keeping in his sight.

"We need to hurry." Jaylynn mounted her bike, as did the others, and they tore off riding down the driveway.

Jimbo and Johnny jumped out to the lead, riding abreast.

Ten minutes later, Jimbo and Johnny came to a stop near a densely wooded area on the right side of the road.

"This is it," Johnny said, almost in a whisper.

"Yeah," Jimbo added, keeping his voice low.

"Why are you guys whispering?" Clayton asked.

"The clown could be nearby," said Jimbo.

"Yeah, *son*, it could be watching us." Johnny's eyes narrowed. "That's where the man lives who claimed that he saw the killer clown."

Scot's eyes followed Johnny's finger, pointing at a small farmhouse built of unfinished wood. It stood weathered and frozen by a hundred winters and baked by a hundred summers. It had a small porch with a three-foot-high railing that ran the width of the house. Several old jam jars and wire crates sat on top of the wall and held dead plants. A clay pot sat on the porch floor and contained a cluster of dandelions. The wooden front door stood centered between two windows on the ground floor. The second floor had a window centered below the peak of the roof. The drapes were open. There was a clean spot on the window as if someone had pressed a forehead against the glass. The windows on the first floor were dusty, dirty, and grimy.

"How are we on time?" asked Jimbo.

"We're okay." Jaylynn peddled her bike over a wooden footbridge. The undercurrent of Paddle Creek swept by at a torrent speed. She dropped down the kickstand and dismounted. "We have eighteen minutes."

"Can't we hear the scream from the road?" Once again, Scot tried to communicate with Clayton by way of his eyes.

Clayton shrugged. "Nothing's going to get you. Come on."

"What about the old man in the house?" Scot glared up at the second-floor window. Did the curtain move?

"*Son*, he's probably older than the dirt we're standing on," Johnny cracked.

"Yeah," said Jimbo. "What's he going to do, eat us?" He broke into a hearty laugh.

"Get moving." Jaylynn pushed her way between her brothers. Scot followed, alternating his attention between where he was stepping and the second-floor window.

8

Upon entering the woods, Scot's eyes kicked into overdrive, scanning left and right, up, and down. Serenity came with mystery. What if the trees were keeping a secret among themselves? A mosquito landed on his hand, and he swatted it. With a finger, he flipped the squashed carcass to the ground. A multitude of birds chirped. Scot sniffed. A wild mixture of scents filled the forest, damp soil and leaves, rotting wood, wildflowers, and pine trees. A single red rose grew at the trunk of a tall walnut tree. His mother loved roses for their beauty and softness. Scot bent down and rubbed a single rose petal between his fingers. He dropped to one knee and sniffed the flower. Weird. No scent. When Scot stood, a chipmunk scampered from the brush. He tapped his brother on the arm. Clayton nodded.

Scot swatted at several insects flying near his face. He took a step back and gazed up at the treetops. It was pretty neat the way they crowded one another, their branches forming a canopy over saplings and smaller trees. Sunlight streaked through the tree limbs in bright and shadowy beams. The sky was a few fragments of blue, scattered like pieces of an impossible jigsaw puzzle, visible through the treetops. Soggy ground supported his tennis shoes. Why hadn't he worn his boots? The earth nourished many shrubs and bushes of honeysuckle, weeds, wildflowers, and shoulder high thickets, some with thorns protruding from them. Two squirrels ran out from under the brush and bolted off, one chasing after the other.

"Eww! A cobweb." Scot rubbed his face with the palm of his hand. He hated whenever that happened. It had to be the worst feeling in the world.

A small brown bird, with a fat-puff roundness, began singing from its perch on a tree branch above Scot, drawing his attention. Its voice was loud, a high-pitched screech.

"That's a Wren," Jaylynn said. "A small bird with a giant voice."

"I was hoping it was the Screaming Thing," said Scot.

"I don't think so." Jimbo smiled.

The bird's voice did little to help soothe Scot's uneasiness. Several times he had gazed out his bedroom window and wished he had the nerve to explore the woods. Now, here he was, smack dab in the middle of towering trees searching for a killer clown. He needed to have his head examined, especially after his first experience in the woods.

"That one's a House Finch." Jaylynn pointed at a red bird sitting on a branch across the way. "The brown one next to it's also a House Finch. It's a female. The pretty one is a male."

A beautiful bird with red feathers, perched on a neighboring tree, cried out, sounding much like short quick bursts of a car security alarm. Scot pointed to it.

"A Northern Cardinal." Jaylynn tossed her hair. "Also, a male."

"How do you know?" Scot had no idea how a person was to tell the gender of a bird.

"Google." Jaylynn glared over to her brothers. "I feed my brain."

"Show off," Johnny cracked.

"Yeah, we don't care about birds." Jimbo gently punched his brother's arm. "Give us mountain lions, coyotes, snakes, and gators."

"You don't have alligators around here...do you?" Clayton's eyes grew as large as half dollars.

"Of course not. Don't listen to them." Jaylynn growled at her brothers.

A new whistling came from somewhere in the treetops.

"You won't believe the name of that one." Jaylynn giggled. "That's a Tufted Titmouse."

"Yeah, right." Clayton brushed her off with a wave of his hand. Scot agreed with his brother. That was a crazy name for a bird.

"Serious." Jaylynn inched forward. "It's really a Tufted Titmouse. It sounds like it's saying, Peter, Peter, Peter."

Scot looked closer at the bird. A light brown covered its entire belly and circled both eyes like a mask. Its back and feathers were dark gray. He would never remember the names of the birds, but it sure beats hunting for a killer clown.

"Enough nature crap." Jimbo kicked the toe of his shoe at a twig on the ground.

"Yeah, *son*," Johnny said. "It's boring."

Scot bit his tongue. He saw no need to hurry and trudge deeper into the woods to search for death. There had to be a way to slow down this expedition. "Aw," he said, pointing at a bird perched on a branch. "That's a sparrow."

"Correct." Jaylynn smiled.

"Watch it!" Clayton grabbed hold of Scot's forearm, stopping him from stepping into a hole. "Probably a groundhog nearby."

If only that was all Scot had to worry about. A groundhog was a far cry from a kid-eating clown.

"And a bunch of other critters, *son*." Johnny chuckled.

"Yeah, but we're looking for Bozo, the killer clown," Jimbo cracked.

Jaylynn whirled on her brothers. "If you guys don't shut up…"

Snap!

"Where did that come from?" Scot rose on his toes. It wouldn't take much for him to bolt back to his bike.

Johnny picked up a tree branch and swung it over his shoulder like a baseball player. "I'm ready, *son*."

"Shhh!" Jaylynn held a finger to her lips and froze. Her eyes darted back and forth, up and down.

Scot shifted his weight. Trees stood everywhere in either direction. The greenery and undergrowth were thick, a bear could be hiding a few feet away, and they wouldn't know it. A cool breeze swept through the trees, swaying branches with it. A whippoorwill sounded from nearby, followed by two or three others. Does a killer clown have a death song?

After a few seconds, Jaylynn motioned to renew their trek by waving her hand.

Scot moved slowly. Anyone or anything could be hiding behind the next tree, which stood no more than an arm's length away. His ears strained to listen. But both Johnny and Jimbo were stepping on fallen branches as if the entire ordeal was a trip to Disneyland.

"We got coyotes and mountain lions down here," Jimbo said.

"Re-re-really?" Scot halted and stared over at Jimbo. A mountain lion was more powerful, more aggressive than a wolf. If his cousin was trying to scare him, it was working.

"They're kidding again, right?" Clayton asked Jaylynn.

"No. I've seen coyotes more than once. I haven't seen a mountain lion, but there've been several reports of them in the area."

"Grrrr!" Johnny leaped forward, waving his arms over his head.

"Not funny." Scot planted his palm to his cousin's chest and shoved him back.

Glancing at her phone, Jaylynn placed a finger to her lips. "It's time." She leaned her backside against the trunk of a big tree and told the others to do the same.

Scot's head cocked back. The question on his mind must have been written on his face because Clayton answered it. "To watch our backs."

Scot positioned the front of his body against a tree and gawked out from behind it. He didn't want to lose sight of anyone.

"Ten seconds," Jaylynn whispered. She held her phone out in front of her and counted, "Five…four…three…two…one."

Scot held his breath and gripped the bark of the tree as though his life depended on it. Now was not the time to die. His entire life lay ahead of him. Could he outrun the others? In all the horror movies that he had seen, it was always the slowest who was the unluckiest.

An eerie calmness came over the forest as if Jaylynn had called upon it to do so, complete utter silence. The wind had ceased. Birds had gone quiet as if someone had shut off the clatter of nature. No one moved.

Coo-woo-woo-woo broke the stillness. Scot whipped his head back.

"A mourning dove," Jaylynn said. "They can fly up to fifty-five miles per hour."

"Wow," Scot whispered. "I had no idea."

The sound of a snapping branch came from somewhere.

From the sound of it, someone or something had stepped closer. Again, Scot rose on his toes. Every kid for themselves!

"Wha…" Clayton's breath was almost a word.

"Shhh!" Jaylynn's eyes scanned the woods.

Yaa, yaa, yaa, yaa! A cry slipped through the trees. A bird with a vast wingspan swooped down and struck foliage alongside a dead tree stump.

Scot's heart raced a mile a minute. "Whoa!" The bird flew like a fighter jet, dipping downward and back up with precision through the treetops. "Did you see that?" Scot pressed his backside against a tree. That was awesome to witness. That was one thing that he never saw in the big city.

"That was a red-shouldered hawk," Jaylynn said.

"Yeah," Scot added. "But-but-but it had a snake in its…"

"Talons," Clayton answered.

"I didn't know there were snakes in here too." Scot's eyes scanned the ground.

"*Son*, what'd you think was in the woods?" Johnny chuckled.

"Winnie the Pooh?" A grin nearly split Jimbo's face in two.

Scot scraped the toe of his shoe across the ground. Why were they searching for a clown when they had two in their group? Maybe he could outrun them both when the time came. Give the killer clown a double portion of brain-dead meat.

Jaylynn shot her brothers a scowl. "We'll wait an hour then leave."

"We can leave now." Scot sucked in a deep breath. "I'm ready to go." He bent down and picked several briars from his jeans. His teeth ached, and he unclenched his jaw. How far was it to his bike?

"*Son*, we need to go deeper into the woods." Johnny waved a hand in front of him.

"What if we get lost?" The entire time Scot had searched for markers, trees with a unique shape to guide him back to their bikes. If it came down to that, the odds were not in his favor. The dense trees with low branches made running nearly impossible, at least at full speed. Off in the distance, a rabbit sat on its rump engaged in a staring contest with him. No doubt getting a kick out of watching stupid humans doing stupid stuff.

"Get lost? No way." Jimbo pumped a thumb at his sister. "Not with the Lady of the Jungle with us."

Scot determined that he would follow Jaylynn should he need to run for his life. Clayton better be smart enough to do the same. There was no way that Scot would be the slowest. He needed to outrun only one other person.

Jaylynn took the lead, and Scot fell in behind her. They continued further into the woods with the others following until they reached a deep, narrow opening in the ground.

"A gully." Jimbo walked out to the edge.

"*Son*, that's a ravine," Johnny said.

"It's more of a gorge." Jaylynn leaned out for a better look. "There's water down there. Must be part of Paddle Creek. Looks deep from the rain last night."

"Yeah, *son*, it's moving swiftly." Johnny hunched down and placed his palms to his knees.

"Don't fall." Jaylynn took hold of her brother's arm.

From Scot's vantage point, the ground sloped on both sides, where the creek rushed by at the bottom. There was no way they could cross from where they were. The gorge stretched as far as Scot could see. Even if there had been no creek, climbing down and back up the steep embankments would be risky.

"Are we going up the creek or down?" Jimbo asked.

Jaylynn jutted out her chin and walked onward. Within minutes they came to a clearing in the woods, formed in a twenty to thirty-yard circle. There had been no sign leading up to the opening—no thinning of the trees.

A heavy fragrance of pine, wild jasmine, and honeysuckle reached Scot's nostrils one second and was gone the next, replaced with the scent of damp earth. The ground was lush green, like a city park.

"Look!" Jaylynn came to an abrupt halt and stared across the way.

Scot stopped in mid-stride. How many hidden wonders were in a forest? He eyed a suspension walk bridge located at the far end of the clearing. A lone tree, dead and withered like it had lost life years ago, stood near the entrance of the bridge, a rusty, dilapidated bridge that was the only link to the other side of the creek. No way! I can't swim! Scot etched the view into his mind. Not often does one get the chance to observe the place of his death.

9

The bridge extended across the ravine. Its wooden planks had long ago fallen victim to leaves, fir needles, vines, sticks, and moss. Metal fencing, rusty and loosely connected, ran the length of the bridge to prevent a person from falling into the ravine below. Little good that was, should the floorboards give way. The creek splashed, sloshed, and cried, challenging a soul to try its luck. The sound alone was enough to deter Scot from trying to cross. Swamp-like vegetation and broken tree limbs created slimy pools of debris. Midway under the walk bridge, the water swirled in the form of a funnel as if it were churning at the hands of the devil. The whirlpool sucked the muddy waters, and its rubbish to its dark depths like the creek hadn't eaten in years.

"Wow." A sick flutter erupted in Scot's stomach. Surely his brother and cousins had no plans of crossing that death trap. "Where does the bridge go?"

Jaylynn shrugged. "I don't know."

"Me either," Jimbo admitted. "Must be fifty to sixty feet long. Maybe longer."

"Hard to tell," Clayton said. "Can't see the end."

Scot's lips tightened. Clayton was right. It wasn't possible to see the end of the bridge. A shadow cast by trees covered the end of the bridge, giving Scot the impression that the walkway led into the unknown. Why were they going deeper into the woods instead of back to their bikes? Was he the only one with half a brain?

"*Son*, it's old," said Johnny.

Scot stared over at Johnny. Good assumption, Einstein.

"Some floorboards are missing. I wonder who built it," said Johnny.

"Adam and Eve?" Jimbo laughed.

Johnny swatted him on the forearm.

"We're not crossing that old thing, are we?" Scot looked over to his brother. Clayton shrugged. Should Scot ever become rich, the first thing he was going to buy was a tutor to teach Clayton how to read eyes.

"There's no shack, cabin, or anything in sight, *son*." Johnny wiped the sweat from his forehead.

"I bet Hansel and Gretel thunk the same thing." Jimbo's eyebrows danced up and down.

Jaylynn rolled her eyes. "Thunk? You need better jokes."

Scot silently agreed. Jimbo's jokes were loopy, but at least, he wasn't picking on Scot—yet.

"There's a sweat bee on my arm!" Jimbo held his arm out for all to see. A second bee landed alongside the other.

"Don't smack them." Jaylynn hurried over to her brother.

"The bees will die if they sting him." Clayton's face beamed like he had won the final episode of Jeopardy.

"Only honeybees die after stinging," Jaylynn replied. "Sweat bees drink the sweat from a body. Once their stinger pierces the skin, the stinger continues to pump venom until you pull it out."

"Eww." Scot moved back a step. "Are we about to get attacked by bees?" His eyes scanned the sky. It would be his luck that if bees did come, they would be killer bees, raised by a clown.

Without replying, Jaylynn motioned for Johnny to join her, and they both simultaneously flipped a bee from their brother's arm.

"Thanks." Jimbo winked.

Jaylynn inspected Jimbo's arm. "Looks good. Lucky they didn't sting you." She made her way over to the entrance of the bridge. Scot stood alongside her. "I've never seen Paddle Creek so wide and deep." To the east, the creek stretched as far as one could see. To the west, the stream rushed around a bend, splashing its wrath upon the bank.

Scot bit his tongue. It would do no good to suggest that they leave the woods by the way that they came. Going any further was downright crazy. It'd been one danger after another: snake, sweat bees, and, now, a rotting bridge. What's next, flying monkeys? Glancing over his shoulder, he gasped and shouted, "Wow! Frogs everywhere!"

Jaylynn spun on her heels, and she screeched. She took a step back and aimed her cell phone out in front of her. "Whoa! It's an army of frogs and toads." She took a photo. The frogs sat on the ground staring at Scot and the others. "Must be thousands of them. Why are they so quiet? Not a peep."

A shadow moved overhead and drew Scot's attention. Several huge birds perched on branches of various dead trees stared downward at the kids. Scot shrieked and stepped back, tripping over his feet and falling to the ground on his rump.

"Red-headed turkey vultures," Jaylynn said. "Big ugly creatures."

Scot wasn't about to argue with her opinion. They were definitely ugly. "Will they attack us?"

"They are more scavengers than anything else." Jaylynn pointed at flourishing trees beyond the dead ones. "Those are black vultures, also called black buzzards. They've been known to attack cattle and other animals. They're not afraid of humans."

"Scot and I are not going any further." Clayton nudged his brother to get behind him.

Scot didn't hesitate. Finally, Clayton saw things his way. Scot kept his eyes on the vultures and buzzards as his legs trembled, and his lungs tried to stay up with his speeding heart. One vulture stood perched in front of the others. It slowly raised its wings and spread them wide. Scot gulped. This trip in the woods was no longer crazy. It was suicidal.

"Look!" Jimbo's cry got Scot's attention. Jimbo grabbed hold of his sister's forearm and nodded once toward the opposite end of the clearing.

"A parliament of owls," Jaylynn said.

Scot whirled on his toes and locked eyes with his brother at the word "parliament." Neither he nor Clayton had shared the name of the dog under the bridge. "Why did you say parliament?" Were his cousins playing a prank on him and Clayton?

"A parliament is a group of owls."

Scot didn't doubt Jaylynn's answer. But it was still weird to hear such a rare word twice in a day. The owls numbered six. They stood side by side, their big yellow eyes gazing at him as if watching his every move.

"They're spotted owls." Jimbo raised his eyebrows. "So much for being nocturnal."

"The frogs are nocturnal. But here they are in broad daylight." Jaylynn turned toward the owls. "They're not spotted owls. They're burrowing owls, active during daylight. They roost and nest in burrows, but they don't usually travel this far to the northeast."

It still wasn't too late for Scot to make a run for it. Maybe Clayton and the others would follow, or perhaps not. He glanced up at the vultures before looking back at the owls and decided to stay put, at least for now.

The owls turned their heads in unison, first to the left, then to the right, and finally fixed their eyes back on Scot and the others. Each owl hissed.

Scot covered his ears with his hands. "They sound like snakes."

"They're good at that," said Jaylynn.

Both Johnny and Jimbo picked up sticks and tossed them at the buzzards. Several birds took to the air. The boys shared a fist bump.

"That was awesome." Jimbo spread his arms wide. "Such massive wingspans."

"*Son*, wish I had brought my BB gun." Johnny pretended to shoot a rifle.

"Stop, you idiots!" Jaylynn stole the words off Scot's tongue. Her face twisted in a knot. "Trust me. You don't want them to attack us." She glared at her brothers in silence for a moment and then asked, "Are we really related?" She released an audible exhale. "Stupider than stupid." She motioned for everyone to get back. "Walk slow."

"I want to go home," Scot whispered. A frog short-hopped out in front of the others and drew his attention. It landed a few feet in front of Scot and gazed up at him. "I thought frogs don't have tails."

"They don't," Jimbo replied. "Only as tadpoles."

Scot stood frozen, pointing at the frog that sat before him. He knew a tail when he saw one, and that frog wiggled a six-inch tail over its back. Its body was green. Its tail was bright orange. Surely, he wasn't the only one to see it.

"That's freaky." Jaylynn raised her phone and snapped a photo.

The frog tilted its head to the side like a human and continued to stare.

"They don't move their heads like that either," Johnny said.

"This one does." Scot gulped. The frog jumped up and landed on Scot's forearm. He shrieked and smacked it with his free hand. The frog fell to the ground on its backside. It flipped onto its feet and returned to staring up at him. The frog raised its tail over its back, curved in a half-circle like it was pointing at him. Slowly, the frog turned its tail toward the bridge before turning it back at Scot.

"No way, *son*," Johnny said.

"What?" The word barely escaped Scot's mouth.

"The frog wants us to cross the bridge." Jimbo picked up a branch from the ground. Johnny did the same.

"How do you know?" Scot would have believed the statement if Jaylynn had said it. But with Jimbo, he wasn't so sure.

"It's pointing its tail toward the bridge." Jimbo grinned.

For a split second, Scot pictured trading places with Jimbo. Let his cousin deal with the frog. It would wipe that stupid grin off Jimbo's face. Did Jimbo think this was a typical day in the woods? Idiot! But his cousin was right. The frog aimed its tail at him for a second and then twisted it in the direction of the bridge before turning it back at him.

"We can't. It's not safe." Clayton grabbed a branch lying nearby and swung it out in front of him. He motioned for his brother to stay back.

Clayton didn't need to tell him twice. Scot was a fast learner in that category. "Do frogs eat meat?" Scot asked Jaylynn.

"Yes, they are carnivores." That was not the answer Scot wanted to hear.

The tailed frog opened its mouth and croaked a high-pitched Tatt-tatt-tatt. A second later, it shrieked a sound, much like a human whistling for a dog.

"Get ready to run," Scot said in a loud whisper, aiming his index finger beyond Jimbo and Johnny. Another hoard of frogs began walking in long lines like soldiers in formation, coming directly at them.

Tatt-tatt-tatt cried the tailed leader, followed by another whistle. The frogs broke their silence, each croaking in different pitches and cries as if chanting, "Kill!" The entire army of frogs leaped forward in a joint attack.

It was time to see who the slowest runner in his group was. Scot tore off like a jackrabbit at a dog track only to trip over a log, landing spread-eagle on the ground, face down. He raised his head. Frogs surrounded him. Little puffs of frog breath warmed his face. Had the frogs dined on vomit? His heart raced and pounded against his chest while his legs, feet, arms, and hands trembled, and his chin quivered. Beads of sweat formed on his forehead. A sudden chill spread from his toes to the tips of his ears, and his lungs screamed for air. Why wouldn't his body stand and run? He gave it a direct order. This was it. He was going to be eaten alive. What was it that Rand-Dock had said? There was only one thing we can be sure of in life. Well, it was about to strike!

The end of a tree branch swooshed past Scot's head. Several frogs went soaring through the air.

"Stand up." Clayton tossed the branch to the ground. He reached down and grabbed Scot by the shirt and yanked him to his feet. "Get behind me."

Jaylynn, Jimbo, and Johnny swung tree limbs out in front of them, smashing frog bodies and heads mercilessly. The army of frogs charged full speed ahead and attacked.

Scot watched as his brother picked up the branch and joined their cousins, swinging the sticks like ball bats, swatting frogs in mid-jump. The onslaught of frogs increased, some striking the youths on the face, chest, and legs.

"Hurry!" Jaylynn bolted toward the bridge.

Clayton clutched Scot's shirt as they ran side by side. A frog struck Scot on the back of the head, causing Scot to fall to the ground. Clayton pulled him to his feet. "Duck as you run."

Johnny pushed past his sister. Jaylynn slipped and fell to the grass, and Jimbo helped her to her feet. Clayton and Scot came running up behind the siblings. Frogs continued their attack, leaping through the air. Several frogs flew over the kids and struck the bridge fencing where the amphibians fell to the creek.

Jimbo took a couple of steps onto the bridge. A floorboard snapped and dropped to the water below. He grabbed hold of the rail and balanced himself with one foot firmly planted on a second board. After shifting his weight, he proceeded onward. Johnny stepped onto the bridge close behind his brother. Clayton and Scot took up the rear with Jaylynn. At the halfway point, a frog had impaled its belly on the metal fencing. Its eyes stayed on Scot as he edged his way along the bridge. Scot slipped and lost his footing, wedging his foot between two planks.

Clayton pulled on his brother's arm. "Lift your leg."

"I'm trying." The board under Scot snapped and fell to the raging creek, and the whirlpool swallowed the slat. Scot's leg fell below the walkway. He landed with his upper body wedged between two boards with a leg dangling below. "Help me!" Scot twisted one way and then the other. The bridge swayed as its supports groaned. Frogs continued their attack, hopping and croaking, striking Scot, and the others from the back.

Jimbo and Johnny began to walk back to help. Jaylynn raised her hand. "Stay there." She slipped off her backpack and removed a rope. Wrapping the rope around Scot's midsection, she tied it off near his underarms. She wrapped the other end of the line around Clayton and herself and tied another knot. "Grab under his arm. We both pull at the same time." Scot remained wedged. Jaylynn removed a hammer from the backpack and handed it to Clayton. "Bust the board."

"But it might…" Clayton held the hammer in one hand and Scot by the arm with the other. Scot sensed his brother's fear through his grip. The three of them may end up in the whirlpool of death. Jaylynn held Scot by the back of his shirt and grasped the railing with her free hand. She nodded, and Clayton swung. The board snapped in two and fell to the creek. Scared out of five years of his life, Scot got to his feet and hunched over, filling his lungs with short labored breaths.

A distant cry, which sounded like a drawn-out guttural 'argh' wafted over the woods, and Scot lost another year. At this rate, he would be an infant in no time flat.

10

"What was that?" Scot's heart hammered his chest. He scanned the outer edge of the woods that they had yet to enter. Jimbo and Johnny stood clinging to the railing near the end of the bridge. The scream hadn't come from one of them. It came from further away, deeper in the woods.

Jaylynn shrugged. "Maybe the Screaming…" She turned to face the frogs, and Scot turned with her. The amphibians were nowhere in sight—not one. The only evidence the frogs had been real was the one impaled on the railing. Its feet wiggled back and forth, trying to free itself.

"Where'd the frogs go?"

"Hard to say, Scotty." Jaylynn picked up her backpack and slipped her arms through the straps, pulling it snug against her back. "Let's get across the bridge."

"Did that scream come from behind us or in front?" asked Jimbo. Jaylynn shrugged.

The speed of Scot's heart was slowly returning to normal, but it still felt as if he had swallowed a vice, and it somehow managed to clamp down on his ribcage. A couple of times, he had glanced over at his brother, expecting fear to be on Clayton's face. But Clayton looked calm. This made Scot think that maybe his brother had been joking at the rear of the skating rink. For if Scot had seen what his brother claimed to have, followed by that horrifying scream, he would have crapped himself. Scot ran a hand across his face and up into his hair. Hadn't he gone through enough already by facing buzzards, vultures, owls, attacked by thousands of frogs with a freaky leader, and nearly falling from a rickety old bridge to the depths of a black, swirling funnel of water and his death? This was all too much. Something told him that the events of weirdness and danger were far from over. And to beat all, Clayton smiled at him. "Can we go home now?" Clayton didn't respond. "We should go back the way we came," Scot added. Going forward was ridiculous, not to mention tempting fate.

"I agree. We need to get out of here, *son*." Johnny took a step on the bridge and froze. "On second thought." The orange-tailed frog reemerged and sat at the far end of the bridge, staring at the kids.

"There's another crossing east of here. Not far." Jimbo pointed. "The school bus bridge that crosses back on Cyrus Mountain."

"Yeah, I forgot about that one, *son*." Johnny lightly slapped the side of his head. "We should have used it from the beginning."

"School bus?" Clayton's mouth dropped open.

"Yeah, old man Cyrus used to drive a school bus. He bought one headed for the scrap yard and took out the seats and used it as a bridge," said Jaylynn.

"I have to see that." Clayton grinned.

"I'm ready to go home," Scot mumbled. It was a miracle he was still alive. As much as he would love to see a school bus out of service, going home was a better choice.

"Let's get moving." Jaylynn stretched her hand out for Scot to take hold.

Scot took a step and heard a squish. Mud coated his shoes up to the shoelaces. "Aw, man, Mom's going to kill me."

"Not if the killer clown gets you first," said Jimbo.

Jaylynn looked at the screen on her phone. "Hush. Listen for another scream."

"It's long after one-thirteen," said Clayton.

"Maybe the clown is going by the Central Time Zone." Jimbo rocked on his heels, grinning.

"Shut up." Jaylynn's nostrils flared.

There was only one thing Scot wanted, and they were miles from it. He calmed his breathing and checked the whereabouts of that bulging-eyed, orange-tailed creature. The frog continued to sit at the edge of the bridge. No way would he fail to spot that crazy amphibian attempting to sneak up and attack him. Scot took a stick to his mud-soaked shoes and scraped off as much sludge as he could. Traction was one thing he needed to have.

As they neared a cluster of pine trees, Jaylynn raised her hand for the others to halt. No one moved. A multitude of birds chirped off in the distance.

Snap.

Scot whirled on his heels. The sound came from behind the pines. "There!"

"What is it?" Clayton's eyes scanned up and down, left and right.

"I-I-I saw clothing, bright colors, like a clow…" Scot went motionless. He wasn't the only one frozen with uncertainty and fear, was he?

A patter of footsteps broke the silence as a rafter of wild turkeys came running from behind the pine trees. Their feathers raised and squawking as if crossed with a mad dog and a demented duck. Scot grabbed a stick, as did the others, and swung them back and forth, yelling at the turkeys.

Amid the cacophony of gobbles, a horrifying scream filled the forest. It almost sounded human, like a screech of a young girl. Scot froze. Whatever had made the sound was definitely close! The turkeys scattered every which way as if they had recognized the cry as one of death.

"What the heck?" Clayton swung his arm out in front of his brother's chest.

"The Screaming Thing?" Scot's lips trembled. His chin quivered, and he fought the urge to pee.

"It might have been," Jaylynn said. "But it could have been a red fox."

"*Son*, that was more awesome than awesome." Johnny quivered with excitement.

"Yeah, that was awesomer," Jimbo said.

Jaylynn shook her head and whispered, "Awesomer? You guys are too stupid to know you're stupid."

When Scot and the others neared a tall oak tree, Jaylynn raised her hand and motioned for everyone to halt. She held her finger to her lips.

Several birds began chirping only to go silent a few seconds into their song. Scot's eyes searched a tree directly in front of him a few feet away. Perched on tree branches was a grouping of sparrows, each looking upon him as if he were bird feed, and they had been singing his death song. His knees wobbled like they were about to give out.

Jaylynn nudged Scot's elbow and pointed at a towering oak. Vines choked the tree from the trunk to its top branches.

A loud, piercing shrill echoed through the woods. Scot covered his ears. The sharp screech was like that of a boatswain whistle used on a ship when the captain orders all hands on deck. This ship was going down! Once again, Scot's heart kicked into overdrive, banging his chest like a drum. Surely, the creature, or whatever it was, could hear it beating. Even worse, it could smell his fear. Where did the squeal come from? What was it? It had to be near! The aroma of roasted peanuts filled his nostrils, and he sneezed.

There it was. The clown! Standing on a thick branch, grasping a tree limb in one hand, and holding a hatchet at his side with the other. He wore a solid yellow jumpsuit with three puffy buttons on its chest. His face was flawless porcelain white, and his mouth was three times the size of average, outlined in blood red, raised into a smile. Black markings lined his eyes, smooth as if an artist had painted it. On his cheek was a glittered gold star. His head was bald with tufts of red hair on either side. His feet bore black canvas tennis shoes, better to track down victims.

The clown raised the hatchet above its head, and as it did so, the branch snapped, sending the clown head over heels. The jumpsuit snagged on a tree limb, ripping the clothing to shreds. On its way down, his ankle caught in a vine, and the hatchet fell harmlessly to the ground. The clown dangled upside down a foot or so from the soil, buck naked to the world.

Scot stood frozen, afraid to run and afraid to stay. Johnny and Jimbo were the first to drop to the ground on their backs and roll in the dirt, holding their guts and sounding like drunken monkeys. Jaylynn picked up a switch and ran over to the clown and spanked him across the bare butt.

"Ouch!"

"Roger!" Jaylynn blurted. She pulled off the clown mask with a yank. "You're not funny."

"And he's not the biggest in everything," Jimbo cracked, pointing at his naked brother. Clayton and Scot joined in, both hooting and screeching at the top of their lungs.

"Get me down!"

Jaylynn glared into her brother's eyes. "I should let you hang there until you turn purple."

"Ouch! The mosquitoes!" Roger squirmed, wiggling side to side, trying to bend upward to pull his foot free of the vine.

Jaylynn giggled briefly and then broke into a loud cackle. She dropped to her knees, holding her midsection.

"Get me down!"

Clayton tucked the hatchet behind his belt and climbed the tree. He cut the vine, and Roger landed on the wet earth with a thud and a squish.

Roger scurried to his feet and crashed back to the ground. "My foot's asleep." He rolled onto his back and twisted his foot in every direction while covering his private parts with his hands.

Scot held his gut. How much more comedy could he take before his stomach muscles choked the life from him? This was great. Sure beat those old movies Dad liked to watch of the *Little Rascals*. This was stupidity at its finest.

After a minute or two, Roger stood and tried to brush bits of mud from his naked body only to look as if he had caked himself in muck. He grumbled under his breath at his giggling brothers.

"*Son*, you have to ride your bike home naked." Johnny shuffled his feet in a quick dance.

"Where'd you park your bike?" Jimbo asked.

"Behind some bushes over there, where I told you I would." Roger pointed to the east.

"What!" Jaylynn barked, turning to face Johnny and Jimbo. "You guys knew he was going to do this?"

"Welcome to West by God Virginia, cousins." Jimbo patted Scot and Clayton on the shoulders. Scot laughed again.

Holding his hands over his groin, Roger faced everyone. "Somebody give me a shirt."

Johnny shook his head and took several steps back.

"No way." Jimbo stepped behind a tree and placed his palms flat against its trunk. He rose on his toes as if he were about to run.

Jaylynn walked over to Johnny, who weighed more than Jimbo. She leaned forward to where her nose was within an inch of his and thrust out her chest. "Give him your shirt," she whispered in a commanding growl.

Johnny mumbled a wordless sound as he removed his shirt and handed it to Roger. The embarrassed clown wrapped it around his waist and tied the arms together, giving the appearance that Roger had on a diaper.

"Stupider than stupid." Jaylynn shook her head. A slight smile crossed her lips.

"Definitely not smart." Scot pressed a hand to his stomach. He couldn't afford to laugh again. He would need a bucket to carry his guts home.

"How did you guys like my scream?" Roger bowed and then dropped to one knee as if he expected to be knighted.

"Sounded really spooky, *son*," said Johnny.

"Awesomer," Jimbo said. Jaylynn rolled her eyes.

"After what we went through back there, we needed that laugh." Scot slapped his palms together. Finally, the woods seemed peaceful again. He silently admitted that hunting for a killer clown had turned out to be a blast. It sure beat staying home.

"I told you guys to come this way. I was waiting forever."

"*Son*, we had to follow Jaylynn. We didn't want her suspicious." Johnny beamed.

"It worked." Roger retrieved his bike.

Jaylynn grumbled under her breath. She led the way to the school bus positioned across the creek. Rust and graffiti coated the yellow vehicle.

"Cool," Clayton said. "All school buses should be like this."

"Yeah." Jimbo patted Clayton on the back. "Out of service."

"Come on." Jaylynn took the lead and stepped through the front door of the bus.

Johnny plopped down behind the steering wheel. "Next stop, Cyrus Mountain." He swung his arm out like he was opening the door. Roger lifted his bike onto the bus. Johnny sneered, "*Son*, you can't go to school dressed like that."

Roger slapped his brother on the head and then pushed the bike down the aisle and out the rear door.

"Stop playing. We have to get home." Jaylynn exited the bus behind Roger. Within minutes they were back at their bikes.

As the kids reached Route 52, a faint scream reached Scot's ears. No one else seemed to have heard it, and he wasn't about to speak up. He shrugged and forced a grin. It had to be the wind, didn't it?

II

The following morning, Clayton prepared to visit Wanda Kitts. If the citizens of Louisa were playing a prank, it was worthy of an Academy Award. No doubt about it. If there indeed was a monster, well, his mom and dad were raising a future Marine.

"Get up and get dressed." Clayton gently poked his brother's stomach.

"Are you crazy?" Scot sat up and cocked his head to the side. His eyes opened wide. "Why do you want to go see a crazy old woman?"

"I want the truth." Clayton crossed his arms against his chest.

"And what if…." Scot grimaced.

"It's not like she's a witch." Clayton squared his stance.

"Maybe."

"Get real and put on your shoes."

"I'm not going." Scot fluffed his pillow.

"We swore to investigate together." Clayton deepened his voice. Scot placed his hands over his ears. "Now, come on." Scot slid off the bed and slipped on his pants and shoes. "Don't worry, little brother. I won't let anything happen to you."

***

The boys brought their bikes to a halt in front of the home of Miss Kitts. It stood tall, three stories. Its white paint was barely existent, revealing the weathered wood panels. Clayton wouldn't have been surprised to learn that the wood to build the house had arrived on the Mayflower. The yard, recently cut, was plush with Kentucky bluegrass. Climber plants grew up the front of the house, choking the drainpipes. Plants grabbed for the little sunlight that strained to reach over the eastern side of the house. Several large windows seemed to stare back at the boys, like the eyes of an empty soul. As if the windows were challenging the brothers to step inside. Tall pine trees stood on either side of a cobblestone walkway leading to the front door made of oak. A brass knocker attached to the door gave the impression it was a gateway to nightmares. The door was ajar, a sign that the woman was home. The porch light flickered on and off as if the wiring had a short in it.

A brisk breeze swept through the pines, bringing with it the laughter of children. Clayton glanced up and down the street. The roadway was bare, not a soul or car anywhere in sight.

Clayton stepped on the moldy board of the porch stairs, and it compressed as if the house was awakening from a deep sleep. A few potted plants sat on the porch, wilted and brown. Sitting a few feet from the plants were two metal chairs. Both painted blue in their beginning but now coated with rust and dust. Grime glazed the windows of the house, creating spookiness about the place. Clayton raised his hand to knock.

Scot grabbed his brother's forearm. "Maybe we should—"

The door opened, causing Scot to go silent. "What do you kids want?" asked a woman in a voice cracked with age. She glared from Clayton to Scot and back to Clayton. A lump lodged in Clayton's throat. The woman stuck her head out beyond the doorway, and her eyes searched the street. "Well," she added. "Out with it. I don't have all day." Her voice was not pleasant.

"Hel-hel-hello, Miss Kitts." Clayton shuffled his feet then rose on his toes. The woman's dark-brown eyes were mysterious and piercing, set in deep sockets above high cheekbones, like drill bits ready to go to work. Her gaze was sharp enough to slice a person, should they dare to get close. She was short, standing in the doorway, and as plump as Santa Claus. Her hair was thinning, wiry, and silver.

"I have no work to be done here." She glimpsed over her shoulder as if she were expecting someone to walk up behind her. "You boys best be moving along."

"We're not here to work," Clayton replied. He introduced himself and his brother.

"You kids are new to Louisa, aren't you? Only a stranger would dare darken my doorway."

"Yes, ma'am," Clayton answered. "Our dad runs Hall's Grocery. We moved here—"

"Old man Boyd's your daddy?" She ran a bony hand down the sleeve of a black wool sweater as if she tried to smooth a wrinkle.

"No, ma'am. He's our grandpa." Scot smiled.

"I get my groceries delivered twice a month from Boyd. Did your daddy send you here to tell me different?" Both boys shook their heads. "Then what is it?"

"My brother wants to tell you something." Scot jabbed his elbow against Clayton's forearm.

The woman cocked her head to the side. "At the rate you boys are going, this may take a moment. My legs don't like standing long. Come inside." She swung the door wide. Both boys hesitated. "I don't bite."

Clayton nudged his brother in the small of the back, and they entered the house. A wooden spiral staircase stood left of the entry. The steps were caked with dust as if no one had ventured up them in years.

"Take a seat in the front room." The woman gestured toward three high back Victorian chairs. "I'll get us a cold drink. Much too hot out there today."

The brothers entered and took a seat. Clayton ran his fingertips across the arm of the chair. The material was rough, like a burlap sack he had once grabbed in his grandfather's store. He sniffed his fingers and found the scent of saddle soap, a compound used for protecting leather boots. The room reeked of medicine, decay, and mold as if the walls themselves were dying. He clamped his mouth shut so as not to swallow the dust particles that danced in the light of the room. A light bulb hung from the ceiling attached with a white wire, clearly not the safest connection to electricity. Fastened to the fixture was a rope, long enough for a short person to turn on or off. For no known reason, at least none he could see, the cord began swaying back and forth.

"Strange how the string moves like that from time to time," Miss Kitts said as she entered the room. She held out a silver tray supporting three china cups of lemonade on saucers. The cord went still. "I keep this old house tight as a sealed tin of Prince Albert."

Scot cocked his head back.

"Prince Albert is a can of tobacco." She took a seat on a third chair and pointed at an end table. A red metal tin sat atop the table. Stenciled across the front of the tin in large yellow letters was the name Prince Albert. Below the lettering was an image of a bearded man dressed in an overcoat. He held a cane in one hand while his other hand was at his side. Alongside the can stood a 5x7 black and white photo of a teenaged boy and girl.

Clayton had not known of such tobacco either, but that was not his concern. Neither was the swinging light cord, but he caught himself glancing at it now and again. He resumed his inspection of the room. The once crisp golden wallpaper showed rips and cracks in places. On the walls were two gilded mirrors. The frames were dusty, and the light that shone off them showed specks of dirt. A pair of frayed orange curtains draped the three large windows that offered a clear view of the street. No doubt, Miss Kitts had watched them approach her home. The hardwood floor had a glossy shine like a person could eat off it, in total contrast with the rest of the house.

A calico cat strolled into the room and curled up near the woman's feet. Clayton ignored it and continued to observe his surroundings. The place had many antique objects, like a living museum, with mirrors, ceramic figurines, and porcelain dolls. A couch with floral print upholstery sat near a window. At the end of the sofa was a black telephone with a rotary dial. A bulky television with two antennas rising out of its backside sat on top of a massive mahogany table. Beyond the table, a ventriloquist doll, three-foot or taller, sat on the floor in the corner, staring at him. Clayton swallowed the lump in his throat. The dummy was in the form of a boy, dressed in a long-sleeved green shirt and jeans and had brown boots on its feet. Its hair was brown, parted down the middle. From somewhere on the doll's clothing, a black bug crawled out and skittered across the puppet's leg, followed by a second and third insect. Clayton squirmed in his seat and glanced over to his brother. Scot held his attention on the cat as it jumped up on the woman's lap.

"This is my old tomcat. His name is Jess." Miss Kitts stroked the cat's back. She sat the cat to the floor, and it walked out of the room. "So, gentlemen, what brings you here?" She pulled a pair of eyeglasses from under her sweater and balanced them on the bridge of her nose.

Clayton took a deep breath to calm his nerves. "I saw something the other night, near the roller rink. An ugly creature." He sipped the lemonade, rattling the cup against the saucer. The drink was refreshing, cold, and sugary.

Miss Kitts leaned forward, peering over the rim of her glasses. A slight smile began to form, and then her lips pressed into a hard line. Her eyes narrowed, and she raised one eyebrow. The woman sat in silence for a long moment and then leaned back in her chair. "I don't take kindly to a childish prank." The tone of her voice was no longer kind.

"N-n-no, ma'am." Clayton stiffened. "I did see something. Honest."

Miss Kitts' brows scrunched together, and her eyes narrowed to the point that she looked to be asleep. "What did you see?"

Trying to find the words, Clayton hesitated. "The creature was skinny and tall, ten feet or more. Its eyes glowed from inside deep sockets with a face that was long and skeletal like a decayed wolf. The ugly form of its body was covered in a pale yellowish skin until it stepped into the beam of a streetlight. It was then that I saw it had long matted hair, twisted like vines."

"I think it's time you boys leave." She slowly lowered her cup to the coffee table and then placed her hands to the armrests of the chair as if to stand.

Clayton continued, "On its head were antlers. Its feet had human-like toes, and its fingers were long, pointy, claws, like giant talons. Yellow fangs and a long purple tongue protruded from its huge mouth."

The woman screeched and fell back onto her seat with a thud. Her upper lip trembled. She crossed her arms, then uncrossed them, and joined them again, finally tucking her hands under her biceps. "I hadn't mentioned to anyone about the creature's yellow fangs and purple tongue." Her eyes bored into Clayton. She released a heavy sigh by blowing out her cheeks. "You claim you saw it at the skating rink, right?"

"Yes, ma'am. I was on my way to our mom's car when I saw a movement near the far corner of the building." Clayton glanced over to Scot. "It locked eyes with me and raised its long arms above its head and—"

"Why did you look at your brother? Did you see it too?" She stared over to Scot.

"No."

"I don't know if you're pulling my leg or not," she added in a weak, timid voice. "But this isn't funny. It's serious, kid. Do you understand? Nothing to play with."

"No, ma'am," Clayton moaned. "I'm telling the truth. Its head had a wide rack like a deer."

Miss Kitts placed a hand to her chin for a few seconds as if she had gone somewhere in her mind. "You better take heed to what I'm about to tell you." She made a steeple of her fingers on her lap. "There are ghosts all over the world. But for some unknown reason, we have plenty here in Louisa. At least we have our share of stories." She cocked her head back and stared into Clayton's eyes, a stern, penetrating look. "What you saw was a Wendigo, a half-beast creature that appears in the legends of Native Americans. At one time, this area belonged to six or seven different tribes. They believed the Wendigo holds an intense craving for human flesh. The beast is linked with murder, greed, and cannibalism."

"Huh?" Scot whispered.

"Cannibalism is when a person eats another person as a source of food," she replied. "After which they become a flesh-eating monster."

"Eeew!" Scot sat back in his chair.

"Whatever you do, don't run from it. Show no fear." She pulled a scrapbook from under a coffee table and placed it on her lap, closed. "Us kids would hang out at a party barn near where the skating rink is. That was back in 1967. I was a mere sixteen years old." Her fingers swept across the leather binding. "Have you ever heard the old saying, be careful of what you wish for?" She fixed her eyes on Clayton.

Both boys nodded. "Our mother says it a lot," Scot said.

"It applies here tenfold. If you seek the spirits, in due time, they'll grant your desire." She rapped her knuckles on the book cover. "I was under the bridge with Jesse, my best friend. He was two years older than me. We liked to sit there and talk about our future together. Well…even way back then kids loved ghost stories, and the Big Sandy has its share. It's said that the bridge and the river have ears. Both are hot spots for spirits. We were young and foolish." She looked down at the floor and then over to the staircase before turning her attention back to Clayton. "Jesse and I stood under the bridge and dared one another to make a wish to see a ghost. We held hands, and together, we wished out loud." Clayton and Scot exchanged a look between them. "Five days later, the creature granted my wish." She opened the book and handed it to Clayton. He read a newspaper clipping that had faded with age.

> *Local Girl Saw Monster!*
> *Wanda Kitts, 16 years old, a student at Louisa*
> *High School, claims to have seen a Wendigo near the*
> *rear of a barn, a favorite hangout for kids.*
> *"I saw a movement at the back of the build-*

ing and walked toward it, thinking it was one of my friends playing a joke. I wasn't about to be scared off. As I stood there, a huge, ugly creature stepped out of the darkness. It had to be over ten feet tall. The creature's body and arms were hairy and matted with parts of tree branches. It had a massive skull that supported a large rack of antlers, and its eyes glowed red. Slowly, it leaned its snout close to me and sniffed. I wanted to run, scream, get out of there, but I couldn't do either. It was as if I had lost complete control of my legs and lungs. After sniffing me, the creature pulled its head back and raised a hand to its chin, as if studying me. That's when I noticed it had hairy fingers with long fingernails, razor-sharp, like talons. It leaned in and sniffed me a second time. That creature ran its fingernail gently down the side of my face, slow, like telling me it was pondering about gutting me.

"I don't know why it didn't. It snarled, a sound like you make when you gargle. Then it screamed an ear-piercing petrified wail. A sound that resembled the brakes of a train applied at full force mixed with the cry of a hyena gone mad. Terror rushed over me, and I couldn't move. I couldn't even feel my lungs or heart pumping, and my eyes wouldn't turn away or shut. And God knows I tried to clear the creature from my sight. It leaned in the third time, and I knew my life was about to end. After sniffing me one last time, the creature lowered its snout within an inch or so of my arm. I could feel its breath blow the hairs on my forearm, sending waves of fear over me. The stench of its breath was rank, decomposed like it had swallowed death, and carried the aftertaste within its lungs. A split second later, it stepped back, turned, and ran off into the darkness in three mighty leaps, like a kangaroo on springs. My friends found me on

my knees, crying and praying, shaking hysterically."

"Wow." Clayton closed the book and handed it to her. Miss Kitts's description of the creature was the same as what he had seen at the skating rink. The monster could actually exist. Either that or there was an offspring of actors carrying on the tradition of a wild prank. He did not doubt that Miss Kitts believed the monster to be real, keeping herself hidden inside this house for so long. "You must have been a hero to the town. To come so close to—"

Miss Kitts broke into a loud cackle. "Hero!" she barked. "Boy, I was labeled a nut, wacko, kook, loony, skitzo, insane. People said I was mentally deranged and that I concocted the entire story."

"Huh?" Scot's head flinched back slightly.

"Concocted means I made up the tale. That I lied."

"Did you?" Scot asked.

"Boy, as sure as you're looking at me now, I saw that monster that evening. It was real. I don't lie." She slammed the book down on the end table. "I began seeing ghosts throughout town—people who were there one second and gone the next. I locked myself away in this house. Haven't been out in years." She nodded toward the window that gave a view of the street. "That window is my connection to the outside world…that and when my groceries are delivered. The same girl cuts my grass. I don't even take the newspaper, for I have no interest in the goings-on out there. Occasionally, I'll see a neighbor, but they don't seem to see me. It's just me, and the glass, clear or rain-splattered. I was born in this house. Guess this is where I will…" Her shoulders slouched, and she grunted.

"What happened to Jesse?" Scot leaned out on the edge of his seat.

Miss Kitts closed her eyes and tilted her head back. Releasing a deep audible sigh, she opened her eyes and stared over at Scot. "Back then was a mighty different time. America was smack dab in the middle of the Vietnam War. There was a thing called the draft, where a young man was forced to go to battle. Jesse received his notice to report to the Army. I had a tough time with that and was afraid for his safety. But Jesse joined the Marines, again without my support." She removed her glasses and took the hankie to her eyes.

The word Marines brought Clayton's head up, and he sat straight.

"Jesse and I would meet under the bridge on Saturday mornings. We didn't care if it was in the dead of winter," she continued, returning the glasses to the bridge of her nose. "I could see by the look on Jesse's face that he'd seen something. But being the gentleman that he was, he insisted I first tell him my encounter with the creature." She took a sip of lemonade.

"Did you tell him?" Scot asked.

Miss Kitts gestured for Scot to wait while she took another swig of the cold refreshment. "Of course, I told him. I showed him this newspaper article." She returned the book to her lap. The light cord swayed twice before going still. "This clipping is the last thing that Jesse and I both touched. I've kept it more for that reason than anything else. That tin of Prince Albert belonged to him too. It was his favorite tobacco." Once more, she dabbed her eyes. "Jesse told me that he and his brother had stood under the bridge the night before, on Friday. Jesse's brother was a year younger than me. Everyone called him Frostie because he loved to drink the root beer of the same name. According to Jesse, his brother wanted to go to the bridge and announce that he wanted to see a ghost. As Frostie was about to make his declaration, he lost his footing and slipped down the embankment." She took another sip of her drink.

"Did he drown?" Scot moved further to the edge of his seat.

"Within inches of landing in the water, Frostie came to a halt as if he had hit an invisible wall. Jesse saw that his brother had slammed against the rear leg of a huge white gelding. The biggest horse Jesse had ever seen. On the back of the horse was a soldier, but the man's form was barely visible, and Jesse couldn't determine who it was. In the next instant, both the soldier and gelding evaporated before his eyes. Frostie never saw the man or the horse, nor did he make his wish."

"Wow," huffed Scot.

"Was that why Frostie never saw the horse?" Clayton asked.

"To make a wish or not, those rivers and that bridge have a connection. As to what, I don't know." Miss Kitts sighed.

"What happened after that?" Scot leaned back in his chair.

"Well…it was late summer, and another week passed. When Saturday morning came, I hurried down under the bridge. I waited and waited. It feels like I'm still under that bridge." She placed a palm to her chest. "His family claimed that he went missing. No one ever did find him. The entire family moved out of town within a few days. Anything could've happened to Jesse. His skin was much darker than mine, and white folks were openly prejudiced back then. A mixed relationship was frowned on. I happen to believe..." She whimpered and dabbed her eye with a hankie. "I imagine he went off to battle and couldn't bring himself to say goodbye since I was set dead against the war." She wiped her eyes once more and then blew her nose. "If only I knew what happened. I've spent a lifetime imagining."

Clayton bit his lip. Her words held an agony of emotion that stirred a need for him to respond. But what was he to do with a grown woman sitting before him crying? Hug her? Say something comforting? No words were coming to the forefront of his mind. Tears were what a three-year-old would produce, nothing but annoying infancy. But here was this aged woman with tears streaming down her face obviously in pain, deep-rooted grief. His chest tightened, and he sucked in a deep breath. One day, he too, would be old. It should be a time of peace and happiness like a second childhood. Clayton never met his grandmother, his father's mother. If she had not passed before his birth, she would appear much like Miss Kitts, plump, gray hair, and hopeful. No doubt, there were many tears shed over his grandmother's death. But his parents and Grandpa Boyd knew what had happened to her, and with it came closure. It hadn't been the monster that kept Miss Kitts behind these walls. She had waited fifty years, five decades of not knowing about the love of her life. How sad it must be to wait for someone for so long. "What was Jesse's last name?"

Miss Kitts's eyes lit up. "Lowes. Jesse Lowes."

The sound of several creaks followed her words as if someone were walking down the stairs. Clayton glanced over at the staircase. No one was there.

"You heard it too, didn't you?" she asked. Both boys nodded. "All these years, he has never shown himself or said a word, if it's Jesse." She stood and picked up the framed black and white photo and handed it to Clayton. "This is Jesse and me back in those days. A handsome young man he was." She grabbed a hairbrush from the coffee table and walked over to a large mirror on the wall and began brushing her hair. "Got to look presentable when my..." She turned and faced her visitors. "What do you boys think? Is my hair okay?"

Both boys smiled. Clayton looked over at the ventriloquist dummy and did a doubletake, nearly falling off his chair. The doll was no longer staring at Clayton. It now had its head turned, as if watching Miss Kitts. Clayton tapped his brother on the arm. "We need to get home."

"You boys can come back anytime. I sleep downstairs. Haven't been up those steps in years." She signaled toward the staircase with her index finger. "I don't want to miss a knock, should Jesse…" She sucked in a deep breath and placed her hand on Clayton's shoulder. "It's been over fifty years since I set eyes on that creature. A lot of folks have died mysteriously or have gone missing. You're the first to have seen it and describe it to a tee. If you see it again, show no fear, no matter how scared you are, and I was petrified. It worked for me."

Clayton said he'd do his best. As he reached the door, his eyes caught a glimpse of the staircase leading to the second floor. Impressions of shoes were on the steps as if someone had descended. He gasped.

"Something wrong?" Miss Kitts asked.

The footprints vanished, leaving the steps covered with dust as before. "No, ma'am," Clayton replied. "Do you ever sit on the porch?"

Miss Kitts cocked her head. "Why would I do that? I must stay near the phone."

"Yes, ma'am." Clayton waved goodbye. As he mounted his bike, he told his brother what he had seen on the stairs.

"I didn't see the footprints," Scot answered. "And I don't want to."

"But what if—"

"Stop!" Scot said. "I didn't think we would be hunting real ghosts."

Clayton chuckled. He loved turning Scot's phrase back on his little brother.

12

Come daybreak, Clayton dressed and then switched on the family computer. How many Vietnam Veterans were in Louisa? The best he could determine from Google, thirty soldiers were living in or near the town. Names were not listed.

Next came Wendigo. Was what he saw behind the skating rink real or a prank? One report on the legend took place during the winter of 1878. A Cree Indian brave named Swift Runner had lived in what is now central Alberta, Canada. The brave murdered his wife, brother, mother-in-law, and six kids. He blamed his actions on a Wendigo. Swift Runner further claimed the creature was a shapeshifter that took different forms. The beast possessed him and forced him to murder his family. He cooked and ate their flesh to keep from starving to death. The Indian was arrested, brought to trial, and in December 1879, hanged at Fort Saskatchewan.

Clayton reread the article. "Swift Runner!" Rand-Dock had said the Sasquatch that roamed the graveyard was a swift runner. Was the caretaker hinting at something?

Clayton read more. According to Wikipedia, the Wendigo was a man-eating monster or evil spirit in Algonquian folklore. Years ago, there had been Indian tribes residing in Kentucky. Among them were the Shawnee, who spoke the Algonquian language. If the Wendigo were real, could one be a cursed Shawnee brave from long ago? The creature was a giant, many times larger than humans. Whenever a Wendigo ate a person, it grew in proportion to the meal it had eaten, so it could never be full. The beast, never satisfied, continually hunted for new victims.

Clayton puffed out his cheeks and exhaled. "If the Wendigo is more than a legend, well…" It sounded far-fetched, and doubt worked its way into his mind. He switched off the computer and chuckled. One has to love Hollywood and special effects. He went to the kitchen, where Scot smiled up from behind an empty plate. Clayton devoured his portion of sausage, eggs, toast, and gulped down a glass of orange juice. Time was running short.

"What's on your agenda today, boys?" Mom poured a cup of coffee.

"I'm going to the library. You want to come along, Scotty?"

Scot held a glass to his lips finishing off his juice. "Yes." His voice was garbled.

"Ride safe, boys." Mom kissed Clayton on top of the head and then did likewise with Scot. "Don't be gone long."

"Afterwards, Jaylynn will help us hunt ghosts," Clayton said.

Mom tipped her coffee mug in a good-hunting gesture.

Scot cocked his head back as Clayton pushed from the table.

"Come on, Scotty. I have your back." Clayton walked to the garage.

Scot hurried after him. "Hunting ghosts seemed fun at first. But the caretaker at the graveyard said there were stories of real spirits in the cemetery." He grabbed Clayton by the forearm. "I think the guy and dog under the bridge were real and not phantoms, nothing to fear. But there's no explanation for the frogs and buzzards. They were freaky, no doubt about it, even if they hurt no one. And Roger posing as a clown was funny. But after talking with Miss Kitts, I'm not sure I want to return to the bridge."

Clayton hugged Scot. "I have your back. You know that."

Scot squinted. "If you get me killed, you're the first one I'm going to haunt."

The boys hopped onto their bikes and rode to the Lawrence County Public Library on Main Street.

The brick building stretched a block long, from Clay Street to the railroad tracks. Clayton paused at the front door and read a flyer taped to the window. Louisa's yearly Fourth of July celebration was a week away. Surely, he would see some Vietnam veterans in the parade. But how much longer did Miss Kitts have to wait? She had waited a lifetime without knowing anything on Jesse. He and Scot entered and made their way over to the information desk.

"May I help you?" The male librarian smiled from his position, seated at a computer screen.

"I'm researching the names of Marines from Louisa who served during the Vietnam War." Clayton crossed his fingers.

The man typed on a keyboard. "We have several books on the war, but none that list the names of Marines or soldiers from that time. Have you tried the internet?" He glanced at several computers across the aisle.

"Yes, sir. No luck." Clayton noticed how the librarian had mentioned both Marines and soldiers. A Marine was a Marine. Period.

"You may want to contact the Kentucky Department of Veterans Affairs located in Catlettsburg." The librarian typed on the keyboard again. A moment later, he scribbled on a notepad, ripped a page from the pad and handed it to Clayton. "That is the phone number." Again, he smiled. "Anything else?"

Clayton shook his head. "Thank you." Before Clayton reached the door, a gray-haired man walking with a cane approached him.

"I overheard," said the man. "You boys are trying to find Vietnam vets from Louisa."

A flutter shot through Clayton's belly. "Yes, sir." Would this stranger be able to help?

"I'm Steve Cooper. Louisa had four brave men who died in Nam."

"Was one of them Jesse Lowes?" Clayton edged closer to the man.

Mr. Cooper looked from Clayton to the librarian and back to Clayton. "How did you hear about this Jesse Lowes?"

"Wanda Kitts," Scot said.

Mr. Cooper glanced over to the librarian again. He took Clayton by the forearm and leaned over and whispered, "Old Wanda is heartbroken. She's never let go of the past." He glared over at Scot. "Best to leave some things alone."

"Were you in Vietnam, sir?" Clayton pulled his arm free of the man's grip.

"Like I said, kid, leave it alone." Mr. Cooper walked over to the restroom door, turned back, and glared at Clayton. The man shook his head, raised his cane, and shook it too, then entered the restroom.

If the man's words were meant to scare Clayton, they didn't. He forced his legs not to follow the man and ask more questions. There was something mysterious about the way the man spoke. What did he mean by shaking the cane? Was the man threatening him? It wasn't like he was trying to gain a government top secret.

Clayton and Scot exited the building and hopped on their bikes.

"That man was spooky." Scot looked back at the library. "What do we do now?"

"Let's go see Dad." Clayton led the way to the grocery store, all the while with Mr. Cooper on his mind. The man had seemed nice at the beginning, but the moment Clayton had said Jesse's name, Cooper's eyes went dark and cold, and his voice went hard.

"Hey, boys, what brings you here?" Dad asked.

"I need you to make a phone call for me." Clayton shared what he had learned at the library. Dad took the number and went to his office, along with Clayton and Scot.

"Okay, thanks." Dad hung up the phone. "I got you an appointment to speak with the Administrator tomorrow, Mr. Green."

"Me?"

"Yes, son. This is on you. It's your mission. You can handle it." Dad slipped the phone number in his desk drawer. "Are you boys heading home now?"

"Jaylynn's going to meet Scot and me under the bridge for another ghost hunt."

Dad smiled. "Be careful. Don't stay long. See you at home."

The bridge was a block and a half away, allowing time for the mysterious Mr. Cooper to creep back into the forefront of Clayton's mind. The way the man had whispered and the tone of his voice. "Leave it alone." Why? How was it that Rand-Dock, the graveyard caretaker, and Mr. Cooper, gave the same warning, "leave it alone" if the entire ordeal wasn't a prank?

Clayton found Jaylynn straddling her bike near the entrance of the bridge. "Don't tell me. Your brothers are doing chores."

"You catch on quick." Jaylynn grinned.

Clayton shared his and Scot's visit with Miss Kitts. "Do you know any Lowes living nearby?"

Jaylynn shook her head. "No. Never heard the name before." She led the way down the embankment.

"Hey there!" Someone shouted at them.

Clayton spun on his toes. A man, dark-skinned, tall, and skinny, aged like he could be old enough to be Grandpa Boyd's grandpa, stood a few feet from the kids.

"Reckon I don't know you young'uns," said the man.

The closer Clayton eyed the man, the more relaxed Clayton became. The guy wore a smile on his creased face. Still, to be on the safe side, Clayton stepped between the man and Scot.

"We better be getting home." Scot stepped back as if to leave.

"Now wait a minute," the man's voice filled with excitement. "We ain't met proper. We ain't know each other a moment ago, but we ain't got to part as strangers." He held out his hand. All three kids took a step back. "I understand," added the man. "I do for sure."

Clayton stepped forward. Grandpa and Dad had demonstrated to him and Scot how men shake hands, firm, and tight. A lot could be told about a man through a handshake. Clayton gripped the man's hand. "My name is Clayton. This is my brother Scot and our cousin Jaylynn." The man's grip was weak. His hand was clammy and cold, eerily cold.

"Good to meet you'uns. My name is John Brown. Many folks in these parts call me Uncle Jim. I've my own little cabin on the property of Mr. Frederick Moore, his wife, and nine children, a short spell back that way in West Virginny." He raised a hand and pumped a thumb over his shoulder. "I is looking for my grandson, many generations removed. His name is A-lee, spelled A-l-e-y…Aley Smith. His birth don't name him a Brown, but he is truly a Brown, same as me, from our direct bloodline. I is hoping to find him, for I desire an early start this morning to be back home readying ourselves for dinner." He cast his eyes out onto the river. "We be partaking of a hearty supper of good, lean bear-meat, sweet milk, some Johnnycake, and cornbread. You kids is welcome to sit with us. The missus never turns away a soul with an empty stomach." A truck passed over the bridge, and he cocked his head upward. "Mighty big wagon. I don't recall this here fancy bridge. I need to get out more often." He gazed over to Scot. "Little Aley is about your size, Negro. I hear he was coming here to swim. The current is too harsh, and I is hoping to stop him before he makes the plunge. He likes to dip in the Tug Fork, but I ain't seen him over there, so I is looking over here."

"No, we haven't seen anyone, sorry." Jaylynn's smile looked forced.

"We had heavy rain three evenings ago. This old river has a tendency of rising a bit too high for comfort during a storm. That boy has the soul of a bird, flying here and there, flapping his wings to be free. I just can't stay up with little Aley. I need to gather him and get us home. Still needing to collect wood for the fire." Mr. Brown's eyes examined the river once more. "You boys got any tobacco? I could sure use a draw."

"No, sir, we don't smoke." Clayton shook his head.

The man revealed a toothless smile. "Mighty good habit not to smoke. Reckon I'll wait till I get home. If you young'uns come across little Aley, tell him Uncle Jim is trying to fetch him." He walked off to the north and out of sight.

"Have you seen him before?" Clayton asked Jaylynn.

Jaylynn shook her head. "Never."

"He took the same path as the man and dog we saw." Scot's jaw dropped open.

"Doesn't mean anything." Clayton playfully jabbed his brother in the ribs.

"Could be a Nightwalker," replied Jaylynn. "A group of souls who roamed the area back in the early 1800s. They haunt the district they most enjoyed during life."

"Shouldn't a Nightwalker be out during the night?" Clayton cocked his head back. The folks of Louisa were doing a bang-up job!

"I don't know everything," she admitted. "Heck, I don't know what to believe anymore."

"I want to go home." Scot turned toward the embankment.

"Okay, Scotty." Clayton took hold of his brother's forearm. "I'm going to Google John Brown and Aley."

"Tell me what you learn." Jaylynn hopped onto her bike. "I have chores to finish."

Clayton and Scot waved goodbye and headed home. When they reached the top of Town Hill Road near the cemetery, Clayton raised his hand for Scot to stop.

"The wolf." Clayton eyed the animal as it stood in the middle of Cemetery Road with its back to him. Rand-Dock stepped out from the woods and walked over to the wolf and rubbed the animal on the top of the head. It was an amazing sight. The animal could be a Siberian husky after all. Either that or the caretaker had a way with wild animals.

Clayton waved. "Hello, Mr. Dockery!" The man and canine turned and faced the boys. The caretaker said nothing and didn't return the gesture. Clayton shrugged and pedaled away, leaving Scot to follow.

Clayton's mind stayed on the creature his dad had called a dog. Nobody loved you as much as a dog, except your mom, maybe. Did the animal need a home, or did it belong to the caretaker?

Clayton guided his bike onto the driveway with Scot behind him. Mom and Dad sat on the porch. "Mom! Dad! We saw the white wolf." Clayton shared the event of Rand-Dock patting the animal on the head.

"I still believe it's a Siberian husky." Dad took a sip of coffee. "No one is going to tame a wolf."

"I don't care what it is," said Mom. "You boys be careful with all dogs."

Clayton bit his tongue. Surely, somewhere, someone has tamed a wolf. First, he would have to make friends with the canine.

***

That evening, Clayton switched on the computer while Scot headed for the shower. "Wow," he whispered. He phoned Jaylynn and shared the information with her. "Fredrick Moore was a Philadelphia merchant who laid out the city of Louisa with its wide streets in 1815. He did have nine children and owned slaves. John Brown, known as Uncle Jim, was a slave that the Moore's treated like family. Uncle Jim died in 1885, said to have been a hundred years old. I can't find anything on Aley Smith."

"If this is a prank by citizens, it's a doozy," Jaylynn said.

"Tell me about it," replied Clayton. "Or making a wish under the bridge is really…"

"I know," Jaylynn answered. "That part is spooky. Which do you believe?"

"Well, Miss Kitts' newspaper clipping was real. Her description matched what I saw behind the skating rink. But I still think it's a prank."

"Time will tell, cousin. Time will tell." Jaylynn hung up the phone.

13

Clayton found it difficult to sleep. Morning was taking its good old time in arriving. Each time he woke during the night, his mind drifted to the upcoming meeting at the Veterans Affairs Building. What if the meeting would be for nothing? Or worse, what if he discovered Jesse was dead? How would he tell Miss Kitts? She's been hanging on, waiting on him for a lifetime.

Finally, sunlight streamed through the window and lit up Clayton's room. He jumped from bed and dressed.

Clayton and Scot climbed inside Dad's truck and buckled their seatbelts.

"Can Clayton sign up for the Marines today?" Scot asked.

Dad chuckled. "That's still a few years off."

"I wish I could join now. That'd be cool. Clayton Hall, the only twelve-year-old Marine in the world!" He performed a crisp salute.

Dad broke into a full-blown laugh. "Just seeking information on this Jesse fellow. Nothing more."

"Dang," said Scot. "I wanted your bedroom." Clayton rolled his eyes. "Just kidding. I wouldn't have anyone to ride bikes with."

"The day your brother joins the Marines will be here far too soon," said Dad. "Let's not rush it."

Scot gazed out the window. "I don't know if I would be brave enough to join."

"Don't worry, son," replied Dad. "The military isn't for everyone."

Clayton stared at the road. Let today be fruitful. Miss Kitts deserves answers.

"Don't get your hopes up, son. The military doesn't give out much information." Dad kept his eyes on the highway.

"I know, Dad. But wouldn't it be cool if…" Clayton rested his head on the headrest and closed his eyes.

"Yes, it would," said Dad. A heavy silence filled the truck.

***

When they arrived, Clayton eyed the building. It stood as grand as a city hall with four big pillars out front. A second-floor walkway connected it with the Boyd County Judicial Center.

"Look, Dad." Scot pointed at the sign on the building. "That's Grandpa's name."

"Yep." Dad nodded. "Even way back when I was a kid, Grandpa would tell me this county was named after him."

"Was it?"

Dad shook his head. "No, son, just Grandpa being goofy."

Clayton, Scot, and their father entered the building and paused at the directory.

"Looks like room 105." Dad tapped a finger on the glass case.

"Are you going with me?"

"This is your mission, son. You can handle it." Dad patted Clayton on the shoulder.

"Can I go with him?"

Dad shook his head. "We'll wait here, Scotty."

Clayton took a deep breath and opened the door. He introduced himself to the receptionist and asked to see the Regional Administrator.

She smiled up at him. "I'll see if he's available." She pressed a button.

"Yes, Tammy?" came a male voice.

"Mr. Clayton Hall is here to see you, Sir."

A moment later, a door opened and out stepped a tall, broad man. "Clayton Hall?"

"Hello, Mr. Green." Clayton held his hand out. The man's grip was tight, firm, a true Marine handshake.

"What can I do for you, young man?" He waved his free hand for Clayton to take a seat in his office.

"I'm hoping you can give me some information on a Marine from the Vietnam War."

Mr. Green plopped down in a chair behind a wooden desk. "What's his name?"

"Jesse Lowes, Sir. L-o-w-e-s."

"What type of information are you after?"

"If he's alive and where he lives."

"Are you kin?"

Clayton hesitated. His answer could determine if he would receive information on Jesse. Without it, he couldn't help Miss Kitts. A lie didn't seem like a lie when it came to this. Right and wrong were all mixed up in his head. It wasn't good to tell a lie, but he wouldn't feel exactly bad, either. If what Grandpa Boyd had told him about heaven and hell was real and liars ended up in hell, then one day, he would face judgment. Grandpa had also claimed that God created love. Life held risk. Surely God would forgive him for a well-intended lie, wouldn't He?

"Well, Clayton, are you related to Mr. Lowes?"

"No, Sir." Clayton slumped back in the chair.

"I can tell you if he served during the war and may be able to say if he's alive or not. However, I'm not permitted to give out his personal information." The man scribbled something on a notepad.

"I'd love to know if he's alive." Clayton rose from the chair. "Please, Sir. It's important." Mr. Green removed his eyeglasses but said nothing. Clayton's heart banged against his chest like a racehorse headed down the home stretch. It was now or never. He shared the story of Jesse and Miss Kitts.

"Are you related to Miss Kitts?" Mr. Green took a sip of coffee.

Clayton lowered his gaze to the floor. Here was another opportunity. "No, Sir." Clayton shook his head.

"Why's this so important to you, Clayton?"

"I'm going to be a Marine, like my dad."

"That's nice, kid. Then you know as a Marine, we deal with battles. The greatest battle is the one for the heart."

Clayton forced himself not to blink. What was he to say to that? "I don't know much about either. But after seeing this woman, I know that she's in a lot of pain. That tells me that the heart that truly loves never forgets."

The administrator's mouth opened as if to speak but said nothing. The man's gaze intensified for a long moment. Was the man about to ask Clayton to leave? Finally, Mr. Green stood and walked over to a file cabinet. He opened the second drawer and pulled out a folder. "Jesse Lowes was…" He turned and faced Clayton. "Jesse was an E-4, a corporal in Vietnam. While his unit was under heavy fire, they lost their Lieutenant and Sergeant. With Corporal Lowes' leadership, his men held their position, eventually capturing six Vietnamese soldiers. Jesse was wounded during the battle and received the Purple Heart. There's no mention of the extent of his injuries." Mr. Green took a sip of his coffee before continuing, "At the Walter Reed Army Medical Center in Washington, D.C., Jesse received a promotion to Sergeant. His unit was the Old Breed." Mr. Green flipped a page. "The Old Breed is the nickname for the 1st Marine Division. The oldest and largest active-duty unit."

Clayton cocked his head to the side. He was aware of Marine groups and how they had slogans. The motto that he had shared with Scot was *Retreat, hell!* It was the cry of the 2nd Battalion, 5th Marines. "What's their motto?"

"No better friend, no worse enemy."

"Oohrah!" Clayton shouted. A division he would be proud to join.

"Sergeant Lowes was quite a hero, awarded the Silver Star, and…well, this is something I've never heard of before…" Mr. Green looked up from the folder and glanced over to Clayton before continuing, "Strange…it seems Sergeant Lowes is slated to receive the Medal of Honor from the President but hasn't stepped forward to claim it." He flipped a page and studied it for a few seconds before he stared over at Clayton. "I can't tell you more, son. It refers to another folder that I don't have access to."

"Who do I have to see?"

"No one, unless you know the POTUS."

"The President of the United States?" Clayton swallowed hard.

Mr. Green nodded. "Sorry. Beyond this, it's marked classified."

"Is Jesse alive?"

Mr. Green held his gaze on the folder and plopped back down in the chair. "There's no notice of death, but I can't guarantee it. The Medal of Honor is a coveted award. It's not likely one would ignore it, unless…"

Heat rushed to Clayton's face. The blood was roaring in his head. A sinking feeling gnawed at his stomach. He took a breath and forced his voice out. It sounded weak and worried. "Can you tell me his last known address?" The walls of the office seemed to be spinning around and around him. He shifted his weight, took a step back, and shifted his weight again. "Please!" the weak and worried voice added.

"You said Miss Kitts still lives in the same house from way back then." Mr. Green leaned back in his chair. Clayton nodded twice. "It seems to me if Sergeant Lowes wanted to see her, he would."

If the walls had been spinning around him before, now they stopped and began to close in on him. "But-but-but, Sir, we're talking about an old woman. I saw her cry…" Clayton's voice cracked with emotion.

Mr. Green raised the cup to his lips only to sit it down without drinking. He nodded. "Love cuts the deepest, son."

Finally, Mr. Green offered Clayton hope without knowing it. "Exactly the reason I'm doing this, Sir."

With raised eyebrows, Mr. Green sat the opened folder on his desk. "I have to go to the restroom. I'll be right back." His eyes went from Clayton to the folder and back to Clayton. "You don't mind waiting a minute or two?" Clayton shook his head rapidly. The man exited the room and left the door open.

Clayton hurried over to the desk and found two addresses listed. He wrote both down and bolted for the door where he and Mr. Green nearly bumped into each other.

"Leaving already?" Mr. Green stepped back, grinning wide.

"Yes, Sir. I'm on a mission." Clayton walked briskly down the hall.

"Hey, kid!"

Clayton spun back to face the administrator. Had Mr. Green changed his mind, or had Clayton misread the man's vibes?

"See you in a few years. Semper Fi!" Mr. Green saluted.

Whew! Clayton clicked his heels and returned the salute. "Semper Fi, Sir!" He marched back to his brother and dad. "Got Jesse's address." He shook the paper out in front of him.

"Great, son." Dad smiled from ear to ear. "Let's get home."

Clayton spent the entire trip home going through scenarios in his mind. He would find Jesse and bring the Marine and Miss Kitts together for a glorious reunion. Jesse might be in hiding. And if so, was it because the police were looking for him? Maybe the Marine was in a hospital suffering from Post-Traumatic Stress Disorder. Many combat veterans suffered from flashbacks, nightmares, and severe anxiety. According to Mr. Green, Jesse received a Purple Heart. How critical had Jesse's injuries been? Worst of all, Jesse could be dead. Then, there was the mysterious Mr. Cooper. The man definitely stirred up his curiosity. Clayton needed to focus on the positive, but it wasn't an easy task. Nothing about his search for Jesse was simple. His meeting with Miss Kitts often came to his mind. He liked the woman. Her tears touched him in a way he had never known. She deserved to know the truth.

As Clayton stared out the windshield, again without seeing the road, her voice came back to him, "If only I knew what happened. I've spent a lifetime imagining."

14

Later that night, Clayton rose from bed and went to the bathroom. The digital clock on his nightstand flashed—11:11 p.m. A sharp wail broke the silence like a dog when it howls, except this was not howling or barking. It was crying. Clayton's breath caught in his throat. He walked over to the window and scanned the woods. Night in Kentucky was as dark as black can be, but tonight, a full moon lit the back yard. The white dog appeared from the cover of the trees. The animal was skinny, downright boney, no doubt starving. A dog may die from hunger, but a wolf would find food. The dog paced back and forth a few times and then fell to the ground as if it had fainted. A moment later, the dog stood and stared up at Clayton. The husky took several steps back, encasing its body up to its head in the shadows of the trees, and continued to stare at Clayton.

His parents had to be asleep by now. There was no way he could wake them for a hungry dog. After slipping into his jeans and tennis shoes, he cracked open his brother's bedroom door. Scot was in bed facing the wall. No need to wake him. He would scare the dog, or the dog would scare him.

Clayton hurried to the kitchen and scooped leftovers onto a paper plate. He opened the garage door. The dog stood completely still with its head cocked sideways and big yellow eyes on Clayton. Maybe he should rethink this? There still was the possibility that the canine was a wolf.

"Here, boy." Clayton held the plate out in front of him. "Here's some food." The dog took a step forward and then two steps back. "Come on, boy. I won't hurt you." The dog bolted into the woods. Clayton sat the plate on the ground and returned to the garage. He closed the door and waited at the window. Ten minutes passed, and nothing. The animal was a male, but maybe he had a mate and pups, and they, too, were starving? Had the dog taken a few steps into the woods and fainted? He should at least try and check on its condition, regardless if it was a wolf or dog. Just keep some distance.

Clayton hurried over to a toolbox along the far wall and opened a metal ammo case, grabbing Dad's night vision thermal monocular and a six-inch LED flashlight. Once outside, he closed the garage door, leaving it unlocked. After shoving the night vision inside his pants pocket, he picked up the plate of food and carried it in one hand and the flashlight in the other. Ample moonlight guided him to the woods. At the edge of the tree line, he aimed the beam of the light into the darkness. Where did the dog go? A whimper broke the silence. There! Straight ahead. The dog poked his head out from behind a tree. "Here, boy. I brought you some chow." The dog's tail zigzagged like windshield wipers at fast speed. "Come on." The dog stepped back behind the tree, out of view. Clayton had a feeling that he should return home, but he wasn't about to let the dog starve. The canine could be indicating that it wanted Clayton to follow him, but why? There was only one way to find out.

He stepped into the woods and fanned the flashlight to the left and right. The wind stirred the trees, and their shadows danced over the path, crossing, and crisscrossing the ground, making it difficult for him to determine if he should be concerned with any of the shadows. Twigs snapped at his feet, and a shudder shot up his spine. The snapping of twigs carried an eeriness walking through the dark even when created by his feet. A rabbit hopped over a branch and darted off, disappearing into a thicket. Tree branches continued to sway in the wind. He came to where the woods ended, and the cemetery began. The wind blew harder across the treeless area, and the moon slid in and out from the clouds, sometimes lighting the course, sometimes casting it into darkness. A curtain of mist rose and hovered above the dark, wet ground as if the grass were cooking in a steamer.

Clayton shivered. His teeth chattered—not because it was cold, which it was, but also because he had traveled farther than he had planned. He should have brought a sweater or jacket. There was a movement up ahead, about twenty yards away, white and the size of a dog. Due to the gray mist spreading across the ground, it was impossible to determine. The form moved further into the darkness and disappeared. Clayton proceeded deeper in the cemetery, groping among the graves, invading the privacy of the dead. From behind came a rustling of bushes. The beam of the flashlight revealed nothing but darkness encasing the trees. A howl drew his attention back to where he thought he had seen the dog. Shadows danced in the breeze. Headstones took on a different look in the dark, appearing like dark silhouettes of waist-high stalkers ready to attack a living soul. Each time the beam of the flashlight scanned a statue, tall spooky shadows developed. Some shadows stood motionless while others scurried away. Moonlight cast plenty of shadows from tree branches. Was the dog or something else in the vicinity? The flag now flapped in the wind. Its rope slapped the metal flagpole. The stench of rotten eggs filled his nostrils.

He froze and scanned the area. Was he being watched? This land belonged to the Angel of Death. It was not the place to be after dark. How stupid could he be? Nonsense. Ghosts don't really exist, and should any such phantoms arise, it had to be humans acting as such. A whimper broke the silence. Is that someone sobbing? Where? Who? His ears strained to pick up the location. The crying was faint. Peering through the night vision, he inspected the area to his right to the tree line and then to his left. A ghostly figure, a woman, clothed in a black dress that reached the ground, stared back at him. She wore a black bonnet on her head. A black shawl draped over her shoulders. She tilted her head to the side and shook a boney finger at Clayton. Her mouth dropped open as if to speak. But instead of words came an audible intake of breath, and with it, a breeze passed from tree to tree, swinging branches. She raised a white hankie to her eyes, her frail body shaking with sobs. As the woman's knees gave way beneath her, two other women appeared alongside her, taking hold of her elbows. The women guided her further into the darkness until all three ladies disappeared. A heavy silence settled over the graveyard.

The hairs on Clayton's head stood on end. He took a deep breath and exhaled slowly. Must calm down. He had not prepared to see the ghostly figures of the women. They hadn't evaporated, as he would expect a spirit to do to prove it was real. But even so, they were spooky, silent, and mysterious. Show no fear while showing respect. Do not belittle any person, specter, or thing, human or not.

The millions of goosebumps prickling at the hairs on his arms were not from fear alone, but also awe. The three women had to be human, part of some elaborate hoax. But if they were real ghosts, then he was witnessing supernatural entities. And that was saying something.

Again, he went stock-still and listened. The wind, flag, and rope had silenced, bringing a substantial calm over the graveyard. Once more, he used the thermal monocular to scan the area. If there were more ghosts or people to see, they were well hidden.

Wait! The ground seemed to have jolted, and with it came a rhythmic thump, thump, thump. The sound grew louder by the second. A shadow came over the crest of the hill—dark and shapeless, like fog or smoke drifting across the graveyard. Was it an entity, a specter, or an animal? Should he hide or run? An instant later, it took the form of a white horse and came trotting toward him. He returned the night vision to his pants pocket, more of a test than anything else. The horse remained visible. It came to a halt within inches of Clayton and whinnied twice, spraying its hot breath over Clayton's forearm. Clayton sneezed at the unpleasant scent of sulfur. The animal stood large, eighteen hands or more. It was a gelding that could have carried the Incredible Hulk into combat.

A soldier clothed in a shell-gray wool jacket, and blue wool trousers sat on the horse. He wore knee-high boots, shined a glossy black. Hanging from around the man's shoulder was a faded cream-colored haversack. Strapped at his side was a long saber, its hilt protruding from a solid brass casing. The handle was a gilded brass cast in three pieces: the grip, pommel, and guard. He wore a slouch hat, creased on top, made of gray wool felt. Gray hair jutted out from under the hat, a tad darker than the cap itself. His face, serene and peaceful, sported a full beard as white and long as the one worn by Santa Claus. The beard extended along his cheeks to his ears, hiding his neck, giving him the distinct appearance of being neckless.

The soldier appeared to be more human than ghostly. This guy must be joining forces with the old caretaker to play a prank on him. "Not funny," Clayton whispered and grinned. What did the soldier expect Clayton to do? Run across the graveyard screaming like a child? He was sure the man would enjoy that, probably fall from the horse laughing.

"Bringing grub to a specter won't bring you any favor, lad." The soldier's voice was flat, lifeless. Despite the warm summer night, waves of vapor radiated from the soldier's mouth like breath in the cold of winter.

Clayton choked back a giggle. Was there no limit as to what the townsfolk would do to prank him? "Did you see a dog?"

"Dog? Is that what you consider it to be?" The man tugged on the brim of his hat.

Clayton's eyebrows shot up. "A wolf?"

The soldier chuckled. "I saw the little scamp run by me. That mutt arrived here last month, I would guess." The soldier raised his head and closed his eyes. "Yep. It was last month. The mongrel starved to death, I reckon." He opened his eyes and ran his fingers through his beard. "The old cur likes to roam the heart of this place, mostly the area between the two flagpoles. It howls something awful, but I ain't never heard it bark. I reckon he had the bark beaten out of him as a pup, and the bark ain't never come back."

Clank! Wham! Snap!

Clayton spun on his heels and choked back a shriek. A man dressed in a dark suit dangled from a tree branch with a rope around his neck. His head lolled sideways as his feet and legs swung back and forth. Wow! No way Clayton would have dreamed up that trick. He turned back to face the soldier, expecting to see a wide grin on the man's face.

The soldier held his gaze on Clayton, but he wasn't smiling. His face held a somber expression. "That's ol' Pud Marcum. The crazy coot shot and killed a cousin or uncle of his. Not sure of which. I heard both versions. He was the last legal hanging in these parts on April 29, 1887. They left him dangling for the longest time, swinging between the heavens and earth. 'Twas no pretty sight to behold. I'd say he's deader than a coffin nail for sure."

Clayton placed the night vision to his eye. Surely the man was wearing a safety harness, but the man vanished too quickly to determine. Clayton took a deep breath and held it. Now that was some great special effects.

"I reckon ol' Pud has gone back to Fallsburg. He died here, but he called that little burg his home. Fallsburg's a village not far from here." The soldier pointed north. "I guess old Marcum keeps going through his departure, hoping the rope will break."

Clayton blinked several times. Steven Spielberg had to be hiding nearby, directing a script written by R. L. Stine.

"I reckon this is a tad much for you to believe, lad. But your eyes aren't lying." The soldier patted the horse on the neck. "You brought that fancy spyglass of yours and got a glimpse of real darkness, conjuring me and several others from our slumber and leisure. Now you must deal with doing so."

"Then how is it I see you without the night vision?"

"Once waken is all it takes, lad. Most of us here are guarded inside." He placed a palm to his chest. "And we are pleasant on the outside. It's that guarded part you need to take heed."

Clayton grinned. His face had to be splitting in two. "You're most certainly not a spirit. You're an actor in costume."

The soldier scrunched his eyebrows. His upper lip twitched. "You know what a woodshed is for, lad?"

"Of course. The title tells you that."

"There's another meaning to it, and I'd love to show you." The soldier leaned out over the horse. "I'm a forgiving sort nowadays. However, don't take my kindness as weakness. Now, let's get down to business. Do you have a pepperbox, lad?"

"A what?"

"A pistol."

Clayton shook his head.

"Shouldn't be here without one. Are you wallpapered?"

"Wallpapered?"

"I'm asking if you're drunk?"

"Of course not."

"Then you must be swimmy-headed. Stupid coming here to be amongst us poor souls when you're not commissioned to be." The soldier leaned back in the saddle and saluted. "I'm Major Ronald Connors of the Confederate States Army." He brushed his fingers across the front of his coat. "I see you staring at my uniform. Pay no heed to the trim and decoration on this jacket," added the rebel. "I assure you, young man, I'm a Major, not a second lieutenant. I took this jacket off a comrade after he arrived here. A scoundrel he was. My original uniform was bloody and torn beyond repair. There was no way I was going to be caught dead in it." He broke into a hearty laugh. And with it, the ground shook beneath Clayton until the man regained his composure.

The horse lowered its head and touched Clayton on the forearm with its muzzle. Then the animal sniffed at the plate of food and turned from it. Clayton rubbed the horse on the bridge of its nose. The gelding was real, no doubt about it. Clayton had a hard time biting back a chuckle. It was a poor attempt at playing a ghostly prank, but he would play along.

"Here, lad, give this to Sir Midnight." The Major held an apple, waving his hand up and down. Clayton sat the plate of food to the ground. The soldier tossed the apple in the air, and Clayton caught it. "You give him that apple, and when you see him in the afterlife, he'll remember you."

In the afterlife! Clayton coughed to disguise a chortle. It was getting harder and harder not to bust out laughing. The caretaker must have paid a hefty price to this Civil War re-enactor riding a horse. Clayton held the apple out in the palm of his hand. The horse took the apple into its mouth and chomped down. Little pieces of apple fell upon the ground. Sir Midnight bent its long neck and tongued up the pieces of fruit. When it raised its head, it was as if its big brown eyes were whispering thanks. "Why is his name Midnight when he's white?"

"So, you believe my faithful companion not to be black?"

Clayton stepped back and eyed the horse. It was white as a bedsheet. Or was it? For a moment, it changed to gray and then black and back to white. "I-I-I don't know." Clayton lived in a time of computers and movies with special effects. How was this done? His eyes scanned the graveyard before turning them back on the soldier.

The Major sat up straight and patted the horse on the rump. "You ever ride a horse, lad?" Clayton shook his head. "You can hop up here, and I'll take you bouncing over the knoll."

"No, thank you, sir."

"I shall bring you back in the utmost safety and urgency."

"I better not, sir." Clayton smiled out of respect, still believing the man and horse to be a prolific prank. "Are there others here?"

"Others?" The Major cocked his head.

"Spirits." Clayton's smile deepened. The prank was too extravagant not to involve more people. Too bad Scot and Jaylynn weren't here. This was drama at its best!

"Aw, I see." The Major leaned over and patted the horse on the neck. "This place is full of specters. My job is nothing more than a glorified sentry." He sat upright and straightened his jacket. "The true power lies in imps, the scamps...the mischievous rascals who roam this sacred ground. They're rough scoundrels, true demons. The Indians among us call the beasts, Wendigos. They love the winter months but do, on occasion, venture out during hot summer nights. Beware of them, for they'll snatch your soul and rejoice in doing so."

Clayton figured there was no harm in going along with the joke. "Why don't these creatures harm you or your horse?"

"They, even with their mighty evilness, cannot bring spoil to my comrades and me. For our fate has already been determined." The soldier waved an arm outward as if he were spreading an invisible cloak over the graveyard. "Besides, those beasts don't appear the same nights us humans do." He raised the middle and forefinger of both hands and made air quotes when he said the word 'human.' "However, it doesn't mean those creatures won't appear at the same time."

Ha! Clayton fought back a smile. Finger quotes didn't date back to the 1800s. Did they? Surely this soldier was no ghost.

"I ask one final time," added the Major. "You want to ride Sir Midnight?" Clayton shook his head. "In that case," the man's voice turned gruff. "I need to know if you're with the Union or with us?"

Confident, Clayton squared his stance. It was time to have some fun. "Union? I don't have a job."

"Are you fighting for the north or the south?" the soldier snarled, leaning out over the side of his horse.

Clayton cocked his head in silence. He had clearly gotten under the Major's skin. The game was on!

"Boy, haven't you heard about the Civil War?" The Major pulled his sword from the sheath and swung it in a circular motion over his head.

Time was up. Game over. Clayton was facing a life-taking weapon in a mental duel. "Yes. President Lincoln."

The soldier lowered the sword, resting the tip of the blade upon the horn of the saddle. "Don't tell me that old scalawag is still the president."

Clayton laughed. "Of course not."

"Well, lad, are you for slavery or not?"

"Slavery?" Clayton squared his stance. "Slavery is wrong. All humans are equal."

A smile crept across the soldier's face. "Glad to hear it, lad. I didn't know it then, but I do now. Death is a mighty, powerful teacher." He slipped the sword back into the casing. "Even a soldier should have the right to change his beliefs. Wouldn't you agree?"

"Yes, sir."

Sir Midnight stomped its front hoof once, and then a second time. The horse flared its nostrils and blew a powerful blast of air on Clayton.

The Major twisted in his saddle and cocked his head. Another rider came into Clayton's view near the flagpole atop the hill, waving a hat over his head. The Major raised his hat in return, and the soldier rode off, disappearing over the knoll.

"Well, lad, it's time for me and Sir Midnight to go. James A. Garfield, General of the Union Army, is waiting to finish our game of chess." The Major slapped his cheek with his hand. "The gallinippers are out tonight."

Clayton's head snapped back. "Huh?"

"Gallinippers…mosquitoes. Dang buggers. Hate 'em. They're about as big as a Georgia thumper."

Clayton rose on his tiptoes. "Georgia thumpers are grasshoppers!"

"Grasshopper is correct. That's good horse sense, lad, yet you venture into this graveyard…at night." Major Connors raised his eyebrows. "I admit most of these souls are molly grubbing, doing nothing to pass eternity. But you ain't bright as an unlit candle coming here after dusk." The Major leaned forward. "Do you know of the Battle of Louisa?" Clayton shook his head. "By golly, that was hunkey-dory, toeing the mark, doing the job. Union soldiers, both races, got in a battle amongst each other and began shooting. Several of the bluecoats bought the ground that day, at their own hand. It was a bad fix for the Yanks. Thought for sure it had opened the door on the hen house for my boys and me. But that was my bad fix…unpleasant situation. Shortly after that skirmish, I found myself assigned to my current duties." He tipped his hat. "Got to go," he continued, still leaning forward. "Got to get back to the game. Wasn't that long ago old Garfield ran my boys and me out of Louisa three years after the battle at Ivy Mountain in 1861, not far from here. But I'll be fried in pork grease before he beats me at chess." The Major leaned back in the saddle, twisted his body, and glared over to the tree line. "Let's go!" He yelled like he was calling someone. "It's time for us to go!"

Clayton peered into the darkness. No one came into view. When he looked back to the horse, it began to fade like it was an apparition. Clayton's knees buckled. The soldier turned back to face him, and he too began to disappear. "Are you a real gho…" Clayton choked on the word.

"Lad, that's something you have to decide. Go home now." A youth came out of nowhere and walked up to Sir Midnight. The kid was near Scot's size and age. The Major leaned down and pulled the kid up by the arm onto the horse to sit behind him. "Let's go, Aley. Need to get you home safe and sound."

Clayton's jaw dropped open and froze there. Aley? Was this the kid that the man under the bridge, known as Uncle Jim, had been seeking? Clayton tried to speak, but his tongue would not move.

The soldier tugged on the reins. "Get home, Clayton Hall. It's not safe out here at night. I suggest you skedaddle!" With those words, the Major, the kid called Aley, and the horse, headed for the hill. The sound of its thunderous hooves rumbled in the distance. Before reaching the top of the knoll, all three evaporated before Clayton's eyes. A flash of lightning shot across the sky, followed by a crack of thunder, loud and sudden as a gunshot.

Clayton stood stock-still. An eerie calm settled over the graveyard. He took a deep breath and held it a moment while giving thanks for being alive before proceeding on across several graves. A few feet from the entrance of the cemetery, Clayton stopped and stared at the sacred ground. He had seen a ghost, actually several. What were the odds? His brother was in for an ear full!

Clayton arrived home to find the garage door unlocked as he had left it. On his way to his bedroom, he checked in on Scot. His brother was sound asleep. As he reached his parents' doorway, his father coughed. Clayton held his breath.

"Clayton, Scot?" Dad called.

"It's me, Dad," replied Clayton. "Going back to bed." It was the truth.

"Okay, goodnight, son."

Clayton slipped into bed. In the morning, he would search the Internet for information on the Major. He might also revisit Miss Kitts.

15

Clayton woke to the aroma of bacon. His stomach growled. Before giving in to his hunger, he switched on the computer. "What the heck. Hey, Mom, we have no Internet!" There was no way his mom would reply. She yelled upstairs only when she wanted something done immediately.

Scot entered Clayton's room. "What's wrong?"

"Man, you missed out on seeing ghosts last night."

"You went to the cemetery? Alone?"

"Shhh, not so loud." Clayton grinned. "Yes, alone, and I saw several spirits."

"Sure you did." Scot giggled. "Must've been a heck of a dream!"

"I'm serious." Clayton grabbed his brother by the forearm. "I followed the white dog into the woods. When I got to the cemetery, I saw several ghosts, including a soldier from the Civil War."

Scot's head snapped back. "Uh-huh, sure." He jerked from his brother's grip and exited the room, giggling.

Clayton hustled after Scot. "It's the truth. I even saw a kid named Aley."

"Uh-huh." Scot snorted like a pig.

Clayton's nostrils flared.

***

After breakfast, Clayton returned to the computer and found the Internet to be working. Jaylynn had been correct. Balcutha became Louisa, and Cassville became Fort Gay. There wasn't anything on Major Ronald Connors of the Confederate States Army. But James A. Garfield of the Union Army did occupy Louisa from December 1861 until the end of the war, and there were several Confederate takeover attempts. The Battle of Louisa was real. Union soldiers had shot and killed each other in 1864. There wasn't anything on a man drowning under the bridge. It didn't mean that it didn't happen. The influenza outbreak in 1918 was factual. Jaylynn was well informed. Was Louisa a hotbed for ghosts? Would he see the Major again? Clayton was about to turn off the computer when he spotted a news article dated from the year 2010.

Fort Gay hit national news when Microsoft suspended an Xbox Live account that belonged to a town resident for writing "Fort Gay, WV" as his location, as Microsoft has language policies that prohibit references to the word gay. Microsoft customer service representatives refused to acknowledge that Fort Gay existed. It took an appeal from the town mayor and media coverage for the issue to be corrected.

Clayton shook his head at the ignorance of some folks. Was Jaylynn aware of the story? All anyone had to do was Google Fort Gay, West Virginia.

Switching off the computer, he stood and stretched. Time to conduct his search for the Marine. He rapped his knuckles on Scot's bedroom door and pushed it open. "I'm going to go look for Jesse. You want to come along?"

"Heck yeah."

The boys entered the garage and hopped on their bikes. Within minutes they were at the intersection of Adams and Lock Streets. Clayton eyed two house trailers positioned a few feet from each other. One painted blue and the other white.

"I don't see an address on either one."

"Try the blue one first." Scot pointed.

Clayton smiled. Blue was his little brother's favorite color. He knocked on the door.

A woman answered. "No one here by that name."

"Thank you." Clayton took a couple of steps toward the white trailer.

"No one named Jesse there either," added the lady. "Three elderly women live there, named Kristel, Puja, and Kusum."

Clayton waved to the woman and mounted his bike. "One other place to check." He and Scot rode away.

A block down the street, a dog barked at the heels of a mailwoman. The lady stood motionless while yelling, "Shoo! Get back!"

Clayton dismounted his bike and called to the beagle, "Here, boy. It's okay. Come here, boy." He patted his leg. The dog stared at Clayton for a moment and then growled. The mailwoman's face took on an expression of terror.

Scot squared his stance and stuck his hand in his pocket, reassured when he felt one of Old Blue's biscuits. "Here, boy." He walked up to the dog showing no fear, holding the treat in the palm of his hand. The beagle sniffed the biscuit, then took it and ran to the side of the house. Clayton stared at his brother. "I got it from Jaylynn's house," said Scot.

"That was five days ago." Clayton rolled his eyes and shook his head. "Don't you ever change your pants?" Scot shrugged.

"Thanks, boys." The mailwoman unclenched a fist. "Guess I need to get some doggie treats."

"Would you know where this address is?" Clayton handed her a slip of paper.

The mailwoman transferred the mailbag from one shoulder to the other. "Sandy Lane isn't far from here. Take Adams to Public Way and turn left. You will come to the Louisa Do It Best Hardware store near Lackey Avenue. There's a string of homes across the railroad tracks. Sandy Lane is across those tracks."

"Do you know which house?"

The woman shook her head. "No, sorry. It's not my route."

"Do you know Jesse Lowes?" Clayton asked with a lift of his chin.

The mailwoman took a step back. Her chest rose and fell with rapid breaths, and she dropped the slip of paper to the ground. "Told you too much already." She put a stick of gum into her mouth. "But I warn you. The folks over there are secretive and protective. They don't take kindly to strangers." She popped a bubble, wheeled on her heels, and walked briskly away.

Clayton picked up the note and chased after her. "What do you mean you said too much?"

The mailwoman shoved several envelopes and a package into a metal mailbox. "I should've asked who you were searching for. I've never met Jesse. He's an unsung hero and values privacy."

"I just want to talk with Mr. Lowes." Clayton jammed his hands in his front pockets.

"I doubt you'll find him at that address. Still, you did me a favor. There's a Marty McCormick who lives next door to Dee's Drive Inn on the second floor. Do you know where Dee's is?" she asked, around her chewing gum. Clayton nodded once. "Marty served with Jesse. He may be able to answer your questions. Marty has handled all matters for Jesse with the government and the like." She pulled several envelopes from the mailbag in preparation for the next house. "Marty's your go-to-guy. I've nothing more to say. Sorry."

"What's your name?" Clayton smiled. "Is it okay if I tell Marty you sent me?"

"If you've been asking about Jesse, I'm certain Marty already knows." The mailwoman cracked the gum with her teeth and waved Clayton off.

"Where to now?" asked Scot.

"To the other address." Clayton hurried over to his bike and hopped onto the seat. The guy named Marty wasn't needed yet. Not when Clayton still had another place to check first.

Scot leaned out over his handlebars. "But she said it wouldn't do any good."

"We don't know that yet." Clayton tore off down the street with Scot riding alongside him.

Clayton came to a halt at the hardware store. On the other side of the railroad tracks stood a row of five houses. None seemed to have a visible address. "Come on."

"Where you boys heading?" came a male voice as the brothers crossed the rails.

A white, middle-aged man stood on the porch of the first house. Clayton slammed on the brakes and skidded to a stop. "Looking for Jesse Lowes."

The man reached into a pocket of his bib overalls and removed a canister of smokeless tobacco. Popping the lid, he placed a pinch of tobacco into his mouth. "You boys ain't from these parts, are you?"

Scot shook his head. "We live across town."

"I would say you are correct, and then some." The man spat to the ground. "There ain't no Jesse Lowes here." He raised his voice when he said Jesse's name.

A stout dark-skinned man, in his mid-sixties, appeared in the doorway and stepped onto the porch. He wore blue jeans and a black muscle shirt and had bulging biceps. "Who's hunting Jesse?"

Clayton's heartbeat quickened, his fingertips tingled, and he felt out of breath. In front of him stood an American hero. "Hello, Mr. Lowes." He saluted.

The man's face went rigid as he stepped off the porch. "What brings you boys barking up my tree?"

"Wanda Kitts." Clayton's knees wobbled. He moistened his lips as he waited for Jesse to speak.

"Did Wanda send you here?"

Clayton's muscles tightened. "She's still waiting for you to come home, sir."

"Me?" Mr. Lowes bellowed. "Shuck no, boys. Wanda isn't waiting for me. She has the notion my brother is going to walk through her door. Not me."

"Frostie!" Scot shouted and grinned so wide that it nearly cut his ears in two.

"Yep, that'll be me. What do you boys want with my brother?"

Clayton puffed out his chest. "To ask why he hasn't seen Wanda. She's still—"

"Boys, you have no idea what you're setting yourselves up for. Jesse went off to war, but my brother didn't return." Clayton lowered his head, feeling his fast-beating heart go up into his throat. He had the sensation of riding his bike down the twisting road of the cemetery and losing his front tire in a curve. "Now, don't get me wrong. Jesse's alive, but a big part of him died in Nam. He has no desire to see anyone, including me. He wants to be left alone."

"Maybe if we—"

"There's no maybe about it, boy," Frostie interrupted. "If I can't get through to him, no one can." The white man whispered something to Frostie, then went inside the house. "How did you find me?" Frostie cocked his head back.

"It wasn't easy, sir." Clayton wasn't about to give up Mr. Green.

"Who are you boys?"

Clayton introduced himself and Scot. "Our dad owns Hall's Grocery."

"I thought old man Boyd owned it."

"He's our grandpa." Scot puffed out his chest.

"Do you think you can get Jesse to meet with Miss Kitts?" Clayton crossed two fingers.

"Son, I've asked, repeatedly. I told him he owed Wanda that much. Jesse never leaves his home, and I doubt he ever will, not until six men carry him out. He's part mule and part jackass."

"Is Jesse inside?" Clayton held his breath.

"No, son, he doesn't live here, and don't ask me where. I love my brother. I would die before I betray him."

"But—"

"Look, Clayton," added Frostie. "It's kinda crazy if you ask me, but what do I know. The level of love Jesse reached with Wanda is one I never experienced in my lifetime."

"If he loved her, why does he stay away?"

"Clayton, war changes men and women in ways you can never fathom. I pray you never know the taste." Frostie frowned. "Now, if you boys will excuse me, I have things to do. And don't continue on your wild goose chase. Let it go. It is what it is."

"But, sir…" Clayton took a sharp breath in response to Frostie waving a hand and walking inside the house. The screen door slammed shut.

"Let's go find Marty McCormick." Clayton rode across the tracks and headed downtown, Scot in tow. There was that phrase again—let it go. Not in this lifetime!

The boys pedaled hard and fast. Dad would be home soon. They locked their tires and skidded to a stop next to Dee's Drive Inn at the front of a two-story building constructed of brick. It had three doors. Two were painted white—the middle door green. The ground floor had seven plate glass windows. The second floor had four windows, each with green shutters. Attached to the outside wall alongside the green door were five small mailboxes.

Clayton tapped a finger on the box tagged with the name Marty McCormick and opened the green door.

"Hey!" yelled a man walking briskly across the street, swinging a walking cane back and forth in the air. Clayton released the door. "You don't give up…do you, kid?" The man was Steve Cooper from the library. He came to a halt a foot from Clayton, shook his head and grunted a wordless sound. "I told you to leave it alone." Cooper's stare intensified.

"Marines don't quit, sir," said Scot.

Mr. Cooper locked eyes with Scot. Judging by the sudden snap of Cooper's teeth and narrowing of his eyes, Scot's statement hadn't helped any. The man didn't bother to mask his annoyance as his chin jutted forward, and he whirled from Scot to face Clayton. "You have a thick skull, boy." Cooper banged the tip of his cane against the ground twice. "Back in my day—"

The green door swung open. A towering figure of a man stepped out. "I hear you want to speak to me." The man's voice was gruff like Clayton imagined a bear would sound if it talked. "I'm Marty."

"Mr. McCormick, I—"

"The name is Marty, and I know all about you boys. You've been making more noise than a Clydesdale in a mortuary." He studied Scot through narrowed eyes before doing the same to Clayton. "You're Clayton Hall. Your brother is Scot, spelled with one 't,' and you boys are looking for Jesse." He leaned down and placed his head near Clayton. "Now, tell me something that I don't know."

Clayton forced himself not to flinch. The man could wrap one hand around both of Clayton's hands and still have room for a baseball. Clayton drew himself up, shoulders stiff. "I'm not giving up my search, sir. No better friend, no worse enemy."

Marty looked over to Mr. Cooper. "What do you think, Coop?"

"Guess it wouldn't hurt to hear him out." Cooper transferred the cane from one hand to the other.

"Yeah," replied Marty. "We both know how persistent a Marine can be."

"Like hemorrhoids," Mr. Cooper growled. "I'll be upstairs when you're done, Marty."

Marty gestured with a thumb up at Mr. Cooper. "Let's go next-door to Dee's for a coke on me." The boys hesitated. "Don't worry. It has a back door in plain sight."

The instant they entered, a half-dozen pairs of eyes fixed on Clayton and Scot. A quick scan revealed the back door, and Clayton relaxed. "Hey, Marty," said a couple of men simultaneously, and they waved. Marty returned the gesture. The restaurant was clean, warmly decorated, with red metal tables and chairs. Black and white tiles covered the front counter where customers placed orders.

"Hello, Karen," Marty raised three fingers as he greeted the waitress behind the counter. "Three Cokes." He nodded toward a booth near a brick wall. "Have a seat, gentlemen. Debbie told me you boys were coming."

"Debbie?" Clayton leaned back.

"The mail carrier." Marty smiled. "So, tell me, why are you looking for Jesse?"

Clayton shared the meeting he and Scot had with Miss Kitts.

"Son, you're not going to find a city friendlier than Louisa. And Fort Gay is the same." Marty took a sip of Coke. "Both towns protect their own. Jesse is what we call homegrown, born and raised right here. If one of us seeks privacy, we get it."

"What about Miss Kitts. She's also homegrown. Doesn't she deserve to know the truth?" Clayton stared into the man's eyes. Blinking was not an option.

Marty's mouth dropped open. Judging by the crevices on his forehead, he wasn't about to agree with Clayton.

Clayton continued to stare despite the urge for his eyes to blink.

After ten seconds or so, Marty chuckled. "Boy, you've got me there." He took another sip of Coke. "Jesse and I are family. Being a Marine is for a lifetime."

"Do you ever see him?" Scot sucked on his straw. The sound told everyone that his glass was near empty.

"I get his groceries every Thursday and deliver them in time to have lunch with him. He wants no visitors. None."

"Why did he turn down the Medal of Honor?" Clayton placed his arms onto the table.

"Well, I see you did your homework." Marty's stare intensified. "Do you think it's easy for a Marine to ignore the President of the United States?" Marty stared at the straw in his glass for a second. When he turned his eyes back on Clayton, they took on a glow as if they had gone somewhere in search of calmness and found it. "All I can say is, some things outrank others. Sorry. There's nothing I can do."

"Will you ask him to visit Miss Kitts?" Clayton cupped his hands together.

"Son, I'm not the only one who has begged Jesse to do so. But as I said, he's a hero. His wish is honored daily, and that's not about to change."

"Meanwhile, Miss Kitts…" Clayton lowered his gaze to the table without seeing it.

"I'll ask him one more time. And I'll tell him that you boys are looking for him. This Thursday is the Fourth of July, and I'll be too busy with the parade. It'll be Friday or Saturday before I'll see him, but I already know his answer." Marty stood, left a tip, and exited.

Clayton and Scot followed and rode their bikes home.

16

The following morning, Clayton rose, stepped in front of the mirror, grinned and shuffled his feet. "How does it feel, Clayton Hall?" he whispered to himself. "You're now a teenager." He dressed and hurried downstairs to the kitchen.

"Happy birthday, Clayton!" Mom, Dad, and Scot shouted in unison and then broke into song.

"When I get home from work, we're going to Dee's for dinner." Dad hugged Clayton. "So, don't wander off too far after you guys cut the grass. Got it?"

"But it's my birthday."

Dad cocked his head, and his lips formed a sly grin. "And?"

Clayton's shoulders slumped, and he nodded.

***

When noon arrived, Clayton and Scot met Jaylynn near the bridge. Clayton shared the event he experienced at the graveyard.

"You really saw a kid named Aley?" Jaylynn rocked back on her heels.

"Yep, and a soldier riding a horse."

"Did they look like spirits?" Jaylynn sucked in a quick breath with a hand against her chest. Fingers splayed out.

"Not at first. But they evaporated." Clayton didn't mention the man hanging from the tree and the weeping lady. He might tell Jaylynn later, but not his brother.

"Uh-huh." Scot yawned, waving a palm to his mouth. "And Harry Potter is real."

"It's the truth." Clayton poked his brother in the ribs.

"Ouch!" Scot swatted Clayton's forearm.

"If you weren't so scared, you could've gone with me." Clayton stepped back and threw his chest out. "I'm still alive."

"Awesome." Jaylynn raised her fist. Clayton bumped his fist against hers. "I'd love to see a soldier from the Civil War. What color was the horse?"

"It was white for a moment, and then changed to gray and then black and back to white. But it was gentle. I fed it an apple."

Scot giggled.

"I did! The soldier tossed me an apple, and I fed it to the horse."

"And then the horse disappeared. Wham!" Scot slapped his palms together. "My brother, the magician!"

"I want to go to the graveyard." Excitement filled Jaylynn's voice.

"Count me out." Scot's face tightened.

"Why are you worried about a magic trick, little brother?"

"Well, what if…"

"It's daylight, Scotty. Nothing's going to appear. Besides, I have your back. Maybe Rand-Dock knows where Jesse is. Plus, we can tell him about our meeting with Miss Kitts."

"Come on, Scot." Jaylynn's eyes glowed. "We're in this together."

Scot puffed out his cheeks and blew out a long breath and fell in line.

***

The threesome entered the graveyard. Clayton came to a halt near the spot where he had met the soldier and horse. Small pieces of apple lay at his feet.

"Gee," Jaylynn exhaled. "You weren't kidding."

Scot bent down and picked up a chunk of apple. It was still moist two days later. "If you honestly saw a ghost, why didn't he hurt you? I thought the Confederate…"

"There were good men on both sides of the war, Scotty. The Major was nice. He even offered me a ride on the horse."

"Look!" Jaylynn pointed. "At the top of the knoll beyond the flagpole."

"Antlers. Two racks. Must be two deer." Clayton watched the antlers duck out of sight. He glanced over at his brother. Scot turned his bike as if he were about to bolt off. "It's okay, Scotty."

Scot scrunched his face and continued to straddle his bike, feet on the pedals. "Howdy, kids!" came the voice of a woman.

Two women came walking down the blacktop road, both middle-aged, slim, wearing jeans and long-sleeved shirts. One carried a gasoline-powered weed trimmer and the other a can of gas.

"Howdy," repeated the shorter of the two. "Are you kids looking for a certain grave?"

"Wasn't that the words Rand-Dock had used?" whispered Scot. "I'm sure some ghosts are women."

Clayton glared at his brother.

"No, thank you," said Jaylynn. "We're looking for Rand-Dock, the caretaker."

The ladies looked at each other.

"Is he busy?" added Clayton.

"Whoa there. Down here, we ease into the questions. First, we say howdy." The taller woman stepped forward, balancing the weed trimmer in both hands. "I'm Mare. This is Jenny Belle."

Jaylynn introduced her cousins and herself.

"Now, what can we help you with?" Jenny sat the gas can to the ground.

"We'd like to speak with Rand-Dock." Clayton shifted from one foot to the other.

"Rand-Dock?" Mare raised her eyebrows. A zero-turn mower topped the hill with a man at the controls. "We're the caretakers. That's our brother Robbie on the mower. We don't know a Rand-Dock."

"What does he look like?" Jenny waved for her brother to come over. The man brought the mower to a halt and shut off the engine. He was plump and clean-shaven and wore a new John Deere cap.

Scot nodded. "He wore a hat like yours."

Robbie removed the cap and fanned his head with it. "John Deere is popular in Kentucky."

Jaylynn described the man. "He said his name was Rand Dockery."

"That's a name I would remember." Robbie wiped his forearm across his sweaty forehead. "But I haven't heard it before now. Sorry."

"From your description, I'd say you're talking about Tony Lee Bellows. An elderly guy who lives beyond this cemetery in the woods." Mare sat the base of the weed trimmer against the ground and aimed her index finger to the west. "Sometimes he walks through here heading for town. That's the best I can tell you. But I don't recall a scar on his face."

"Tony Lee had a brother who lived with him a spell." Jenny bent down and picked up the gas can. "But I don't think his name was Rand."

"Yeah, but the brother died four or five years ago, give or take," added Robbie.

"Is he buried here?" Scot's voice carried a hint of nervousness.

"Possibly." Robbie leaned out over the steering wheel. "Don't know. I've seen Mr. Bellows stop at the top of the hill near the flagpole and stare at the ground, sometimes for several minutes. Could be an unmarked grave he's paying respects to."

"Or…" said Jenny, drawing attention her way.

"Or what?" asked Jaylynn.

"Tony Lee is speaking with the devil." Jenny winked and broke into a cackle that sounded like the clucking of a crazed hen.

"Not funny, Jen." Robbie frowned as Scot stepped behind Clayton. "My sister has a warped sense of humor."

"Sorry." Jenny smiled. "Just having a little fun."

"Do you know where his house is?" asked Clayton.

"I doubt anyone knows exactly." Mare shrugged.

"Do you know where Cemetery Road turns left leading to the church?" Robbie placed the cap on his head.

"Yes." Clayton nodded. "We live nearby."

"There's a dirt road that turns off to the right at the bend. You proceed on the dirt road a short distance. There you will see a trail that goes straight while the dirt road continues to the right. If you take the way to the right, it leads to Riverbend Road and the Lawrence County Judicial Center. You need to go straight instead. It's a path marked by a four-wheeler leading deeper into the woods. Bellows likes to park his ATV near there and walk into the graveyard. Just so you kids know, Bellows is not a friendly sort." Robbie started the motor on the mower and drove away.

"Maybe you kids should rethink your notion of finding Mr. Bellows." Jenny scratched the back of her hand that held the container of gas.

"We'll be careful." Clayton smiled. "My brother and I live near the church."

"Don't make us call the sheriff to go hunting for you kids." Mare raised her chin. "You hear?"

"Yes, ma'am." Jaylynn nodded. The kids rode away and headed for the woods.

When they reached the path, they parked their bikes and entered the woods. About a hundred yards in, they came to a hut. The windowless structure had seen better days, built with rough timber, and covered with moss. Coarse straw covered the roof. A gray stone chimney stuck up like a single eye watching for the coming of a trespasser. Trees hugged its foundation and towered over it like protective guards. If not for the smoke coming out of the chimney, the shack would have passed as abandoned. Strewn across the small clearing in front of the hut were junk motors, scrap metal, and aluminum cans. Wood planks spread on the ground formed a sidewalk that led from the path to the front door. Clayton pointed at an ATV parked near the hut. Jaylynn and Scot nodded.

"What's that smell?" Jaylynn pinched her nose.

"Smells like raw sewage." Clayton clamped a hand over his mouth. How could anyone live near such a stench?

Scot spat to the ground. "He's cooking a dead…" He made a gagging sound.

"This place gives me the creeps." Jaylynn continued to squeeze her nose.

"Look," Scot whispered. Clayton's eyes followed his brother's finger.

Nailed to the trunk of a tree, was a form of a man dressed in ragged and torn clothing, arms spread outward like it was about to grant all visitors a bear hug. Its face bore the mask Jason wore in *Friday the 13th.* The eye sockets were dark like they were hollow.

"It's just a scarecrow, little brother."

Scot rose on his toes. "Real or not, it's spooky."

A rustling charged through the underbrush from behind the shack, crunching twigs and branches. A chicken emerged running wildly, squawking as if it was a guard dog. Clayton tossed a stick, and it landed within inches of the hen. The bird ran off, cackling as if it had laid an egg.

"I have to pee." Scot ran over to a tree. Clayton and Jaylynn laughed harder.

The front door opened, and a short, chubby man appeared in the doorway with a face creased with age and a scowl. A white bandanna, stained with blotches of red, covered the top of his head. He held a pickaxe in one hand and a butcher knife in the other. "You kids are trespassing." His voice was as gruff as his appearance.

Clayton shifted uneasily. "Hello, Mr. Bellows. Is Rand Dockery here?"

The man walked out and came to a halt a few feet from the kids. "I ran him off long ago, and he's not coming back."

"Do you know where we can find him?" Jaylynn stared the man straight on. Clayton figured her Bowie knife was on her mind.

"Look in the graveyard." The man raised the knife out in front of him and shook it in the general direction of the cemetery. "He hangs out there a lot."

"Thank you, sir." Clayton gestured for Scot to come out from behind a tree. Not everyone could be a Marine.

"What ya'll want with old Rand?" The man took a step forward.

"Just to see him," said Jaylynn. "We spoke with him the other day."

The man raised one eyebrow. "You don't say?" sneered Bellows. "Did you use a Ouija board?" Clayton and Jaylynn shook their heads. Scot edged further behind the tree. "Ya'll accomplished something I ain't done in a spell," added the man. "When you see him, tell him his brother said hey."

"Are you saying he's…" Jaylynn looked over to Clayton.

"I'm saying he hangs out in the cemetery for a reason." The man scraped the knife blade across the stubble on his face. "Be aware. Old Rand isn't always pleasant. That boy is known for having a temper."

Jaylynn waved goodbye and strolled down the path, repeatedly glancing over her shoulder.

Clayton took Scot by the arm and hurried after Jaylynn, kicking his peripheral vision on high alert.

"Forgive me for not being neighborly!" Mr. Bellows called out. "You kids want to come inside and sit a spell? I'm baking gingerbread." The man burst into a loud, witch cackle.

The kids dashed to their bikes.

"That was creepy." Jaylynn's lip trembled.

"Do you think Rand-Dock is a ghost?" Scot climbed onto his bike.

"I don't know," Clayton said. "Let's go see Marty McCormick."

"Stop at your house first." Jaylynn crossed her legs and grunted. "I need to go to the restroom."

"Me too." Scot moaned. Clayton agreed.

The kids rode down Cemetery Road. Robbie waved from his position on the mower. Clayton returned the gesture and fell in behind his cousin and brother. Should anyone come up from behind, they would have to go through him first.

17

"Grandpa!" Clayton parked in the driveway and dismounted his bike. He hustled over to where his grandfather sat on a porch swing. Grandpa removed his pipe from his mouth and placed it beside his leg.

Jaylynn hugged her grandfather, then entered the house.

"Happy birthday, son." Grandpa handed Clayton an envelope.

"Thanks, Grandpa. There's cake in the house." Clayton tucked the envelope into his pants pocket.

"Got to go easy on sweets." Grandpa ruffled Clayton's hair.

Clayton took a seat and placed his hands on his knees. "Have you ever seen thousands of frogs gather and attack humans?"

Grandpa banged the bowl of his pipe against the edge of a large metal coffee can. "No, can't say I have. Was it in a horror movie?"

"We saw it," Scot said.

"In the woods off Paddle Creek." Clayton straightened his back. "Not far from the McGee house."

Grandpa gazed down at the floor while he packed his pipe with tobacco. Shifting his weight, he picked up a Zippo lighter and flipped it open. Raising his head, he lit his pipe, taking a deep draw and blowing smoke from his mouth. Two smoke rings floated in the air and evaporated. "Was this while you kids were hunting the Screaming Thing?"

"Yes." Scot squirmed in his seat.

Grandpa took another draw on his pipe. "Thousands of frogs, eh?"

"And vultures, buzzards, owls, and wild turkeys." Scot stood and sat beside his grandfather.

"Have you ever seen them gather at the same time?" Clayton leaned back in the chair.

"There are many wild creatures in the woods." Grandpa clamped his teeth on the pipe's mouthpiece. "Who knows what God has put in the woods for us to admire and fear?" he said out the side of his mouth. "As far as thousands of frogs, I may have an explanation for them." He removed the pipe from his mouth and looked over to the front door. Clayton imagined he was making certain Mom wasn't in earshot. "McGee was a frog farmer. He bred the critters like they were guard dogs. I never saw his so-called pets, but he boasted of having hundreds of them. Even as a kid, McGee was an outsider, strange in his ways. He liked to experiment, taking part in weird science, mixing chemicals, catching butterflies, removing their wings, and electrocuting them. The last time I saw McGee was at the VA hospital. He had dyed his hair orange and was talking out of his head. Two years later, on a humid day in August, his skeleton was found on the ground near his back door, picked naked by wildlife...or wild frogs."

Clayton and Scot stared at each other. Clayton nearly told his grandfather about the Wendigo, Major, horse, Aley, Pud Marcum, the weeping lady, and her two companions, but he bit his tongue. How much would his grandfather be willing to believe?

"Guess I shouldn't have told you that story." Once more, Grandpa looked at the front door. "But it's the truth. As far as vultures, buzzards, owls, and wild turkeys appearing together, that is indeed a strange occurrence."

"Spooky, too," said Scot.

Jaylynn walked onto the porch carrying a piece of cake on a saucer and handed it to Grandpa.

"I guess one small piece won't hurt." Grandpa placed his pipe on the seat of the swing.

Clayton turned toward Jaylynn. "You took photos of the frogs. Show Grandpa."

Jaylynn pulled out her phone. "I tried to show Pa, but the photos never took. I don't know what happened to them." She sat on the chair that Scot had vacated and told the story of Roger's attempt to scare them.

Grandpa hunched over and held his gut, laughing that turned into a hacking cough. He raised a hand until he regained his voice. "I would've loved to have seen that. Roger is goofy. Did you kids see the school bus bridge?"

"Yes." Scot grinned. "It was cool."

"I helped Robert Cyrus to put it there along with six other men." Grandpa closed his eyes. "We built cranes with pulleys and heavy chains. Reckon that was over twenty-five years ago. I haven't been back there since."

"We can go back if you want to come with us." Scot's face beamed.

"Nah, these old bones ain't up to that walk."

"Grandma Pernie was alive back then." Clayton enjoyed hearing stories of his grandmother. He couldn't come close to counting how many times he wished she were around.

Grandpa raised his head. "Yes, she was. I miss that woman," his voice broke with emotion. "Wish that you kids could've met her." His chest rose and fell with rapid breaths, and his chin trembled. He glanced down at his hands. "Sorry." He sniffled and then cleared his throat. "I think about her every day."

"She's been gone a long time." Scot hugged Grandpa.

"Yes, she has." Grandpa broke from the embrace and pulled his wallet from his back pocket. His hand quivered. "This is the last photo taken of Grandma and me together."

"Wow," Scot sighed. "You were young, Grandpa."

Grandpa chuckled. "Yes, we were. I reckon we both were in our forties then. Believe it or not, I used to be a boy too."

"Did you hunt ghosts?" Scot handed the photo to Clayton. Grandma smiled in every picture, even while she was on her hands and knees tilling her vegetable garden.

"Nah," said Grandpa. "The story of Wanda Kitts seeing a creature was scary enough to keep kids from doing such. Many of us poked fun at her, but none of us dared to challenge if what she claimed was true or not." He paused for a few seconds before he spoke again. "In fact, at our forty-fifth high school reunion, three years ago, a classmate poked fun at Wanda's claim. He tried to renew the teasing, but none of us participated. It wasn't right to speak of Wanda, without her present to defend herself. The classmate went on to say, if he had met the creature, he would've killed it with his bare hands. Three days later, that old boy went missing as if he vanished off the face of the earth. No one has seen him since. His name was Rand Dockery."

Clayton gasped and dropped the photo to the floor. Scot slammed back in the swing, and Jaylynn squealed. No one moved. No one spoke. The only sound was the squeak, squeak, squeak of the porch swing.

"Did I say something wrong?" Grandpa leaned back and crossed his legs. "You kids look like you've seen a poltergeist."

Jaylynn placed her palm against her chest. "Are-are-are you saying Rand Dockery is a ghost?"

"No. All I'm saying is no one has seen the old boy in three years. One should not tempt the hands of fate."

"Do you believe in ghosts?" Clayton retrieved the photo and handed it to his grandfather. He looked over to Scot and Jaylynn, hoping they would read his eyes. Now was not the time to mention their meeting Rand-Dock.

"Funny thing about spirits, not everyone can see them." Grandpa returned the photo to his wallet. "And those who claim they have, swear that they did. I do admit there are times I hear noises at home. I find myself wishing it were Grandma checking in on me from time to time."

"Cool," Scot said. "As long as she's friendly."

"There was no one friendlier, son." Grandpa laughed and ran his hand through Scot's hair.

"What about ghosts in the cemetery?" Clayton had to ask.

Grandpa's eyes lingered on the door of the house for a few seconds before turning back to face Clayton. "I have heard stories of such from a few of my friends," he whispered. "They said spirits of soldiers from the Civil War roam the grounds." Grandpa took a bite of the cake and swallowed it.

Clayton looked over to Scot. His brother's eyes went wide open, but Clayton still wasn't sure if Scot believed his story about the Major.

"I went to the cemetery a few times but never saw a thing." Grandpa wiped his brow with the back of his hand. "You and Scot are from Columbus, Ohio. Did you boys know we have a city named Columbus here in Kentucky?" Both boys shook their heads. "We sure do. It's a small city in Hickman County and borders Missouri. The Mississippi River separates both states. Like the Big Sandy River runs between Kentucky and West Virginia." Grandpa pointed to the east in the direction of downtown Louisa. "I bet that little town of Columbus has plenty of ghosts being near to the Mississippi. When the Civil War began, it appeared that the United States had become three countries—the Union, the Confederacy, and Kentucky."

"What do you mean?" Scot straightened his body.

"Kentucky was neutral. The state didn't side with the North or the South. But when the Confederates invaded Columbus in the fall of 1861,

Kentucky joined the Union. Two days later, Union Brigadier General Ulysses Grant entered Paducah, Kentucky, to rid the state of Confederate soldiers. Some 74,000 Kentuckians fought for the North while 35,000 joined the South. Several families had brother fight against brother."

"I'm glad times have changed." Clayton glanced over to Scot.

Grandpa chuckled.

"We can't go that far to hunt ghosts, Grandpa." Jaylynn tilted her head back. "Did you ever stand under the tri-bridge and make a wish to see a ghost?"

"No. I never made such a wish." Grandpa took another bite of cake.

Clayton studied his grandfather. His concern wasn't on Columbus, Kentucky, and the Civil War, nor was it on the bridge. Grandpa was like a rock, the foundation of the family. Clayton couldn't throw off the image of Grandpa shaking from the memory of Grandma. A time that was long gone. It brought back the event when he had watched tears stream down the face of Miss Kitts. "Grandpa, can I ask you something?"

"Sure, son."

"Why do old people cry?"

Grandpa did a double take at Clayton, and he released a bark of surprise.

"I mean, after living so long, and seeing so many tough times," added Clayton. "Why does it seem that the older one gets, the more they cry?"

"When one gets old, son, tears come quicker, and they come deeper," replied Grandpa. "At old age, you realize how short life is." He puffed out his cheeks and released an audible sigh. "Both types of tears."

"Huh?" Scot's face scrunched like a bulldog.

"Happy tears and sad. Both types run profoundly." Grandpa finished the piece of cake and set the saucer on the swing.

"Why would someone cry if they're happy?" Scot beat Clayton to the question.

"Yeah," added Jaylynn. "It seems silly if you ask me."

"Time will answer that." Grandpa laughed. "Enough of this sad talk. What else happened today?"

"Have you ever heard of Jesse Lowes?" Clayton was certain of the answer. But would Grandpa admit it? He was also homegrown and near the same ages as Jesse and Wanda.

Grandpa raised an eyebrow. He banged the bowl of his pipe against the metal can again. "Your father told me about your trip to the VA. I was wondering when you were going to ask me." He packed tobacco in his pipe and lit it. "I knew of Jesse in school."

"You did?" Scot twisted sideways on the swing. Clayton got to his feet. Jaylynn leaned out to the edge of her seat.

"Jesse was three years ahead of me in school. He had his friends. I had mine. We didn't know each other personally. He played on the basketball, baseball, and football teams. He was talented. But, due to the war, he got a draft notice shortly after high school. He joined the Marines and shipped off to Vietnam."

"Do you know where he is now?" Clayton pulled his chair closer to the swing, and it scraped against the floor.

Grandpa leaned back. "I love Louisa. You're not going to find a better class of folks. But when they protect one of their own, they don't take the task lightly."

"But do you know where Jesse is?" Clayton felt that his grandfather was dodging the question.

"Son, you kids are looking for a ghost of a different kind."

"He's dead?" blurted Scot. Clayton cocked his head and stared over to his brother. Frostie had stated that Jesse was alive.

"I didn't say that. But it's clear Jesse doesn't want to be found." Grandpa's voice hardened. "A matchmaker isn't always successful."

"I'm just trying to find Jesse." Why didn't the grownups understand that about Clayton's search? He just wanted to find the man and relay the information to Wanda. Nothing more.

"You're banging your head against a wall, son," said Grandpa. "We all must lose what we love sometimes."

Clayton drummed his foot against the porch floor. He needed a new approach. "Do you know Marty McCormick?"

"Yeah, I know Marty. How'd you hear of him?" Grandpa took a long draw on his pipe, but the fire had gone out. He relit the tobacco and blew the smoke from his mouth.

Clayton shared his meeting with Marty and Frostie.

"Marty and Jesse were best friends in school." Grandpa dumped the tobacco into the metal can and placed the pipe in his shirt pocket.

"Can you ask Marty for us?" Clayton hardened his stare. He wasn't about to give up the mission.

Grandpa stood and stretched. "Time I be heading home. I was hoping to see your dad. He's a tad late tonight." He opened the screen door. "See you later, Lola. Tell Gary I will stop by again tomorrow."

"Okay, Boyd. Drive safe," Mom shouted from somewhere inside the house.

As Grandpa stepped from the porch, Clayton took hold of his arm. "Will you ask Marty where Jesse is?"

Grandpa rubbed two fingers across Clayton's forehead. "Watch out for those walls, Clayton. They're mighty hard." He walked to his pickup truck and drove away.

"Do you think…" Scot sat back in his chair.

"Yeah," said Clayton and Jaylynn simultaneously.

"Grandpa knows more than what he's saying," added Clayton. No doubt, Grandpa was a friend with most everyone in Louisa and Fort Gay, but what was the purpose of the secrecy? It had to be something profound—a reason that ran deeper than love, if there was such a thing. This hunt for Jesse began as a desire to bring closure to Wanda, but the more Clayton requested information from others, and with the way they had shut him down, the more his curiosity flared.

"I've got to head home." Jaylynn walked over to her bike.

"Hold on." Clayton opened the screen door and asked his mother if he and Scot could ride with Jaylynn to the bridge.

"Hurry back, boys. Your father will be home soon."

The threesome tore off down Town Hill Road and came to a halt in front of the building where Marty lived. Mr. Cooper stood out front leaning on his cane.

"Hello, Mr. Cooper. Is Marty home?" Clayton placed his feet on the ground and balanced his bike between his legs.

"No. Sorry. What do you kids need?"

"Jesse Lowes." Clayton puffed out his chest.

Once more, Mr. Cooper leaned out over his cane and faced Clayton. "You already know that answer." He leaned back and stared Clayton in the eye. "Tell me something, kid. What makes you think, with you being a stranger, you can come to our town and discover a fifty-year secret?"

"After I saw Miss Kitts cry." Clayton's grip tightened on the handlebars. Mr. Cooper cocked his head to the side. "May I ask you something, sir?" continued Clayton. "In all the years you have cried, which has been the deepest? As a kid or at the age you are now?"

Mr. Cooper took a step back and shook his head. At the entrance door to Dee's Drive Inn, he stopped and stared at Clayton. He shook his head again and went inside.

A pickup truck pulled alongside the kids. Marty climbed out. "Hello, Clayton, Scot and…" he paused and squinted. "Bentley," he said to Jaylynn. "You're one of the Bentley kids. Right? Brian and Lucille's kid?"

"Yes, I'm Jaylynn."

"How's your mom and dad?"

"They're fine. Thank you."

Clayton cleared his throat.

Marty turned and faced Clayton. "Son, I wish I had good news, but I don't."

Clayton's lip trembled. He tugged on his shirt. "Did you tell Jesse that we're looking for him?"

Marty nodded once. "I spoke with him on the phone. Getting ready for tomorrow's parade has put us all behind schedule. But Jesse made it clear. He's not willing to see you kids, now or ever. Period."

The door of Dee's opened, and Mr. Cooper stepped out, holding a Styrofoam cup. "Watch that one there, Marty." He shook his cane at Clayton. "That boy believes he's privileged."

Clayton bit his tongue. It was doubtful that Mr. Cooper had a tear in his entire body. Clayton forced a smile. "Thank you, Marty, for trying."

"Happy birthday, Clayton." Marty strolled over to Mr. Cooper. "I hope to see you kids at the festivities tomorrow."

Clayton cocked his head and took a step back. How did Marty know it was his birthday? Had Grandpa told him? It seemed Marty knew everything about everyone. Regardless of how nice Marty appeared to be, the man wasn't willing to help Miss Kitts get to the truth. The Marine was willing to let an old woman die without knowing. Clayton grumbled under his breath.

Clayton led the way to the bridge and stopped near the entrance.

"I want to see Rand-Dock again." Jaylynn glanced at the screen on her phone.

"Yeah," Clayton agreed. "I want to ask him if he's a ghost."

"You guys are crazy," said Scot. "Count me out."

"If he's a ghost, Scotty, he didn't hurt us." Jaylynn wiggled her eyebrows.

"Doesn't mean he won't." Scot pedaled off on his bike. Clayton waved goodbye to Jaylynn and chased after his brother.

Clayton and Scot arrived home and found Dad climbing out of his pickup truck. "Hey, boys, any luck with finding ghosts or Jesse today?"

Clayton shared the event of meeting Mr. Bellows.

Dad glared into Clayton's eyes until Clayton blinked. He then did the same to Scot until Scot gazed down at the ground. "Do I need to say anything?" he finally whispered.

Both boys shook their heads.

"We won't go back." Clayton frowned and told his father the news from Marty.

"It's time you give up your search for Jesse." Dad grabbed a bag of groceries from the truck seat and shut the door. "If he doesn't appear at the Fourth of July parade tomorrow, then your quest is over. Understood?"

Clayton took the sack from his father, but he didn't answer.

"Understood?" Dad repeated, taking hold of Clayton's elbow.

"I heard you, Dad." Clayton's answer had to be enough. Lies kept mounting, and he was far from reaching his goal of finding the Marine. He hurried inside the house and placed the groceries on the table.

Mom entered the kitchen. "You boys get changed. We're going to Dee's."

"Yes! Chili dogs and a chocolate shake."

18

The Fourth of July showed the promise of beautiful weather, mid-eighties, and sunny—perfect for a parade and celebration. Clayton climbed into Mom's van ahead of everyone else. Today had to be better. With several Vietnam War veterans at the ceremony, there had to be, at the very least, one who would speak with Clayton on the whereabouts of Jesse. He did not doubt that one or all knew the Marine.

Mom slipped behind the steering wheel and guided the van to town. Banners, streamers, and flags swayed in the wind. Folks lined the main thoroughfare from Pocahontas Street to Vinson Avenue. Mom turned on a side street and parked near the library where Jaylynn and her family stood waiting.

Clayton hustled out in front of everyone, taking a position at the curb. A Louisa police car with emergency lights flashing and siren blaring led the parade. Behind the police vehicle, marched a group of military men and women dressed in uniforms. Several of the soldiers were near the age of Marty. Which one should he approach first? The group of soldiers turned their heads at the same time and looked back at him, in a scowling way. He swallowed hard. Not one soldier wore a smile. It was as if Clayton had stepped over the line of military brotherhood, in the wrong direction.

A pickup hauling the Grand Marshal followed. The next vehicle carried the mayor and several other folks. Then came an ambulance, two rescue vehicles, and five large fire trucks with emergency lights on and sirens shrilling. The first responders represented several departments, Louisa, Cherryville, Fort Gay, and Fallsburg.

"Pud Marcum," whispered Clayton, remembering what the Major had said about the ghost he witnessed hanging from the tree. "Rest in peace."

A short line of classic cars and farm tractors were next in line. People stood on floats, tossing candy to the ground. Then came riding mowers, golf carts, go-carts, motor scooters, motorcycles, and kids on bicycles. The General Lee from the TV series *The Dukes of Hazzard* drove by tooting its trademark Dixie horn. Behind the General Lee was a four-wheeler with a fiberglass body. It had a ghostly figure and the words, Grave Digger painted on its side. The windows were small and narrow. Whoever sat behind the steering wheel stayed hidden in the darkness of the cab.

The final vehicle was another Louisa police car with lights flashing, but it was the Grave Digger vehicle that held Clayton's interest. A hand tugged on his elbow from behind. An aged woman stood within inches of him with a firm grip on his arm. She wore a black wool sweater with a veil over her face. Had the woman confused Independence Day with Halloween? A stench swept over him, much like the awful breath-stealing odor in the woods at the shack of Mr. Bellows. Clayton coughed and blinked several times.

"Stop looking," snarled the woman, raising the veil and removing it from her head. Her hair was as white as ivory, brushed back over her head and covered her ears. Wrinkles ran every which way across her face, and the age spots gave her skin a coffee-stained tone. The woman's jowls hung below the chin that she jutted outward. Her thin, pink lips matched the color under her cold, dark, mysterious eyes. She poked Clayton in the stomach with a finger of her withered hand. "Stop looking," she repeated.

Clayton stepped back and covered his nose and mouth with his palm. "Huh?" He glanced to his left and then to his right. Where had his family gone? "I wasn't looking at you, ma'am," he said through his hand.

The woman spat to the ground, cocked her head back, revealed a toothless grin, and raised one eyebrow. "Consequences, boy. You're searching for consequences. You better be ready for 'em, for they are seeking payment." The woman's voice made fingernails on a blackboard sound good. She winked.

"Clayton!" Mom yelled from across the street. "Come on. We're leaving."

Clayton glanced and waved at his mother then turned back to face the woman. "Do you know Jesse Lowes?" His hand remained over his nose and mouth.

The woman glared and leaned forward, shaking her finger. "I know who *you* are."

Clayton removed his hand from his face and waved her off. As he stepped into the street, a car blew its horn. His heart leaped in his throat.

"Be careful, son!" yelled Mom.

Clayton checked both ways and crossed the road. When he peered back across the street, the woman was nowhere in sight. His heart raced as his eyes searched the crowd. It was as if the woman had vanished like a—

"What were you doing standing there by yourself?" Mom asked.

"You didn't see the woman talking to me?"

Mom placed her palm to his forehead. "Are you feeling okay?" She fluffed his hair with her hand. "Stop pulling my leg. You know there wasn't anyone else."

Yes, there was. The woman was real. Remnants of her gut-wrenching odor remained in his nostrils. But where did she disappear? What did she want, and who was she? Was she another Nightwalker on a daytime outing? Scot and Jaylynn also claimed not to have seen the woman. He shook the remnants of the encounter with the woman from his mind when he spotted a group of retired soldiers wearing military dress uniforms standing near his mother's van. Would one of the men talk to him? Before he could reach the soldiers, the men looked to Clayton and broke from their group and scattered.

Dad pulled Clayton in close. "It's okay, son. Their reason runs deep. It's over. You can stop your quest to find Jesse."

Clayton bit his tongue. Words would do him no good unless they guided him to the Marine. He may not like what he discovered, but he wasn't about to quit. His reason also ran deep. And it was far from being over.

***

The Halls followed Jaylynn and her parents across the bridge to their farm for a family cookout. Uncle Gary had bought fireworks to put on a display, but Clayton wasn't into the festivities. His mind raced from one idea to the next. The pressure inside his ribcage was like a mule sitting on his chest. Every new plan was no better than the previous one. Louisa might be a great town filled with friendly citizens, but he had yet to agree. Didn't seem to be anyone willing to help him discover the whereabouts of Jesse. What was the big deal anyway? What harm could come from a simple meet and greet? A simple explanation was all he was after. Or was it? He was chasing fifty years of answers.

Clayton called Jaylynn to the side and told her that he saw Pud Marcum hanging from a tree.

"Let's Google him." Jaylynn led Clayton to the computer.

"It's true." Clayton leaned back in the chair the moment he read the information on the computer screen. "Pud Marcum was the last person to be legally hanged in Lawrence County, Kentucky. It took place near Pine Hill cemetery in 1887."

"Let's check out the habits and routines of ghosts." Jaylynn typed on the keyboard. "Says here that not all spirits are tied to where their bones are buried. Some roam the place where he or she died."

"Makes sense. The Major said that Pud was buried in Fallsburg, not far from Louisa. And Pud often returns to Pine Hill to relive his last moment."

"Fallsburg is seven miles north, just a spit and giggle off Route 23. If you sneeze driving through town, you will miss seeing a thing."

A spit and giggle? Clayton grinned. Sometimes it was evident that Jaylynn and the triplets were siblings.

"Maybe the Major also died near Pine Hill?"

"Could be," said Clayton. "General Garfield became our twentieth president. He was the second to be assassinated. But why does the spirit of President Garfield haunt Pine Hill, according to the Major?"

"Maybe Garfield continues to protect Louisa." Jaylynn typed on the keyboard. "Let's check on a weeping lady in Kentucky."

"Whoa!" Clayton lightly tapped the computer screen. "According to this article, there's a statue in the middle of Ashland Cemetery in Ashland, Kentucky. It's of a weeping woman. Dad took me to Catlettsburg a few days ago. The cities border each other."

"Yep." Jaylynn read the article. "She sits on a bench, loosely holding a rose in her right hand. She leans over two graves, grasping her left breast while mourning the two souls buried beneath her sight. Several visitors have claimed to have heard weeping coming from the statue and seeing tears run down its cheeks."

"When I saw the lady in Pine Hill, two other women appeared and helped her to walk away." Clayton leaned in closer to the screen. "I wonder if the two graves near the statue belong to those women?"

"Spirits can travel to where they want." Jaylynn sipped her root beer and switched off the computer.

Clayton agreed. There was no way of knowing for sure why any of the ghosts haunted Pine Hill. "I guess every cemetery has spirits. I don't know if we're lucky or cursed to be able to see them."

Back outside, as the festivities ended, one idea came to Clayton in his search of Jesse. True, it could backfire and land him in a deep heap of trouble. But what else was he to do?

19

When morning broke, Clayton dressed in a hurry. He hustled over to Scot's bedroom, knocked once, and opened the door. Scot was on his side, snoring.

"Get up." Clayton shook his brother.

Scot rubbed his eyes. "What now?"

"We find Jesse."

"We've checked everywhere." Scot placed a pillow over his face.

Clayton poked his brother's leg. "I have a plan. Get dressed."

Scot swung his legs over the side of the bed. "It better work. You messed up a good dream. Do you want to know what it was about?"

"No." Clayton walked over to Scot's window. "Come here, quick."

Scot hurried over alongside his brother. "The white dog. What's that in its mouth?"

"The paper plate I used to give it food. He wants more to eat."

"That dog is super smart." Scot pressed his forehead against the glass. "He's watching us."

"I'm back to thinking it may be a wolf."

"Why?" Scot cocked his head back and turned toward Clayton.

"Just do." Clayton wasn't about to tell Scotty what the Major had said about the canine.

"Either way, we should name him. He keeps coming to the house."

Clayton silently agreed. His little brother made sense. "Thor or Titus?"

"Titus?"

"Short for titanium. A strong metal."

"I like it, but what about Togo?"

Clayton nodded. "After the sled dog in Alaska that made the serum run in 1925. I like Togo. He was a great dog, but this guy needs his own name."

"How about Cagey?"

Clayton gave a double thumbs-up. "Perfect for him. I'm going to feed Cagey again while you're getting dressed."

"No! Wait for me." Scot jumped into his jeans and laced up his shoes. "What are we going to tell mom? She won't let us get near it."

"You keep her busy while I slip outside."

"No way." Scot shoved his brother in the small of the back. "You keep her busy."

Clayton shook his head. First, they had to succeed at getting food out of the fridge without Mom becoming suspicious. "Come on."

The boys entered the kitchen and discovered Dad had already left for work, and Mom was elsewhere in the house. "Shhh," Clayton placed a finger to his lips. The brothers stood motionless and listened for a sign as to where their mother could be. There was nothing but silence. Scot set a paper plate on the counter. Clayton grabbed a pack of bologna from the fridge and opened it. He placed half of the contents on the plate and returned the package to the fridge.

"What are you boys up to?" Mom appeared at the kitchen doorway.

Clayton nearly yelped as his heart skipped a beat. Scot whirled to face his mother and positioned his body in front of the plate.

"Getting ready to take out the trash." Scot pointed over to a trash bag sitting in the corner near the door leading to the garage.

"Without me telling you to do so?" Mom raised a hand and fanned herself. "What's on your schedule today?"

Clayton looked Mom in the eye. "Going to visit Dad at the store." It was the truth.

"Anything else?" Mom raised her eyebrows. Clayton shifted his weight. Was she trying to read his mind? At the kitchen counter, she poured a cup of coffee.

Clayton hesitated. Please don't look out the window!

"What else are you two up to?" Mom turned around, cup in hand, and faced Clayton.

There were two ways of telling a lie. By speaking or not saying anything at all. "Nothing else, Mom." If the town wasn't full of secrets, maybe Clayton could be more honest.

"Be careful." Mom made her way to the living room.

Clayton carried the plate outside. Scot followed, dragging the bag of trash behind him. Cagey stood near the edge of the woods. It still held the previous paper plate clutched in its teeth. The animal stood frozen with its cold dark eyes fixed on the boys.

"Here, boy." Clayton held the food out in front of him. "Got you some meat." He took a step closer and stopped. "Come and get it, Cagey." Clayton squatted and sat the plate to the ground.

The animal cocked its head to the right and then to the left.

"Did you see that? I think he knows you called him Cagey."

Clayton didn't know if Scot was correct or not. Maybe the canine picked up on the name, or perhaps he didn't. "Come on, Cagey."

The animal cocked its head again in both directions.

Scot stepped sideways closer to his brother. "Do you think Cagey is really a wolf?"

"I don't know. But if it is, Rand-Dock rubbed it on the head."

"Yeah, but for all we know, that caretaker could be a ghost," said Scot.

"He could be, and so could Cagey. According to the Major, it's a wolf and roams the graveyard." Clayton scolded himself for letting it slip.

"You never told me that." Scot inched forward. "Maybe it's friendly."

Clayton grabbed his brother by the elbow. "Don't even think about it."

"He's starving."

"He'll eat when he's ready. Let's get to the grocery store." Clayton tugged on Scot's arm.

Cagey dropped the used plate to the ground and inched its way over to the bologna. It sniffed the meat then strolled toward the boys.

"I'm going to try to pet him." Scot held out his hand.

"No. Don't move. You'll startle him."

"It would be awesome."

"Don't touch him."

Cagey crossed in front of Clayton and stopped within inches of Scot, where it sniffed the boy's pant leg. Scot gingerly reached down and patted the animal on top of the head.

"No," whispered Clayton. If the animal was a wolf, it was strange how it stayed quiet, not a whimper or growl. Maybe it was the calm before the storm, as Grandpa often said about the weather. "No," he repeated. "He could bite before you blink."

"What are you doing?" came Mom's voice from behind. Clayton whirled on his toes, his heart blasted out of his chest and landed somewhere on the other side of the earth. Mom stood in the doorway of the garage with her hands raised above her head. Like a flash, she bolted inside the garage. A split second later, she reappeared, holding a tire iron at her side. Slowly, she approached her sons. Scot dropped to his knees and hugged the animal's neck. Mom shrieked.

"Can we keep it, Mom?" Scot's eyes pleaded.

"Let him go, Scotty," Mom whispered harshly. "Now." Scot released Cagey, and the canine ran off into the woods. "I should ground you, young man!"

"It's not mean, Mom. It just doesn't have a family." Scot hung his head.

"Well, it's not living here." Mom placed her fingers under Scot's chin and raised his head. "Understand?" Scot nodded once. "And be careful on those bikes." Mom released him and returned to the house.

"I told you not to pet it." Clayton shoved Scot in the small of his back.

"It's not a ghost." Scot thrust his chest out. "I held him in my arms. It's as real as you and me."

Clayton bit his tongue. No need to remind his brother that the horse he had touched felt real before it evaporated before his eyes. "Come on. Let's go to Marty's."

***

They arrived at Marty's apartment building and took cover across the street in a parking lot between a barbershop and pawnbroker. They had a clear view of Marty's truck.

Within minutes, Marty came outside, carrying a box of items. As he placed the box inside the bed of his truck, Mr. Cooper exited Dee's and climbed in the passenger side. Marty slipped in behind the steering wheel and drove away. Clayton and Scot chased after him, peddling as fast as they could.

Marty drove past Dad's grocery and parked in front of the NAPA Auto Parts Store. He climbed out and went inside while Cooper stayed in the truck. The boys cut around the corner and took a position near bushes at the edge of Inez Deposit Bank.

"Do you think Marty is on to us?" Scot leaned out over his handlebars.

"I don't know. Stay behind the bushes. They have to come this way."

"Unless Marty makes a U-turn," said Scot.

Clayton chanced a peek as Marty exited the NAPA store. Marty glanced in his direction, and Clayton ducked back. At the sound of an engine starting, Clayton stuck his head out once more. Marty made a U-turn and slowly drove a block down the street and parked in front of Wellman's Hardware. He climbed out and stretched his arms on the hood of the truck. A woman exited the Lawrence County Sheriff's Office and strolled over to Marty.

Clayton's jaw dropped open. "Scotty, do you see that woman?"

"Of course. Why?"

"She's the one who spoke to me at the parade."

"Really?" Scot leaned further out over his handlebars. "She doesn't look spooky to me."

Clayton said nothing. What were Marty and the woman talking about? It was one thing to play a joke on him, but not at the expense of Miss Kitts. She had a right to know Jesse's whereabouts.

The woman handed something to Marty, then made her way toward the courthouse. Marty climbed into the cab of the truck and drove down South Main Cross Street.

"Follow that truck!" Clayton took the lead. "This is our chance to find Jesse."

At the midway point on the bridge, Clayton slammed on his brakes. Scot nearly hit his bike from behind. Marty's truck turned left onto Court Street in Fort Gay and out of sight.

"I never thought…"

"What?" Scot asked.

"That Jesse could be living in Fort Gay."

"What are we going to do now?"

Clayton shrugged and aimed his bike toward Louisa.

***

Later that evening, while preparing for bed, Clayton shared his new plan with Scotty.

"I like it, but what if Mom and Dad find out?" Scot sat on his mattress and leaned his back against the bedroom wall. "We could be grounded for life."

"We have to try." Clayton held out his pinky finger.

Scot interlocked his little finger with his brother's. "Oorah!"

20

It was eleven in the morning when Clayton and Scot reached the courthouse, taking cover behind a shrub in the courtyard with a clear view of Dad's store.

Clayton studied Dad's building. Three connected gables gave the roof and building a unique form. Engraved in a cement block over the main entrance was the year 1892. "Imagine the spirits that roam the second floor after 127 years."

"Huh?" Scot's face went blank.

"The upper floor of Dad's store is empty. It was built over a hundred years ago. I wonder if..."

Scot grimaced. "No. I'm not ever going up there."

Clayton laughed to himself. He held his cell phone out in front of him. "Is yours on?"

"Yes."

"Call me the minute Marty walks out with groceries."

"But how am I going to catch up with you?"

"I'll wait for you before I confront Jesse. Don't worry." Clayton rode off.

***

Scot dropped his bike prone on the ground and kept watch on the store. Marty arrived in his pickup and parked on Main Street. Scot grabbed his phone and called his brother. There was no answer.

***

Clayton crossed the bridge. There was no time to walk his bike across the railroad tracks. He pedaled fast, down Broadway Street, around the curve to Court Street, and into the heart of Fort Gay. He had no idea how far Marty would travel. If Clayton went too far, Marty could turn without Clayton seeing the man do so. And if Clayton didn't go far enough, he may not be able to stay up with Marty until he did turn somewhere in town. Then there was the possibility that Marty could end up driving through Fort Gay and go someplace in the country. Trying to stay up with the speed of a truck on a bicycle was impossible outside of town.

Clayton came to the intersection of High Street and Court Street, where an empty lot sat catty-corner from Meredith's Marathon Service Center. Along one edge of the lot were overgrown bushes and trees. He pushed his bike up the incline and took cover behind the greenery where he checked his cell phone. He had a missed call from Scot. Quickly, he called his brother.

***

Marty exited the store carrying a box of groceries. Scot's phone rang. Marty cocked his head and stared in Scot's direction. Scotty ducked behind the bush, and the phone rang again. He pressed the talk button. In his haste to place the phone to his ear, he dropped it, and it bounced a couple of feet beyond his reach.

"Scot?" came Clayton's voice from the phone.

Scot rose to his knees and whispered, "Clayton. Marty is leaving."

"Scot! Can you hear me?"

"Marty is leaving," repeated Scotty, keeping his voice low.

"Scot? Scot?"

Scot fought the urge to retrieve the phone. What if Marty should spot him? Finally, Marty's truck pulled out and headed down South Main Cross Street. Scot pounced from behind the bush and grabbed his phone. "Marty left the store and is heading your way."

"Good. Follow the main road through Fort Gay. I'm at the corner of High Street. If you don't see me when you get here, call me." Clayton hung up.

***

Clayton positioned himself at the edge of the bushes and waited. A few minutes later, Marty's truck came into view. Clayton placed his forearm across his face at the bridge of his nose. Marty shouldn't be able to recognize him from afar. Once Marty reached Vancouver Street, Clayton ran up the embankment to his bike. Vancouver was the last possible turnoff if Marty were to stop before reaching High Street.

The moment Marty drove past, Clayton tore off down the embankment, riding on the berm of the road.

Marty came to the Exxon Gas Station and turned right onto Pauley Court, a mobile home park.

Could this be it? Clayton guided his bike into the Exxon station. Here he had a clear view of Pauley Court and the trailers lined on either side of the street. Marty got out of his truck and walked over to a man standing nearby. Clayton couldn't get a clear view of the man. Was he Jesse?

Clayton had to get closer. But Pauley Court was wide open and offered no cover. A building constructed of cinder block stood at the entrance. It stretched a couple of hundred feet deep. The first mobile home on the left stood where the building came to an end, the exact location where Marty stood talking with the man. Clayton eyed the front of the building. It was as wide as it was deep and appeared abandoned. The roof had fallen upon itself in several places. An extended area of land stretched alongside the building east of the trailer park. He rode his bike across the street and eyed the area. The field ran deep enough to get him as far as the first trailer and keep him hidden behind brush and shrubs. But that could bring on a new problem, a charge of trespassing. A house stood where the field ended with two cars parked in the driveway. The occupants of the house may own the land, especially since the yard was well maintained.

Clayton's success hinged on two things, timing and not blowing his cover. He scanned to the west on Court Street. What was taking Scot so long to arrive? There was a good chance Marty could leave at any second. Clayton had to act fast. He pushed his bike up the embankment leading to the field and laid it on the ground. The front door of the house opened, and a woman stepped onto the porch.

"May I help you?"

"I-I-I…" Clayton's mind raced for an excuse. "My dog ran back here a few moments ago. Is it okay if I look for him?" That was a flat-out lie. It seemed one lie was leading to another.

"Sure. No problem." The lady smiled.

"My brother will show up any minute to help me."

"Okay." The woman looked over to a van as it pulled into her driveway.

Clayton caught his breath. The driver was the delivery girl at Dad's store. He spun in a one-eighty. Had she seen him? This mission was about to bring more trouble for him than he ever imagined. Slowly, Clayton dared to look back at the delivery girl. She handed the lady a bag and hopped back inside the van and drove away. The woman reentered the residence, closing the door behind her.

Clayton wandered along the property line between the house and the abandoned building like he was searching for a dog. Thick brush and green Virginia Creeper vines stretched from the ground to the top of the structure. He paused when he reached the first trailer and eyed the surroundings. A vine-covered chain-link fence stood at the rear of the building, providing him a shield to hide behind. He stepped around the corner and spotted Marty and the man. The man was Hispanic.

Clayton's phone rang. Marty spun on his heels. Clayton's breath caught in his throat as he fell back and landed on his butt. Scotty was calling. Why hadn't he put his dang phone on vibrate? Whispering, he directed his brother to his location with instructions to be quiet.

Scot joined Clayton, and they forced their way through an opening in the fence. They crawled on the ground to where they could watch the front door of the trailer and stay hidden behind the ivy.

"Dad will kill us if we get caught." Scot blinked rapidly.

Clayton placed a finger to his lips. He didn't know the penalty for trespassing, but he couldn't worry about it now.

The Hispanic man and Marty shook hands and parted. Marty grabbed the box of groceries from his truck and climbed the stairs of the first trailer. The steps creaked under his weight. He knocked on the door. His knock was like a code, five rapid taps followed by a pause and then two more taps.

"Come in, Marty," came a man's voice from within the home.

Marty opened the door and entered, shutting the door behind him.

"How long are we going to wait here? Marty might be in there all day."

"Be quiet, Scot." Clayton silently admitted his brother was right, and it was getting late. If Mom had called Dad to check on them, trespassing would be the least of their problems.

The door of the trailer opened. Marty stepped out and straddled the doorway.

Clayton's phone rang, and he scolded himself. Vibrate, dummy. Put it on vibrate! Clayton switched his phone to quiet mode. Mom was calling. No way could he answer.

"That's the third time today that I've heard a phone ringing. The second time out here by your trailer." Marty pulled a cell phone from his back pocket and glimpsed at the screen. "It's not my phone."

"Someone must be talking about you, Marty," came the voice from inside. "Ha!"

"My ears are ringing, Sergeant. Not burning."

Clayton and Scot giggled, both with a hand over their mouth. Pay dirt!

"See you next week. Peace, my brother." Marty closed the door, made his way to his truck, and drove away.

Clayton and Scot squeezed through an opening in the fence and paused to pick briars from their clothes.

"You better call Mom."

"Yeah." Clayton's mind raced to form another lie.

21

Clayton checked his phone. He blew out his cheeks and released an audible sigh.

"What are you going to tell Mom?" Scot rubbed the back of his neck.

Clayton shrugged and pressed a fingertip to the cell phone.

"What took you so long to return my call, son?"

Clayton crossed his fingers. "Sorry, Mom. I just now saw that I'd missed your call." Another lie.

"Tell your father to bring home a bottle of olive oil."

"Okay." Clayton made a mental note and hung up.

The boys walked over to the door of the mobile home and knocked, the same pattern of taps Marty had used.

"What'd you forget, Marty?" came the man's voice from inside.

Clayton opened the door and entered. A man, clean-shaven and bald, sat on a brown leather couch with his back against the armrest. His skin reflected the overhead light. The man's head jerked back, and he scowled. "What are you boys doing in my house?" A comforter stretched the length of the couch and covered the man's feet and legs. He wore a white tee shirt and had muscular biceps with the numbers 8-8-68 tattooed on a forearm. The man slipped a hand under the blanket. "Well?"

Clayton took a deep breath and forced his voice out. It sounded faint and scared, like no one he had ever heard before. "Jes-Jes-Jesse Lowes?" He cleared his throat and tried again. "Sorry, sir, my brother and I…" He swallowed the lump in his throat. The man's gaze narrowed, and Clayton snapped his mouth shut before his babbling got worse. Clayton's eyes followed the man's hand as it came out from under the quilt. Thank God his hand was empty.

"We've been searching everywhere for you, sir." Scot stepped forward, grinning like he had found a long-lost friend.

"Who gave you my secret knock?" Jesse's hand returned under the bedspread.

Clayton stiffened. "I heard Marty use it."

Jesse pulled his hand from under the blanket and folded his arms across his chest. "So, you boys are Clayton and Scot. I advise you to leave. Now."

"Without telling you why we're here?" Clayton widened his stance.

"I know why. Because you both lack intelligence."

"It took us a long time, but we found you." Scot continued to grin.

"Wipe that smirk off your face, boy. You think this is funny?"

"No, sir." Scot frowned.

"Wanda Kitts." Clayton didn't dare look away. Marines held their ground, even in enemy territory.

Jesse's head snapped back. His hand slipped under the comforter a third time as his eyes narrowed down to little slits. He took a deep breath and exhaled slowly. "Don't know her."

"You never met with her secretly under the bridge as teenagers?" Clayton advanced one step.

The Marine scowled. From the intensity of his stare, if eyes were flaming arrows, Clayton would be no more. When Jesse pulled his hand from under the blanket, it held a fourteen-ounce can of Prince Albert Tobacco. "I asked you once to leave. Don't make me ask again."

"Wanda still has one of your old tins of Prince Albert on her coffee table." Clayton thrust his chest out. He still wouldn't dare blink.

Jesse's grip tightened on the canister for a split second before fixing his eyes on a framed black and white photo of a teenage girl on his end table. Reaching into his shirt pocket, he removed a package of Top cigarette rolling papers. He placed the pack on his stomach and grumbled under his breath.

"She never married," added Clayton.

Jesse removed the lid on the canister and placed a pinch of tobacco onto a piece of rolling paper. After licking the sheet, he dropped the cigarette into his shirt pocket. He repeated the process, slipping the new cigarette between his lips. "That tells me she's in love with a memory. I have caused her enough pain. No need to add more with my condition."

"Your condition?" Scot's chin shot up.

Jesse grunted and grimaced. "You boys wouldn't understand. Now, leave."

"Try us." Clayton came too far to walk away. He wasn't leaving without a reason as to why the man never returned to see Miss Kitts.

Jesse crossed his arms over his chest. "How old are you, boy?"

"Thirteen. My brother is eleven."

"I'm almost twelve!" blurted Scot as if it mattered.

"What happened to kids being kids?" Jesse removed a Zippo lighter from his shirt pocket and flipped it open. "The problem with kids nowadays, too smart for their britches." He lit the cigarette and blew a puff of smoke out the side of his mouth and dropped the lighter back inside the shirt pocket. "How did you find me? I know there's no information about me on the Internet."

Clayton forced a smile. He wasn't about to reveal Mr. Green. "It wasn't easy." For the first time, his eyes scanned the trailer. A large TV sat on a stand at the far end of the living room. In front of the television stood parallel bars, six-foot-long and three-foot-high. Green vinyl tiles covered the floor. The walls were wood paneling, vacant of photos.

"For the last time, you boys were not invited here." Jesse pulled a cell phone out from under the blanket, held it out in front of him and shook it once. "Fort Gay does have a police department."

"Wanda would love to see you." Clayton glanced over at the photo of the girl.

Jesse looked down at the floor before bringing his eyes up to meet Clayton's straight on. He dropped the phone to his lap and cracked his knuckles.

"She thinks you're dead." Clayton blinked. The Marine's eyes pierced holes in Clayton's confidence.

"Then, she's a wise woman." Jesse picked up the phone, touched the screen, and it lit up. Once more, he shook it toward Clayton. "Leave. I'm busy."

"Doing what? Lying to yourself?" Clayton whirled around and faced the door.

"How is she?" Jesse asked. Clayton didn't respond. "I asked how's she doing?"

"Go see for yourself." Clayton spun back to face the Marine. Had he finally made a breakthrough?

"It's not happening, kid." Jesse pulled out a blue ceramic ashtray from under the blanket, half-filled with burned butts of hand-rolled smokes, and snuffed the cigarette.

Clayton scanned the trailer once more. "Unreal. You've been hiding in a box for fifty years. Don't you get lonely?"

"I know the taste, kid. But loneliness and I have an understanding. And more times than not, I want to dwell in it. It's my right to do so."

"Really?" Clayton had seen denial before, but this Marine had long ago passed that stage. "Is it your right to pass that loneliness on to Miss Kitts without an explanation?"

Jesse's nostrils flared. He growled and again cracked his knuckles. "Look, kid!" He yanked the comforter from his lower body. Clayton took a step back, and his breath caught in his throat. The Marine was legless from the knees down. "I went off to war, came home half a man. There was no welcoming party for a soldier returning from Vietnam. Our people were not happy with the military back then. I couldn't ask her to live with that." He pointed at his partial legs. "And this…now could I?"

"She-she-she has a right to know." Clayton gulped and squared his stance.

"Then you tell her." Jesse reached over and pulled out a wheelchair from behind the couch.

"It's not my job." Clayton thrust out his chest.

Jesse rammed his fists into the couch. He raised his body upward and guided himself onto the wheelchair. "Go. Now!"

"It's amazing." Clayton held his ground. "You have no legs, yet you're still running."

Jesse cocked his head to the side. "Boy, I'm running from nothing, except making that sweet girl more heart-broke." Jesse removed another cigarette from his shirt pocket and lit it.

Clayton and Scot's parents raised them to show respect to others, especially adults. Clayton couldn't imagine living without legs. The Marine had to be tougher than what the man was letting on. Jesse was a hero, no doubt about it. But Clayton couldn't stop the heat that had rushed to his cheeks, nor the flapping his tongue was about to make. "Keep telling yourself that, Sergeant." He stared the man in the eyes. "Too bad that Purple Heart you got can't replace the one in your chest." He tugged on Scotty's shirt. "We're wasting our time."

Scot stepped back and faced the Marine. "Sir, my brother wants to be a Marine. Even after…" He glanced over to where the man's legs should have been. "Right?" he added, looking up at Clayton.

"Of course," replied Clayton. "A Marine is always a Marine…so I believed."

Jesse took a long draw on the cigarette. "A Marine can handle disappointment."

Clayton crossed his arms against his chest and cocked his head to the side. "Really?" He blinked. "How did that work out for you?"

Jesse squinted and snorted, pointing at the door.

Clayton heaved a heavy sigh. "I suppose this is where I should give up. But I can tell you one thing, Sergeant. Should I live to be old, I won't forget this meeting. I'll use it to remind myself how not to be." Clayton spun on his toes. "You care only about yourself." He slammed the door on his way out.

Clayton stepped onto the ground and grabbed his stomach. He kicked at the gravel driveway. This was not how the meeting had played out in his mind. He looked at the window near the door of the mobile home. The curtain moved, followed by the sound of a deadbolt.

"Come on, Scotty. I want to check something." Clayton made his way to the other side of the trailer. "I knew it…a wheelchair ramp. I wonder how many times he had someone drive him past Wanda's house without stopping?"

"We'll never know that answer."

Clayton needed a second meeting, but the Marine wouldn't fall for the same pattern of knocks on his door. He had failed Wanda Kitts, Jesse, and himself. There had to be another way to reach Jesse, but how? His cell phone beeped, drawing his attention. It was a text message from Jaylynn. He called her and explained what had taken place. "I want to visit Wanda tomorrow."

"Great," Jaylynn replied. "I'll meet you and Scot at the bridge at eleven."

Clayton agreed and hung up. He and Scot climbed on their bikes and rode to Dad's store. With a wave of his hand, Dad called the boys to his office and closed the door.

"Were you boys in Fort Gay a few minutes ago?" Dad leaned against the front of his desk.

"Yes, sir." Clayton stared at the floor. Busted by the delivery girl. He couldn't lie this time.

"Did you ask your mother first?"

"No, sir." Clayton raised his head and locked eyes with his father. "We didn't have time. We followed Marty from here and found Jesse."

"He wasn't friendly, either," added Scot.

Dad pushed himself from the table and walked over to a file cabinet. He opened the top drawer and slammed it shut without looking inside. His father was venting to keep from exploding.

"We were careful, Dad." Scot lowered his gaze to his feet.

"That's not the point, son. Go straight home. We'll continue this later." He pointed to the door.

Clayton stopped at the door and faced his dad. "Mom needs a bottle of olive oil."

"Aisle three." Dad's voice snapped with impatience.

The boys rode home in silence.

***

When Dad arrived home, he called the boys down to eat supper. Occasionally, Dad's eyes met the eyes of his sons at the dinner table without saying a word. Mom's silence assured Clayton that she was aware of what her sons had done.

After dinner, the family watched a movie. Once the film ended, Dad continued the silent treatment and sent the boys to bed with a simple hug good night.

Scot paused at his bedroom door. "Why is Dad quiet?"

Clayton shrugged. The few times he and Scot had screwed up in the big city, the sentence came swift. Was this quiet treatment Dad's new approach to something more severe? "I guess he wants us to think about it for a while." Clayton did not doubt that punishment was coming—it was a matter of time. He went to his room, got undressed, and climbed into bed.

"I'll be seeing you soon, Jesse," he whispered and closed his eyes.

22

During the middle of the night, Clayton gasped and sat up in bed. Sweat dripped off his forehead. His palms were clammy, and his heart pounded against his chest. He filled his lungs with deep breaths, releasing the air slowly. The dream had felt real, too real. He and Scot had been walking through the woods when Cagey came up to them from nowhere. Scot patted the wolf on the head. As Clayton reached out to do the same, the animal bit him on the wrist, snapping Clayton awake. He blew out his cheeks and muttered, "It was just a dream."

Clayton glanced at his digital clock. 11:11 p.m. Rising from bed, he went to the bathroom and got a drink of water. He returned to his bedroom and stood at the window. Nothing seemed out of the ordinary. Wait! There was movement near the tree line. The wolf! Cagey cocked its head back and gazed up at him. "Not tonight," Clayton whispered and shook his head. "I'm not feeding you anymore." The animal stepped back, turned, and ran off, disappearing into the woods. Clayton climbed back into bed and stared up at the ceiling. There had to be a way to see Jesse again.

"Maybe if I…no, that won't work." Clayton sprang from bed and ran his fingers through his hair. He paced from one end of the room to the other, back and forth. "Maybe…" He grasped his skull with all ten fingers and grunted, "Damn." His head snapped back and he threw his hands up in an "I give up" gesture. "Except I'm not giving up. You hear me, Jesse? I'm not giving up. I'll think of something." He plopped back in bed and continued staring up at the ceiling.

***

When morning broke, the sunlight penetrated Clayton's bedroom and warmed his face. He sat up and quickly scanned his room, thankful that the dream hadn't been real. He leaned back against the headboard. This was going to be a great day. First on his schedule, was a second visit with Miss Kitts.

He slid out of bed, dressed, and reached for his cell phone atop the dresser.

His phone wasn't there!

"Dad," huffed Clayton. "Of course." Punishment had begun. But what was the big deal in trying to bring closure to an aged woman? How many times had he seen a news report on the death of an individual, and the family spoke of finding closure? How was this any different? Okay, Jesse wasn't dead, but Miss Kitts still deserved closure. True, he and Scot had crossed the bridge without consent. But how could Mom and Dad not see the importance of his mission?

Clayton walked to Scot's room and opened the door. His brother stood at his bedroom window, looking out.

"Did you see Cagey?" Scot glanced at Clayton before turning back to the window.

"Yes. Stay away from him. He bit me last night."

Scot spun on his heels. "What?"

"In my dream. You were patting Cagey on the head, and he bit me."

"I think he's friendly." Scot slipped into his blue jeans. "What are we doing today?"

"I want to visit Wanda."

"What are you going to tell her?" Scot looked up from tying his shoes.

"I don't know yet." Clayton shrugged, glancing over at Scot's dresser. "I see your phone is missing too."

"Huh?" Scot stared over at the chest of drawers.

"I think I know why." A sour taste reached Clayton's tongue. "Let's get this over with."

The boys made their way to the kitchen. Mom sat at the table, drinking a cup of coffee. Clayton and Scot greeted her good morning. She looked over at them, smiled, and tipped her cup but said nothing. Clayton checked inside the microwave and then the stove. Both empty. Yep, Mom was aware that they crossed the bridge yesterday. He grabbed two bowls from the cabinet and a box of Cheerios.

Scot grabbed the milk from the fridge. "Dad at work?"

Mom rose and went over to the sink, rinsed her cup, and then walked to the living room.

"Why's Mom not talking?" Scot asked between bites.

"You're not that stupid, are you?" Clayton finished his cereal and then washed his bowl. He joined his mother in the living room, where she sat on the couch reading a novel. "Can Scot and I ride our bikes to town? We'll stay in Louisa." She held her attention on the book and flipped a page as if he had not spoken. "Mom, is it okay?"

Mom lowered the book. Her gaze ping-ponged between Clayton and Scot. "Since when do you boys need permission to do what you please?"

"We're sorry, Mom. But Scot and I found Jesse, and we had to meet him. We didn't have time to—"

"You *had* to?" Mom bared her teeth. She gave Clayton that steady look that always preceded a stern punishment, and he braced himself. Her lips tightened but remained still, and she turned back to her book.

"Can we go?" Scot begged. Mom's head snapped up, and fire flashed in the stare that once again ping-ponged between Clayton and Scot.

Clayton blew out his cheeks. Grandpa was withholding information on Jesse's whereabouts, and Dad wanted him to quit his search for the Marine. And now Mom was about to lay down the law. Finding words to lower Mom's sudden blast of anger wasn't going to be easy. But it was worth a try—his mission lay in the balance. It was time to tell Mom the whole story. Blowing out another sigh, he went into detail of how he, Scot, and Jaylynn had met Rand-Dock that led to their meeting Wanda Kitts and her story of Jesse.

Mom patted the couch cushion for Clayton and Scot to sit beside her. "Boys, love is the greatest gift in the world. I'm all in for the sake of love. Even so, it's not our place to stick our noses in the business of others. Did Wanda or Jesse ask for your involvement?"

Scot stared down at the floor.

Clayton shook his head. "No, but—"

Mom raised her hand. "It seems to me one doesn't know you tried and the other you managed to upset. Have you done either one of them any good?"

The heat from Clayton's chest erupted upwards, his face on fire. There was only one answer for that because she would hear no other. "No, ma'am."

"You boys need to cut the grass and weed my garden. No bike riding today." Mom reopened her book. "This is my relax time. Now get to work."

And just like that, his entire mission had been dismissed. How could Mom say, on the one hand, how incredible love is while, on the other hand, dish out a yard chore? Was he the only one concerned with the tears of an old woman? True, maybe it was none of his business, but there was that one thing—closure. Clayton's curiosity as to the whereabouts of Jesse had reached its peak. Giving up was not an option, regardless of the consequences.

Clayton waved to Scot to follow him. The instant he opened the garage door, he froze, and a knot formed in his stomach. Their bikes were missing! Clayton wheeled on his heels to reenter the house. Mom stood in the doorway with her arms crossed in front of her chest.

"You boys will be lucky if that's all your father and I take from you. He put them in the back of his truck. He'll let you know how long they will stay there, and I have your phones." She entered the house, shutting the door behind her.

Clayton faced his brother. Scot was glaring at him. "Sorry for involving you, Scotty."

"No, you're not." Scot grabbed the hoe from the corner of the garage as he continued to grumble under his breath.

Clayton supposed Scot was right. It was terrible that his brother had received punishment along with him, but he wasn't sorry for finding Jesse. Maybe a second visit would turn out different? He started the mower and went to work. A few minutes later, the mower ran out of gas. While he refilled the tank, Jaylynn came riding up the driveway.

"I waited at the bridge for an hour." She slammed the brakes on her rear tire and brought her bike to a skidding halt.

Clayton explained his and Scot's jam.

"I might as well help you guys." Jaylynn started the mower and took a turn at cutting the grass.

Clayton grabbed the battery-operated weed eater. After he trimmed the grass along the sidewalk and driveway, he plopped down on the top step of the porch.

Mom appeared in the doorway with three root beers. She sat the cans on the porch floor. "What brings you here today, Jaylynn?"

"Hi, Aunt Lola. We were going to hunt ghosts."

"Not today. I'm sure the boys told you why."

Jaylynn nodded. She opened a can of root beer and sat alongside Clayton. "Thank you for the pop."

Scot dropped the hoe to the ground. Loose dirt caked his tennis shoes. "I'm going to have blisters." He frowned and held his palms out in front of him.

"Good." Mom bared her teeth in a wide grin. "I wouldn't want you to make them worse by grabbing the handlebars on your bike." Scot rolled his eyes. Mom entered the house, laughing.

The wolf stepped out of the woods. "Cagey!"

Jaylynn's head snapped back, and her eyebrows shot up.

"We named him." Scot stepped forward as if he were about to walk over to the animal.

Clayton grabbed hold of his brother by the elbow. "No!"

Jaylynn took hold of Scot's other elbow. "Wow, it's beautiful. But it looks skinny."

"I fed it once. Not doing that again." Clayton shared his dream with his cousin.

"Not a good dream to have." Jaylynn held her attention on the wolf. It continued to stand motionless with its eyes looking in their direction. "Regardless if it's a dog or wolf, it's wild."

A whistle came from the woods, the sound a person makes when calling a dog. Cagey cocked his head back, and another squeal followed. Clayton glimpsed over to his brother. Scot continued to stare at the animal as a third shriek ensued, louder.

"Someone's coming." Jaylynn pointed at the woods. "There. By the walnut tree."

Clayton spat pop to the ground. He was taking a drink when he spotted an arm stretched outward with the hand waving for the animal to come. A walnut tree obscured the person's body. Cagey scampered over to the person, and both disappeared within the cover of the trees.

"Was that Rand-Dock?" Jaylynn jumped to the ground.

"I bet it was." Scot downed his pop and sat the empty can on the porch.

"Are you thinking what I'm thinking?" Clayton scurried to his feet.

"Mom will kill us."

"Not if we stay within hearing distance." Clayton dropped his pop can in Dad's recycling container. Scot and Jaylynn did likewise.

The kids bolted to where Cagey had entered the woods, and they went stock-still. Beams of sunlight pierced the treetops, creating shadows amongst the trees.

"Look," Jaylynn whispered. Briar bushes rustled thirty feet from where they stood.

"Let's go." Clayton nudged Scot behind him and took the lead. Twigs and branches snapped under their feet. In mid-stride, Clayton stopped and held up his hand. Was that the sound of someone clearing his or her throat? There was no one to his right, and no one to his left. A light breeze swept through the trees.

"Kids," a voice called out, faintly.

"Did you hear that?" Clayton aimed his words at Jaylynn. She gave a nervous smile.

Scot poked Clayton in the ribs. He tilted his head as a signal for his brother to look straight ahead.

Clayton rolled his eyes and shrugged. A squirrel jumped from the base of a tree and scurried into the underbrush.

Scot shook his head and repeatedly stabbed his forefinger out in front of him. A shadow loomed on the ground between two trees like it could be a man in hiding.

Clayton picked up a stick and held it to his side. Jaylynn did likewise.

Reaching out and taking hold of Scot's shirt, Clayton guided his brother to stand behind him. A twig snapped, and Clayton spun on his heels.

Mom stood at the edge of the trees with her hands on her hips. "Get back to the house. *Now!*"

23

If there was one thing Clayton could credit his parents for, it was their firmness in dishing out punishment. He and Scot stayed grounded for nearly the rest of July. No bike riding, no cell phones, and no visits from cousins. Two days shy of August, Dad announced they could return to riding bikes and hunting ghosts.

During those three weeks, Clayton thought long and hard on how to bring about a second meeting with Jesse. One plan kept returning to him, and all he could do was give it a try. He asked his grandfather's opinion on his idea.

"It might work, Clayton." Grandpa leaned back against the porch swing. He took a draw from his pipe and blew the smoke out the side of his mouth. "But it could also backfire."

Clayton cocked his head to the side. "How?"

"Well…" Grandpa took a deep breath. "Your plan definitely would inform the entire town of your quest. The folks in Louisa are friendly, but they may not take kindly to you meddling in the business of a local hero."

"I know. A few in town have already chastised me."

"Being told off is one thing, son. But being blackballed is another." Grandpa looked over to Scot, who was walking out onto the porch.

"What's blackballed?" Scot took a seat alongside Grandpa on the swing.

"That's when a person is excluded, shut out, ignored. I'd hate for you boys to make enemies before you even get started in your new school." Grandpa banged his pipe against a metal bucket that he used for an ashtray. Clayton slumped back in his chair. "But then again, there's a large group of younger folks here who haven't heard of Jesse. They may find your goal to be interesting."

Clayton raised his head and moved to the edge of his seat. A rush of excitement shot through him. "Yeah. Scot and I do."

Scot's head bobbled. "Sure do."

"Have you asked around at the VFW?" Grandpa packed his pipe with tobacco.

"VFW?" Scot rubbed his chin.

"Veterans of Foreign Wars. They're located behind the courthouse on Vinson Avenue, not far from the grocery store. The American Legion is in the same building. Talk with the commander. He may be able to help you."

"But they are military. Everyone I have met has been against me, including you, Grandpa." Clayton swallowed hard. He hadn't meant to say it quite like that. His grandfather leaned back against the swing and stared down at the floor. "Sorry, Grandpa."

"It's okay, son." Grandpa smiled. "I understand your position. But you need to understand that I made a promise to Marty years before you were born. A promise is a promise, but I also agree with your father. This is your goal. Succeed or not, your heart's in the right place. A Marine doesn't turn his back on his comrades." Grandpa took hold of Clayton's shirt and pulled the boy in close. "Remember, this could backfire."

Clayton hugged Grandpa, then he and Scot entered the house and grabbed their cell phones. "Mom, can me and Scot ride our bikes downtown?"

"Don't cross the bridge." Mom made firm eye contact with both boys.

Clayton and Scot agreed. Clayton called Jaylynn to meet up with them on Vinson. Jaylynn's brothers had chores to do, but she would be there. The boys said goodbye to Grandpa and tore off on their bikes. When they reached the stone and brick VFW building, they parked their bikes on the sidewalk near the stairs.

Clayton eyed the structure. He wasn't sure if it was three stories or two with a basement. There were windows at ground level that could be for an underground room. Plywood covered the windows on the top level. If the top floor was in use, no sunlight penetrated the area. The stairs were eight high and led to large double doors.

Clayton gazed up at two flags that were flapping against a metal pole. The American flag and a POW/MIA flag. "The black and white flag is for Prisoners of War and Missing in Action."

Scot nodded. "A silhouette of a prisoner standing before a guard tower and barbed wire, and the words, *You Are Not Forgotten.*"

"The flag was created in 1972 during the Vietnam War."

"It must have been a wicked war." Scot kicked the toe of his tennis shoe at a pebble.

"All wars are wicked." Clayton climbed the stairs and rapped his knuckles against the door.

Jaylynn rolled up on her bike and joined her cousins.

The door swung open, revealing a middle-aged blonde woman. "How can I help you?"

"Is the commander in?" Clayton shifted his weight.

The woman shook her head. "Not at the moment. Is there something I can help you with?"

"Do you know Jesse Lowes?" Scot asked.

The woman cocked her head to the side. "No, can't say I do."

Clayton introduced himself, Scot, and Jaylynn. He explained his idea without telling her that he knew the whereabouts of the Marine. It didn't matter if withholding information was the same as lying. His plan wasn't about finding Jesse. It was to draw the man out from hiding.

"I like your idea." The lady grinned. "I love anything to do with the history of Louisa. Go for it."

Jaylynn agreed. "Even if it backfires, no one can blame you for trying. The kids at school wouldn't hold it against you. Not the friends I know."

"But you don't go to school in Louisa," said Scot.

"I know a lot of them from the skating rink. They're cool."

Jaylynn's words were clear, but they had no bearing on Clayton's mission. He wasn't about to change his mind.

As the kids descended the stairs, the woman called out, "The best place for you to get it done is at the library. It's also the cheapest."

Clayton waved thanks to the lady. He led the way to the home of Miss Kitts. "You guys wait on the sidewalk," he said to Jaylynn and Scot. Clayton scaled the porch stairs. The door opened before he could knock.

"Hello, Clayton. What brings you here today? Did you see the Wendigo again?"

Clayton shook his head. "No, ma'am. I would like to know if I could borrow something?"

When he told her what the item was, her head snapped back. "What in the dickens do you want with my prized possession?"

Clayton's throat tightened like a clenched fist, a familiar feeling lately, as an answer crept its way up to his tongue. "I'd like to show it to my grandpa." There it was, another big, fat, outright lie. How was he to tell her the truth? Not with Jesse's stern refusal to see her. It wasn't worth the risk of hurting her further.

"Do you understand how much I value it?"

"Yes, ma'am. I'll bring it back to you in a few minutes. I promise." That was the truth.

Miss Kitts strolled into the living room and returned a moment later. She handed Clayton the black and white photo. "Son, all I have left is my faith, and I'm trusting you."

"I'll hurry." Clayton rushed down the stairs and mounted his bike. Tucking the picture frame under his armpit, he tore off with Scot and Jaylynn in hot pursuit.

***

At the library, Clayton typed a letter. He then removed the photo and scanned it into the computer. Once he had the image, he added the words and printed a copy.

Jaylynn held the flyer out in front of her and read it aloud.

> *What Happened to Jesse Lowes?*
> *By Clayton Hall*
> *I wasn't born in Louisa, but now it's my home. My family moved from a big city where one neighbor may not know the other. Louisa is a tight-knit community. But in being so, has the town lost track of a hero? I first learned of Jesse Lowes from a meeting with an unnamed lifelong Louisa resident. "The last time I saw Jesse," said the woman, "was in the summer of 1968. I have not stopped waiting to see him again."*
> *Jesse was born and raised in Louisa. He graduated from Louisa High School in 1967 at the age of eighteen. The following year Jesse joined the Marines and deployed to Vietnam. Sergeant Lowes received injuries in a fierce battle where he saved the*

*lives of several men in his unit. Jesse left the Walter
Reed Army Medical Center in Washington, D.C., in
1969. The extent of Sergeant Lowes' injuries is unknown. Sergeant Lowes declined the Medal of Honor
from the President of the United States.*

*August 12th marks the fifty-first anniversary of
Sergeant Lowes' departure.*

*Did Jesse return to Louisa? Is Mr. Lowes alive
and well?*

It's time to come home to your town, your people.

*I salute you, Sergeant Jesse Lowes, wherever you
may be.*

Your high school sweetheart and I are waiting.

Clayton printed fifteen more copies. "We have work to do!" He rushed out of the library with his brother and cousin and returned the photo to Miss Kitts.

"Thank you, Clayton, for keeping your promise. What did your grandpa say?"

Clayton crossed his fingers behind his back. "He wasn't home." Another lie.

After bidding goodbye to Miss Kitts, he, Jaylynn, and Scot called on several businesses in town. Each granted permission to display the flyer. The lady at the American Legion and VFW building taped the notice to the door. Clayton took it a step further. He asked the Big Sandy News, the local newspaper, to print it in the editorial section. The editor agreed. The weekly newspaper was due out tomorrow.

"There's one left." Clayton shook the leaflet out in front of him. "Let's go see Dad."

24

"Son, I'm not sure I agree with this." Dad looked up from the flyer. "Where did you get the photo?"

"From Miss Kitts." Clayton smiled. Please don't ask if Miss Kitts was aware of how he used the photo. "I kept her name out of the article."

Dad pressed his lips together and glanced toward the front of the store. "Go ahead. Tape it on the panel of glass alongside the front door. But if I get one complaint…"

Clayton nodded. All to do now was to wait.

***

The following morning, Clayton sat at the kitchen table. What if the flyers had been a bad idea? He would need to walk through town with his head lowered for the rest of his life.

"Clayton!" Grandpa called from the front porch. "You and Scot come here."

Clayton walked across the front room and exited the front door faster than usual. There was urgency in Grandpa's voice. Scot followed.

Grandpa sat on the swing with several copies of the newspaper on his lap. He handed a copy to both boys while taking a long draw on his pipe. "Boys, this is the first that I've seen this town split down the middle." He released the smoke with his words. "You have the younger generation curious and the older veterans in an uproar." He tapped his fingers on the top newspaper. "However, several of the older vets are admitting fifty years is a mighty long time." He locked his eyes with Clayton. "That's a well-worded article, son."

"Thanks, Grandpa." Clayton's cheeks filled with warmth.

"Because of your flyer, folks have tied yellow ribbons to trees, doorknobs, mailboxes, and car mirrors," added Grandpa. "It's an amazing sight."

"Yellow ribbons?" Scot sat up straight.

"It shows support for our troops. There was a song back in 1973 near the end of the Vietnam War, "Tie a Yellow Ribbon 'Round the Ole Oak Tree" by Tony Orlando and Dawn," replied Grandpa. "It's a song about a prisoner returning home."

Clayton leaned forward. "Just like Jesse."

"In a sense." Grandpa's lips formed a half-smile. "But we don't know how Jesse will respond, if at all."

A pickup truck pulled into the driveway, drawing everyone's attention to it. Dad climbed out and shut the door. His gaze stayed on Clayton from the moment he parked until he reached the porch. "You need to return a call to Catlettsburg." Dad waved his cell phone in the air.

Clayton's heart skipped a beat. His eyes rapidly blinked as he ran his fingers through his hair. Only one person in Catlettsburg came to mind. "Why?"

"He didn't say why. Just that he needed to speak with you."

"How did Mr. Green get your number, Dad?" Clayton raised his eyebrows.

"I'd say by caller ID. They're a government agency," Grandpa said.

Clayton sighed. That made sense. Here he had been so worried about Jesse's response that he had forgotten Mr. Green. Was he about to be blackballed from the Marines, kicked out before he could get in? A lump lodged in his throat about the size of Mount Rushmore.

"Click on my last call." Dad handed Clayton the phone.

Clayton pressed on the number and waited. When Mr. Green answered the phone, Clayton swallowed hard. If his stomach had held a church bell, it would be clanging from now until doomsday. "Good morning, Sir. This is Clayton Hall."

"Clayton! I get a copy of the newspaper each week to stay in the know. Did you find Sergeant Lowes?"

Clayton hesitated. No more lies. "Yes, Sir. But he refuses to come out of hiding." Clayton went into detail about the meeting and Jesse's condition.

"If anything changes, good or bad, please let me know, Clayton. I like to stay up to date with all veterans."

Clayton agreed and ended the call.

"Are you kicked out of the Marines before you even join?" Scot fidgeted in his seat.

Grandpa laughed.

Clayton shared the conversation.

"Wow." Scot snapped his fingers. "You're about to become a celebrity."

Clayton quickly learned that Grandpa and Scot were right. He couldn't go anywhere without seeing a yellow ribbon. They were everywhere: mailboxes, flowerpots, fences, telephone poles, street signs, doorknobs, display windows, even on barns in the countryside. The same afternoon a reporter from a local radio station came to Clayton's home and interviewed him. Television stations from Huntington, West Virginia, and Ashland, Kentucky, sent news crews. How was it that so many newscasters had no idea a Marine had declined the Medal of Honor from the President? Clayton spoke carefully, making sure to keep secret his meeting with Jesse. No way would he out the Marine. The reporters fed off the love story between the Sergeant and the woman. They ate it up. The newscasters asked several times for the name of the lady. Clayton refused to provide the information. It seemed every broadcast for the following two days asked what happened to Jesse Lowes and who was the mystery woman.

It was on the third day after the newspaper article that the one person Clayton had expected to appear at his doorstep did so.

The expression on Marty McCormick's face was not friendly. "Have a word with you, kid." Marty pointed to the porch swing.

Clayton stepped onto the porch and took a seat.

Scot appeared at the screen door.

"This is private." Marty pressed his palm against the door.

Scot ducked somewhere beyond the doorway.

If there was one person Clayton knew well, it was his little brother. No doubt, Scotty remained within earshot.

"Young man, on the one hand, I don't see you ever making it as a Marine. You don't seem able to follow orders. On the other, you're stubborn as a mule." Marty furrowed his brow. "Jesse wants to see you and you alone—and no cell phone."

"Why alone and no phone?" Clayton held his breath.

"No interruptions. No recordings. It's to be a meeting between two Marines. Unless you're ready to quit?"

"Quit?" Clayton's head snapped back. "Did you not see the other person in the photo? She's never given up even after fifty years. I'm just beginning."

Marty pressed his back against the swing and crossed his arms against his chest. He took a deep breath of air and released it in an audible sigh. "Tomorrow morning, between ten and noon at Jesse's. Come alone. And if you're late, don't come at all."

"Will you be there, Marty?"

Marty said nothing. He climbed into his truck and sped off.

Clayton plopped down in the spot where Marty had been sitting. He closed his eyes and rocked slowly. Why alone? Would he survive such a meeting? What had he gotten himself into? Clayton recalled the meeting he had had with Jesse. One detail suddenly stood out. How had he missed recognizing it sooner? His eyes shot open, and he slapped his knee. Tomorrow couldn't come too soon. He was ready to see the Marine again, alone or not.

25

Clayton received permission from his parents to visit with Jesse, providing that he took Scot, and they walked their bikes across the bridge.

The moment the brothers arrived at the Exxon station in Fort Gay, Clayton handed his phone to Scot. "Wait for me here." With a deep sigh, Clayton crossed the street and brought his bike to a halt at Jesse's trailer. This was it. No turning back even if he had wanted to. Today would be his last chance with the Marine, no doubt about it. All his efforts, the time spent from his summer vacation, could be for nothing. It was that one thing that kept him going: closure for Miss Kitts. But what if he couldn't get through the Marine's protective wall? Should he tell Miss Kitts that the love of her life was alive and living no more than a mile away? No, he couldn't do that to her, could he? Either way, it was cruel and unusual punishment.

Yesterday, after Marty's visit, Clayton had remembered a small detail from his first meeting with Jesse, and it had given him hope. So much hope that Clayton couldn't wait for this moment. But now, he wasn't so confident. He blew out his cheeks, and his legs trembled. Someone needed to stop his head from spinning and clear up the tingling in his fingers. A bottle of cold water would be great about now, quench his sudden thirst and calm his guts from quivering. No, there was no turning back. Let's get this over with.

As he climbed the wooden stairs, they creaked under his weight. The front door was ajar. He knocked.

"Come in, kid."

Clayton pushed the door open and stepped inside.

Jesse sat in a wheelchair facing him. The Marine pointed at a high-back chair. "Sit."

Clayton took a seat and fixed his eyes on the man.

"Boy, why are you harassing me? Don't you have other things to do?"

"We both know why, sir." Clayton forced himself not to blink.

"Kid, as you grow old, you'll come to know that there are many things you have no answer for. Things happen. You move on." Jesse cocked his head back and raised his chin.

There was a tone of seriousness about Jesse that unnerved Clayton. The way the man stared at him in silence, gripping the arms of the wheelchair as if they were alive and he was choking the life from them.

"You had no right to put my name in the newspaper."

Clayton forced himself to remain quiet. He had one thing to say, and it wasn't the right time to speak. The Marine was right about one thing. He had failed to take Jesse's feelings into account.

"Kid, I have the right to live under self-imposed house arrest. And if Wanda wants to do the same, it's her right."

Clayton continued to bite his tongue. Again, the Marine was right.

"Wanda could've gone on with her life. I even expected that she had. For the first twenty years, I imagined she was married." Jesse rolled a cigarette and placed it between his lips. "I hadn't known she stayed single until 1990 when Marty retired from the corps and informed me. But what could I do?" Jesse flipped open the Zippo lighter and lit the cigarette. He blew the smoke out the corner of his mouth away from Clayton.

It still wasn't the time for Clayton to speak.

"Forgive me for smoking." Jesse mashed the cigarette in an ashtray.

"It's okay," Clayton broke his silence.

"No, it's not, kid. It seems everything I've ever done in my life has been wrong. Wanda was the only thing I did right, and I screwed that up, too."

"She isn't dead, and neither are you." Clayton locked eyes with the Marine and gave no thought of his next words. It was as if his heart had taken control of his tongue. "When I look at you, Sergeant, I see a Marine. A man who knows what it is to give to others." Clayton paused. Jesse's upper lip quivered as if he had something to say, but he said nothing. "For fifty years, you've been giving to her without her knowing it."

Jesse glanced at the ceiling before turning his eyes back to the kid who sat before him speaking like an adult.

"Sergeant, you both may be in love with the past. But how will either of you know, without seeing each other again?"

"How old did you say you are?"

"Thirteen." Clayton leaned back and gripped the arms of the chair. Now was the time to say what he came to say. He looked at the numbers tattooed on the man's arm before fixing his eyes back on Jesse. "Eight, eight, sixty-eight. The last day you spent with Miss Kitts."

Jesse's chin dropped. His nostrils flared, and his chest rose and collapsed, followed by an audible sigh.

"I'm sorry for printing your name. I wanted—"

Jesse raised his palm for Clayton to hush. "It's time to go, kid. And please leave me alone." He pointed to the door.

Clayton squared his stance. He hadn't completed his mission.

Jesse leaned forward in the wheelchair and took hold of the door. "There's nothing more to say, kid." He shoved the door against Clayton's leg. "Go before I show you another side of me."

Clayton lowered his head and locked eyes with the man. "Which side would that be, Sergeant? Human?" He stepped onto the porch. The door slammed shut behind him. As he reached the bottom step, something pricked his ankle. Clayton fell to the ground, eye-level with a snake. The snake hissed, and Clayton screamed.

Jesse opened the door and powered his wheelchair onto the wooden deck.

"A snake bit me!" Clayton grimaced.

Without hesitating, Jesse locked the wheels on his wheelchair. He pushed from the chair and dropped onto the porch, where he scaled the stairs on his rump and made his way to Clayton. A cottonmouth snake hissed nearby. Jesse grabbed the snake by the tail and swung it back and forth, smashing its head repeatedly against the stairs. He flung it to the ground where it lay motionless.

Jesse stretched Clayton's leg out. "Keep your leg lower than your heart. Stay calm. You're going to be okay."

"My leg hurts. I feel sick." Clayton whispered. His forehead drenched with sweat. Was that an earthquake beneath him? Were the clouds falling from the sky? "Suck...out...the...venom..." Clayton panted.

"Never suck out the venom." Jesse patted his shirt pocket. "I left my phone on my couch." Grumbling under his breath, he pushed himself out onto the road. "Help!" he screamed. "Help me!"

A neighbor lady opened her door and stuck her head out.

"Angie! Miss Angie!" Jesse flailed his arms in the air. "Call the squad. Now!"

Clayton raised his head. Was that Cagey, the white wolf, standing near bushes at the far end of the driveway staring at him? Clayton sucked in a deep breath, and it crackled when he exhaled.

"Stay with me, kid!" Jesse cradled Clayton's head in his arms. "Stay with me!"

26

Marty wheeled Jesse down the corridor of Three Rivers Medical Center in Louisa. It was time to bring this nonsense to an end. That crazy kid had gone way too far, and it was up to Jesse to set the kid straight.

Up ahead stood Clayton's parents, Grandpa, and Scot in the hallway.

"Jesse, we can't thank you enough," said Grandpa.

Jesse leaned back and looked over to Clayton's parents. "That kid of yours is stubborn as a mule."

Grandpa chuckled. "For sure, he is."

Heat rushed to Jesse's face. "It's not funny, Boyd."

Grandpa's face flushed, and he frowned.

Dad shook Jesse's hand. Mom hugged the Marine.

A doctor walked up to the group. "Your son's a lucky young man. We expect a full recovery in a few days."

Clayton's parents embraced and verbally thanked God.

Jesse leaned back and watched the family. It was good news, but he still had to face the boy and lay down the law. It wasn't going to be easy, but enough was enough! "Is it okay for me to speak with your son? Alone?" Jesse sat straight with his hands clutched together resting on his lap.

"Of course." Dad opened the door leading to Clayton's room and stepped back.

Jesse guided the wheelchair into the room. Dad closed the door.

***

Clayton smiled. "Thanks for saving my life, Sergeant Lowes."

Jesse leaned back in his chair, and his expression hardened. "Boy, I never dreamed you'd stoop so low to prove your point that you would resort to being bitten by a snake." He cracked his knuckles with fire in his eyes.

Clayton bit his lip, clutched the bed sheet, and glanced around the room. His mouth dropped open. Where were his parents? He swallowed the lump in his throat and blinked rapidly. The air between him and the Marine dropped an icy twenty degrees.

"I figured you out, boy," whispered Jesse like he was doing a podcast for a horror novel.

Heat filled Clayton's face, and his chin trembled. "I didn't intend to be bitten."

Jesse sat in silence for a few seconds, then the Marine slapped his hands together. "Got you, kid!" Jesse spun the wheelchair in a complete circle. "I had you going."

Clayton cocked his head and forced a grin. "I don't understand."

Jesse wheeled his chair over to the side of Clayton's bed. "I know you didn't get bit on purpose. But it was then that several things became clear to me. You were a new kid in town, standing up to face a stubborn Marine for a woman who you didn't know. And the determination that you have shown told me that the snake bite wasn't about to get you off my back." Jesse glanced down to the floor before continuing, "Plus, the knowledge that I had deprived the love of my life from knowing the truth of my condition brings me here tonight." He held out a handkerchief, folded and tied with a faded pink ribbon. "I see how much you care for Wanda. I'll meet her on one condition."

Clayton blew out his cheeks. He straightened his body in a sitting position, grunting and moaning as he did so. The sound that fingernails make by scratching across glass came to his ears. He looked over to the window in his room. With its yellow eyes boring into Clayton, Cagey cocked its head and held its paw against the glass. Clayton's stomach turned rock hard. "Do you see that?" He pointed at the wolf.

"See what?" Jesse glanced over to the window. "There's nothing there."

Clayton blinked. The wolf had gone. Had Cagey been there at all?

"Back to my requirement," continued Jesse. "Show Wanda that handkerchief. Tell her the situation with my legs. If she still wants to see me, I'm game. Guess I owe you both something." Jesse held out his hand.

Clayton clasped hands with the Marine, and they shook.

"Do not unwrap the handkerchief. It's for Wanda's eyes. Not yours. Understand?"

Warmth filled Clayton's face. "I won't look, Sergeant. I promise."

Jesse wheeled over to the door and invited Clayton's family inside. Jaylynn, the triplets, and their parents had also arrived.

"May I, Sergeant?" Clayton looked over at the Marine. Jesse nodded. "Sergeant Lowes has agreed to see Miss Kitts."

Grandpa bent down in front of Jesse. "I'll set up the meeting."

"No." Jesse shook his head. "Clayton started this. He'll take care of the details. If that's alright with you two." He looked over to Mom and Dad. They agreed.

Scot and Jaylynn shared a fist bump.

Jesse excused himself and motioned for Marty to take him home.

"Oohrah!" Clayton yelled as Jesse neared the door.

Jesse raised his hand and called out, "Oohrah!"

***

During the night, Clayton rose to use the restroom. He pulled the IV pole with him over to the window. His room was on the second floor. How had Cagey managed to appear at the window? The first floor extended outward beyond the second and third floors. But it would take a ladder for a human to reach the roof. How would a wolf be able to do it? And if Cagey had really been there, why was it watching him and Jesse? No need to say anything about the wolf to anyone. The notion sounded ridiculous.

27

After three days in the hospital, the doctor sent Clayton home. For a person to recover from a cottonmouth bite usually took a week or more. Clayton credited the visit from Jesse as the reason for his quick improvement. Mom and Dad wanted him to rest on the couch or in his bed, but Clayton wouldn't stand for it. Summer had flown by, and he still had a mission to complete. The first day of school was in two days. Why didn't Louisa use the same schedule as his old school back in Ohio? Columbus City Schools didn't start until August 22nd. Having classes begin on August 7th was way too soon.

"I wonder what's inside the handkerchief." Scot stared over to where Clayton had placed it on his dresser.

"Not for us to know." Clayton slipped into a fresh pair of jeans. He started to place the handkerchief inside his front pocket. No, it might be breakable. "Are you riding with me to see Miss Kitts?"

"Of course."

"Let's get going. I still have a lot to do."

"Like what?" Scot cocked his head to the side.

"Telling Jesse what Miss Kitts has to say about meeting with him."

"It's not like she's going to say no." Scot tossed his head back.

"True, but I'll need to make sure they agree on the time and place."

"Probably be easier to meet at Jesse's." Scot thrust his chest out.

"That wheelchair doesn't stop Jesse from getting out. He saved my life." Heat rushed to Clayton's face. "It may take him longer to do something, but he can do it!"

"Sorry." Scot glanced at his phone. "When are Jaylynn and her brothers coming?"

Clayton shrugged. Uncle Brian and Aunt Lucille had to take a trip out of town and would be gone two nights. Jaylynn and her brothers were to spend the night with Clayton and Scot. "I don't know. Soon I hope."

"Let's get going." Scot hurried over to the door.

Clayton dropped the handkerchief into a plastic Walmart sack and led the way to the garage. Pushing the bike onto the driveway, he slipped the bag on the handlebars. He rubbed a hand over his back pants pocket. "Dang, I left my phone on my dresser. Be right back."

***

Scot balanced his bike between his legs and eyed the woods. Wouldn't it be great if...No way! Cagey stepped from behind a tree and stared at him. Scot held out his hand. "Come here, boy. Come to me, Cagey."

The wolf looked over to the woods for a moment and then walked toward Scot.

"Come on. Nothing to be afraid of." Scot hunched over the handlebars, holding both hands out in front of him, twiddling his fingers.

As the wolf reached within inches of Scot, Clayton came sprinting out of the garage.

In a flash, the wolf snatched the Walmart bag with its teeth and ripped it from the bike.

"Hey!" yelled Clayton. The animal ran into the woods with the bag swinging back and forth from its mouth. "No, Cagey! Drop the bag!"

Scot sighed. "Now what?"

"We go after it. I can't lose the hankie." Leaving the bikes behind, Clayton ran into the woods with Scot following him. When they reached the cemetery, they observed several folks visiting graves. But there was no sight of the wolf.

"We need to get home, Clayton."

"Yeah. I have a feeling that Cagey roams here mostly at night."

"And?" Scot rolled his eyes.

"You know what it means, Scotty. Don't play stupid."

"Count me out."

"We'll see."

***

As dusk settled over the Hall household, Clayton and Scot's cousins arrived. Everyone said the traditional hellos and goodbyes. The kids went upstairs to Clayton's bedroom. The boys would bunk together in two rooms while Jaylynn slept alone in the spare bedroom.

"Roger, where'd your parents go for two nights?" asked Clayton.

"To buy a new combine at the farm conference in Parkersburg."

"Why did your mom go?" Scot plopped onto his bed.

"Are you kidding, *son*? Mom drives our old combine more than Dad." Johnny slapped his knee.

"I'd love to see that." Scot fluffed a pillow and placed it behind his head.

Clayton stepped over to his bedroom window. He paid no mind to the voices of his brother and cousins. There was no sign of Cagey. The wolf could be anywhere in those woods. The handkerchief may be buried or ripped and scattered. Clayton turned and faced the triplets. "I need a favor from you guys." He shared how Cagey had run off with Jesse's hankie.

"*Son*, we can't catch a wolf." Johnny paced the floor. "It's nearly impossible catching a chicken."

"Not going to try and catch it. If we find it, we may discover its den. I've got to get that handkerchief back."

"How do you expect to find the wolf?" Roger plopped down on the edge of Scot's bed.

"It roams the cemetery at night," said Clayton.

"How do you know?" Jimbo leaned against the wall.

"Trust me." Clayton looked once more out the window. "We'll cut through the woods."

"I'll wait here," said Johnny.

"Think again." Jaylynn entered the room, drawing the attention of Clayton and the others. She slipped her Bowie knife in a leather sheath and strapped it to her belt. Judging by the look on her face, the matter was over. "You're going, Johnny."

"Why can't I stay here with Scotty?"

"Forget it." Jaylynn struck her brother across the knees with a pillow. Johnny continued pacing the floor without missing stride. "Scot's going too," added Jaylynn.

"I am?" Scot's eyes swelled the size of melons. Clayton nodded. "Are you going, Roger?"

"Yep. I have to see this for myself." Roger got to his feet and joined Clayton at the window. "See anything out there?"

"Darkness," Clayton said without turning to look. He glanced over at the digital clock on his dresser. 11:11 p.m. There was that number again, eleven,

196 | EDWARD C. HARTSHORN

eleven. Were the numbers supposed to represent something? "Remember to walk softly. Can't afford to have Mom or Dad hear us. Let's go."

Clayton had no doubt what he had to do. There was no way he could tell his parents that the wolf had run off with Jesse's hankie. It would be the end of the mission with apologies to the Marine. Saying he was sorry wouldn't cut it. Jesse had fifty years of emotions wrapped in that handkerchief. Clayton could at least try to get it back from the wolf.

28

The kids entered the garage, where Clayton listened for any sign of his parents. The house was quiet. He motioned with a nod for them to go outside. A deep purple twilight descended upon them. Clayton led the way through the woods, careful of his step as he went along. Crickets and other insects in the forest were sending out their song of clicks, tweets, clacks, and murmurs. Upon exiting the woods, Clayton's eyes scanned the area between him and the church. All seemed normal. He stepped onto Cemetery Road and proceeded to the graveyard. The moonlight shone bright, and it was possible to see clearly. He came to a halt and waited for the others to flank him.

"We keep going." Clayton raised a hand over his head, motioning like he was giving instructions to the cavalry.

"The wolf is long gone," whispered Jimbo.

"*Son*," said Johnny. "We should go back to the house."

"I agree." Scot pointed at several headstones to their left. "There's nothing here."

"Shhh." Clayton stood near the flagpole at the top of the mound. This had been the spot he, Scot, and Jaylynn had first spotted Rand-Dock approaching them. But this time, the kids were on the opposite side of the hill. "There's a second flagpole at the bottom. The area between the poles is what the Major called the heart of this place. Where the wolf likes to roam."

"I don't like it here." Scot moved behind his brother. "I want to go home."

Clayton spun on his heels and took hold of Scot's shirt. "You know I need that handkerchief."

"Jesse will understand."

"Stop being a baby. There're six of us here. You're the only one whining. Nothing's going to happen." Clayton gently shoved the back of his brother's head.

"Yeah, *son*," Johnny chuckled. "Look at the bright side. If we die, our folks won't have far to go to bury us."

"Stop joking!" Jaylynn's voice echoed through the graveyard.

"Are you trying to wake the dead?" Johnny snorted like a pig.

"Not funny." Jimbo punched his brother's arm.

A heavy silence followed.

"Is that..." Jaylynn broke the silence. A silhouette of a human sat on a two-foot-high wall of stone that circled the flagpole.

"Yeah, I think so," said Clayton.

"Who?" Roger stared off in the distance.

"The old man named Rand-Dock. The caretaker." Jaylynn took hold of Scot's hand.

"Let's find out." But the closer Clayton drew to the figure, the more it seemed to be nothing more than moonlight, mist, and shadow.

"Where'd he go?" Jimbo spun in a circle. "Not that I really want to know."

"Hey, kids," came a whisper on the wind rustling through briar bushes and trees.

"Did you hear that?" At first, it sounded like one of the triplets. But their eyes told Clayton differently.

"I didn't hear anything." Johnny shrugged.

A twig snapped to the right of them. Johnny spun on his heels. "Who's there?"

"I heard it too." Clayton stared over to a cluster of pine trees.

Jaylynn aimed the beam of her flashlight across the way. A dark figure darted from one tree to another.

"Someone's there." Jimbo pointed.

"Let's go home." Scot released his grip on Jaylynn's hand and grasped his brother's forearm.

Clayton guided Scot over to Roger, placing his brother's hand into his cousin's. Scotty could have been experiencing an earthquake the way his knees trembled. "Might have been the wolf." Clayton stepped onto the grassy area and proceeded to the spot midway between the two flagpoles.

A fog sprung up from near where the road descended. It came ankle high at first and crept across the graveyard like it was targeting the kids. Within seconds it increased to waist high and moved fast.

"Not good," said Roger. "This is like a Stephen King book. How far are we from Bangor, Maine?"

"Or Ludlow," said Johnny.

"Or Bridgton," Jimbo added.

"Shut up!" Once more, Jaylynn's voice echoed.

Clayton headed for the lower flagpole, panning the flashlight left to right. The beam passed over an object on the ground. "The caretaker's rake."

"Yeah. Heck of a place to leave it." Scot kicked at it and missed.

Everything went quiet as the air turned thick and dull. Clayton raised his hand out for the others to halt. The patter of footsteps came from behind. Clayton spun on his heels and aimed the light at several headstones that stood near a cliff facing the Louisa Plaza. The hairs on his arms stood erect. Was someone or something watching him? The fog drifted up, covering everything in sight—a deathly quiet spread over the graveyard. Clayton took a step forward, holding the flashlight out in front of him. He pulled the hood of his hoodie over his head.

"Clayton," came a whisper.

Was the voice male or female? Clayton turned and faced his brother and cousins. "Did one of you call my name?" As he shined the beam of the flashlight in their faces one at a time, they each shook their head.

"Clayton," came the voice a second time.

Did it come from the tree line at the edge of the graveyard behind the flagpole? Pale forms moved among the trees. Was the Major nearby, watching the group of crazy kids tramp the sacred land of the dead?

"What's that smell?" Jimbo pinched his nose.

"*Son*, it smells like King Kong took a dump." Johnny covered his mouth and nose with his hand.

"And Godzilla," added Roger. "After eating a truckload of eggs."

Clayton held his breath and renewed his trek across the grounds, holding the light out in front of him, panning back and forth. As he drew near the tree line, the fog cleared in a tight circle, and the wolf came into view, lying on its belly under a mass of branches of a felled tree. Hot air streamed from its nostrils. Clayton held out his palm. "Come here, Cagey." Wait! A branch moved! Clayton stopped in his tracks. "Do you guys see that?"

"See what?" Roger pivoted toward the light.

The others gathered alongside Roger, each looking to the tree line.

Clayton aimed the beam of light on the mass. "What the heck?" An inhuman face rose from the branches with dark eyes, black orbs. Blood caked the corners of its mouth. The creature's head resembled the skull of a deer, complete with antlers. It had to be the same monster that he had seen at the skating rink unless there was more than one roaming the area.

Jaylynn shrieked. Scotty moved behind his brother and planted his head against Clayton's backside. Jimbo and Johnny screamed. Roger stepped back.

Cagey stood, snarled, and stared up at the Wendigo. The creature lowered its head and moved into a defensive stance, raising its long, bony arms over its head. The fingers on its hands were long and spindly and ended in spiky claws. With a swift swipe of its forearm, the Wendigo smacked the wolf on a front shoulder. The impact drove the wolf soaring a foot off the ground, and it landed with a thud several feet away. The wolf stood and looked over to Clayton before hobbling away, whimpering. Clayton whirled back to face the creature. This was not a human in a costume! The monster emitted a high-pitched screech, exposing its razor-sharp teeth, and its eyes shone bright red.

The triplets screamed a sound that resembled a helium-filled shriek. Clayton looked over to his cousins. Each boy had wet himself. After a second squeal, this time sounding like air escaping pinched balloons, the triplets fainted and dropped to the ground, face first.

Once more, Clayton turned and faced the monster. He could not speak. What was he to say if his tongue managed to comply? White spots spun before his eyes. His vision was going hazy. Was he about to pass out like his cousins? His heart hammered as he took a breath and forced his voice out. "Don't run from it," Clayton reminded Jaylynn and Scot. "Show no fear." The words were easier for Clayton to speak than to follow. He should grab his brother and cousin and run for their lives, but what about the triplets? This was not the time to flee.

"The Hairy Man's a Wendigo," whispered Jaylynn. "Its twisted branches look like bushy hair from a distance."

"We're going to die." Scot peered out from behind his brother.

"It's only an entity, nothing more than a spirit. Stay calm." A hint of dread crept into Jaylynn's voice.

"It looks real to me." Scot grabbed his brother's shirt. "Can a spirit kill?"

A second creature stepped out of the darkness into view. Both stood near eight feet tall, gaunt to the state of being skeletal. Ash-gray skin tightly covered their bones. The span of each of their foreheads was three feet or more, like that of a vast, monstrous buffalo. A towering rack of antlers protruded from the top of their heads. Their eyes glowed orange and peered at the kids from deep sockets. Both had tattered and bloody lips as if they had been feasting. Their feet were human-like, covered in hair, and their arms stretched below their knees with basketball-sized hands. The creatures' fingers bore ten-inch razor-sharp talons as fingernails. The beast exchanged glares with the first. There may have been mutters between them, which Clayton couldn't hear at this distance.

The monster nearest Clayton, just to his left, stepped forward, leaning its snout within inches of him, where it took a deep, audible sniff. A long, purple tongue emerged from its mouth and licked its lips with a smack. It snapped its head back and snarled. The second monster stepped alongside the first. It stood a tad shorter in height. Attached to the base of its antlers was a single red rose. The creature bellowed a sound that resembled that of a cat having its tail stepped on. It raised one of its long, bony arms above its head.

Clayton reached back and rubbed Scot on the forearm. "Show no fear, Scotty."

Jaylynn stepped next to Clayton and planted her feet. Clayton's hands curled into fists at his side.

The rose-wearing Wendigo slowly advanced, arm still raised over its head.

"Wait, Night Dove!" growled a heavy voice from somewhere in the darkness. The bellow might have had words in it, but the yell had come so fast that Clayton wasn't sure. When it repeated, the words were clear, "Wait, Night Dove!"

"They can talk?" Bewilderment spread over Jaylynn's face.

"Yeah. According to legend, Wendigos had once been human, transformed after acts of cannibalism. They can speak like a human and even imitate voices."

A third creature came into view, much larger and taller than the other two. Its rib cage was skeletal, but its arms and legs were hairy, matted, and intertwined with small tree branches. The creature stood over ten feet tall. Its skinless skull was like the other two, but bigger and broader, four-foot or more. A humongous rack of antlers protruded from the top of its head. Its eyes glowed red and peered at Clayton from deep sockets as well, but its tattered lips were not bloody.

The stench of decay and decomposition reached Clayton's nostrils, and he choked back a gag. "Are you Swift Runner?" Clayton squared his stance. This creature had to be the leader of the Wendigos. Show no fear. Who was he kidding? Clayton's entire body shook. It took all of his willpower not to allow his legs to flee like a yellow-bellied track star.

The leader cocked its head to the side and stared at the boy. Then it motioned with a wave of its long arm to the rose-wearing creature. "Go ahead, Night Dove," it said, speaking and growling at the same time.

Night Dove screeched and smacked Clayton to the ground on his back. Clayton yelped and then panted. The creature bent over and placed its long snout close to the boy's face and took a long, deeper sniff.

Jaylynn picked up a rock from the ground and threw it with a deadly aim, striking the beast on the side of the neck. The creature glanced at the girl before turning its attention back to Clayton. It was if the impact from the rock was nothing more than a pesky insect.

The second monster jumped out in front of Jaylynn. Slowly, it raised its hand as if it were about to snatch hold of her.

"No, Lone Horn!" growled the leader.

The Wendigo that the leader had called Lone Horn took a step back. It indeed had a horn that stood taller from the others on its monstrous head. Lone Horn widened its stance and growled. It extended its long arms above its head and kicked at the ground. With a grunt of disappointment or anger, Lone Horn stormed off and disappeared within the darkness.

Jaylynn turned on the flashlight of her cell phone and aimed the beam on the face of Night Dove. The creature raised its hand and covered its eyes. With her free hand, Jaylynn plunged the blade of her Bowie knife into the knee of Night Dove. The blow squished loud, like smacking a melon with a hammer. Green slime squirted out, and Jaylynn ducked away from the splatter. Jaylynn ran over to the creature and tugged on the knife handle in an attempt for a second strike, but the knife, buried to the hilt, wouldn't budge. Lone Horn sprinted from the darkness and slapped the phone from Jaylynn's hand. Then with the back of its hand, Lone Horn smacked Jaylynn upside the head. She went sprawling across the grass, slamming against a tree where she lay.

"Jaylynn! Get up!" Clayton kicked his legs in an attempt to break free. He had to reach Jaylynn. Was she knocked out cold, or worse? "Get up!"

Lone Horn made its way to Jaylynn and stood over her. The creature growled again, deeper, like that of a boat motor churning water. It bolted off into the darkness.

The rose-wearing beast grabbed Clayton by the neck and lifted him off the ground. The creature bent down, opened its mouth wide, and snarled.

***

Voices and screams penetrated the boiling blood pounding in Scot's ears as he stood a few feet away. He blinked repeatedly.

"Run, Scotty! Run!" Clayton yelled.

His brother squirmed and kicked in the grasp of a monster. What could Scot do? He had to do something, but what if…

"Run, Scotty! Run!"

Scot had never known fear in this form. It overwhelmed him. Thunder and lightning were nothing compared to this. His stomach twisted into a thousand knots, choking him with a boulder in his throat. Hot tears welled from deep inside and coursed down his cheeks. He opened his mouth to scream but produced only a whimper. He clenched his clammy palms into fists. Numbness shot up his arms, and sweat dripped from his forehead. A drop seeped into the corner of his eye, and it stung.

Clayton screamed, "Run, Scotty! Run!"

Scot's first couple of steps were made like he was trudging through quicksand, but then he bolted across the black, sloped ground, in the direction of the road without seeing it, darting between headstones. He tripped. His foot caught something, and he went down hard.

Rand-Dock's rake! Scot picked it up and ran back to face the beast. "Retreat, hell!" He forced a grin to keep the expression of fear from developing on his face and swung the rake, metal prongs outward, striking the creature across its hand, snapping off one of its razor-sharp fingernails. The monster roared, in anger or pain, Scot wasn't sure of which. The ear-piercing cry was enough to cause him to drop the weapon. Quickly, Scot retrieved it and swung again, missing the beast completely. He spun in a complete circle.

The Wendigo placed its foot to Clayton's chest and pressed down. Clayton moaned. Scot flipped the rake around and rammed the tip of the handle into the stomach of the creature. It released another horrifying cry. The beast tilted its head downward and gestured with a single talon for Scot to walk to it.

"Yeah, right!" Flipping the metal prongs of the rake out in front of him, Scot closed his eyes and swung with all his might. Wham! He had struck a solid mass. Scot opened his eyes to find the metal prongs embedded in the creature's thigh.

The monster snapped the wooden handle in half then pulled the metal prongs from its leg. A gob of green slime oozed out of the wound for a mere second before going dry, and the gash closed. The Wendigo cocked its head as if it were weighing which boy it wanted most. It removed its foot from Clayton's chest, bent down, and took hold of Clayton by the arm, dragging him, heading for a darker part of the graveyard.

"No!" Scot yelled at the top of his lungs and charged the beast. He was his brother's protector now, a thing he would never have dreamed possible minutes ago. "Not on my watch!" He leaped up and slammed his full weight against the monster, knocking the Wendigo to the ground. Scot landed atop the flesh-eating giant and stared down into its blazing orange eyes. Scot shuddered. Was the creature stealing his soul? Scot looked over at his brother. Clayton lay several feet away, gasping for air. The beast took hold of Scot's chin and slowly turned his head to face it. This graveyard was where Scot was going to die. He was sure of it.

The creature opened its mouth, revealing long, sharp teeth, able to snap bones in half with one bite. Its hot, bloody breath polluted the air like a decaying pig. Scot choked and then gagged, tossing the contents of his stomach onto the face of the creature.

"Wait, Night Dove!" The leader leaped over to the rose-wearing creature, lowered its head, and moved within inches of Scot's face. The eyes of the leader went from red to brown, and its head moved as if it nodded once.

Scot held his breath. Had the beast smiled? Was that even possible?

"Release the boy," said the leader.

Night Dove cocked its head to the side as if in disbelief.

The leader aimed a talon at Scot. "Worthy."

Night Dove relaxed its grip. Scot fell to the ground on his knees, where he repeatedly spat out the taste of stench. His lungs kicked into overdrive. He got to his feet and ran over to his brother and embraced him. "Are you okay?"

"Yeah…little…brother," Clayton said between breaths. "Tell me something."

Scot blinked and raised his head back.

"Not on my watch?" Clayton cracked a huge grin. "You have Marine in your blood."

Scot chuckled, wanting to laugh, but his lungs weren't up to it yet.

Jaylynn came to her senses, stood, and retrieved her phone. "Hey, Ugly! I want my knife back!"

Yanking the knife from its leg, Night Dove tossed it to her feet.

The fog plunged below the ground as if on demand and cleared. Lone Horn came bounding over the knoll and joined Night Dove and the leader. The three Wendigos walked to the tree line and out of sight. A moment later, Rand-Dock emerged from the same spot the Wendigos had gone. He waved to Clayton, Scot, and Jaylynn. Two ladies followed the groundskeeper.

Clayton shined the beam of his flashlight upon them. "Mare and Jenny Bell?"

"No way!" Scot glared up at his brother. Clayton shrugged.

"Around here, anything is possible." Jaylynn slipped the knife in the sheath and then barked, "Whewie!"

The wolf came out from the tree line and hobbled up to Clayton, dropping the handkerchief at his feet. It lowered its head and limped off, headed for the woods.

"Wow." Clayton bent over and picked up the handkerchief.

"Yeah, that was something," said Scot. "I hope Cagey is okay."

"He will be." Jaylynn nodded.

Roger, Johnny, and Jimbo moaned. The triplets got to their feet, where they each staggered and wobbled for a few moments.

"What happened?" Johnny rubbed his temples.

"I have no idea." Jimbo rocked back and forth.

"I was about to smack a monster between the eyes and, wham! The lights went out." Roger slapped his hands together.

"You guys passed out, like babies." Clayton stuck a thumb in his mouth and pretended to suck.

"After they screamed like baby monkeys that fell in a mineshaft and landed in a puddle." Scot giggled as he pointed at his cousins and their wet pants.

"Yada yada yada." Roger swept a hand in front of his face like he was swatting a bug. "So, who played the prank on us?"

"Is that what you think it was?" Clayton grinned. "Let's get home."

"Yada yada yada," Roger repeated.

"I bet you passed out too, Scot," said Jimbo.

Scot shook his head.

"Then, *son*, you must have found a great hiding spot." Johnny snapped his fingers. "In a jiffy."

Again, Scot shook his head.

"Then what did you do?" A wrinkle shot across Roger's forehead.

Scot's chest expanded as he drew a slow, deep breath. "Nothing that a Marine wouldn't do." Scot skipped away. Clayton and Jaylynn hopped alongside him. Scot was okay with his cousins not knowing that he had faced the Wendigo. Some things were meant to be secrets, and some secrets remained between brothers.

29

The following morning, Grandpa arrived and drove Jaylynn and her brothers to their home to feed livestock. Clayton and Scot rode their bikes to Wanda's house.

As Clayton climbed the stairs leading to the porch, a sudden blast of wind swept through the pine trees in her yard, swaying the treetops back and forth.

"Not good. Could be a storm coming."

"Not a cloud in sight. It's just the wind." Clayton knocked on the door and waited. He knocked again.

"She's not home."

"The curtain moved." Clayton knocked a third time. "Miss Kitts. It's us, Clayton and Scot."

The door opened. "Hello, boys. What brings you here today?"

Clayton opened his mouth to speak, but the words jammed in his throat. Should he first tell her about the Wendigos at the cemetery or the hankie?

"That handkerchief in your hand. It looks like the one I…" Miss Kitts swung open the door. "Where'd you get it?"

"We were told to bring it to you," said Scot.

"Told? By whom?" Miss Kitts scanned the street.

"Jesse." Clayton held the handkerchief out to her.

Miss Kitts scowled. "How dare you boys come here with such a painful joke!"

"It's no joke, ma'am." Scot smiled. "We found Jesse. He lives in Fort Gay."

"And to think I liked you boys. Get off my porch!"

"Please take it, Miss Kitts." Clayton placed his free hand against the small of his back and crossed the fingers. "Jesse put something inside of it, for your eyes only."

Her hardened gaze went from Clayton to Scot and back to Clayton. "I may be old, but I'm not stupid." She turned up her nose and stepped onto the porch, pointing to the street. "Go! Now!"

Clayton untied the ribbon and opened the handkerchief, holding it out for her to examine.

Miss Kitts lowered her head and stared at it. She planted her palms against her chest, shrieked, and then gasped before slumping over.

Each brother grabbed her by an elbow. Tears poured down her cheeks. "I-I-I..." She gasped again, followed by panting as if she had sprinted in a marathon. The boys helped her over to the nearest metal chair. Scot brushed the dust from the seat with his hand before he and Clayton helped her to sit. Scot plopped onto the other chair.

Clayton gently sat the handkerchief onto Miss Kitts' lap. For the first time, he got a glimpse of the items inside the hankie—a chain necklace supporting military dog tags and a ring.

"He's alive?" Miss Kitts placed her palms to her knees and hunched over. "My Jesse is alive?"

"Yes, ma'am." Clayton nodded. "He lives in a house trailer in Fort Gay."

Miss Kitts pulled a Kleenex from her bosom and dabbed her eyes. She sniffled, and her lip trembled. "He's been there for fifty years?" Her hands formed fists, and her expression hardened. "Why'd he do such a thing to me?"

Clayton bit his tongue and glimpsed over to his brother. Scot lowered his head and stared at the floor.

"How is he?" Miss Kitts raised her chin and then crossed her arms against her chest as if she were doing her best to remain calm. She released a heavy sigh. "Is he on his way here to see me?" Her eyes searched up and down the street.

"Jesse looked good, ma'am. He really wants to see you." Clayton widened his stance. "He wants to know the best time to meet with you."

"Nonsense!" growled Miss Kitts. "If he truly wanted to see me, he would've done it years ago!"

Clayton took a long breath. Her frustration and anger were all over her face and in her voice. How was he to explain Jesse's condition? She might decline the meeting. "Jesse doesn't get out much."

"Why? Is he in bad health?" She locked eyes with Clayton.

"No." Clayton shared how Jesse had saved his life without mentioning that the Marine was legless below the knees. There was no way he could tell her that. Not yet.

"I'm grateful that he saved your life, but how could he let my life go to rot for fifty years? Is he married?"

"No, ma'am." Clayton hadn't seen a sign of anyone living with Jesse, but anything was possible.

"I don't want to talk to him!" Her face flared red.

Clayton needed to say something, but what? "Jesse still smokes Prince Albert."

Wanda tilted her head to the side and released a long, low sigh. She lowered her arms and relaxed her hands. "This is my high school class ring." She held the necklace out for the boys to see.

"He has the numbers eight, eight, sixty-eight tattooed on his arm," added Clayton.

Her eyes brightened, and her lips formed a slight smile. "Our last day together. August 8th, 1968." She lowered her head and placed the necklace around her neck. Warmth radiated throughout Clayton's body. "Can you boys take me to him?"

"On our bikes?" Scot's voice squeaked.

"That would be a spectacle." She laughed. "How about your parents? Can one of them give me a ride?"

Clayton shrugged, cheeks on fire. Glancing at Scot, he bit down on his lower lip. He should've asked the Marine when and where the meeting would take place. "I think Jesse wants to come to you," replied Clayton. "It's a man thing."

"I guess it is at that." Miss Kitts placed a palm to her chest. "My Jesse was always a gentleman. Please tell him to wear his dress blues. He left as a Marine and should come home the same way."

"I will tell him." Boy, would he! It took nearly all summer for Clayton to get this far. "What'd be the best time for him to arrive?"

"Immediately! Oh, I need to brush my hair." Wanda's hands moved to the arms of the chair as if she were about to stand.

Clayton cleared his throat. He had to speak with Jesse again to make sure the Marine remained willing to meet. "Scot, and I'll ride over to Jesse's and inform him."

"We'll be right back." Scot leaped to his feet.

"Hold on, Scotty." Clayton held out his hand to Miss Kitts. "Do you want help in going inside?"

"I'm not dead, young man. I haven't felt this good in half a century."

The boys jumped from the porch, hopped onto their bikes, and rode off. They rode to Dad's store and got permission to cross the bridge. When they reached Jesse's trailer, they found a van parked in the driveway. A wheelchair ramp extended from its side doors and sat upon the ground. Marty was wheeling Jesse toward the vehicle.

"Hello, boys." Jesse waved.

"Are you leaving?" asked Clayton as he and Scot's bikes skidded to a stop. "Miss Kitts is waiting. You haven't changed your mind?"

"Changed my mind?" Jesse chuckled. "Son, I've been torn for fifty-one years. One part of me hiding, while another part of me screaming for it to happen. I gave you my word, Marine to Marine. Except..." he puffed out his cheeks and released a sigh. "Marty and I are on our way to Chicago. A buddy of ours from our tour in Nam died. His burial is in the morning. We should return home tomorrow evening. Set up the meeting for Thursday morning at eleven."

"But what about—" Scot stopped in mid-sentence when Clayton elbowed him.

"Leave no man behind." Clayton saluted Jesse and Marty. Both men returned the gesture. "I'll inform Miss Kitts, Sergeant. By the way, she wants you to wear your dress blues."

Jesse cocked his head back. "Why?"

"She said you left as a Marine, and you should come home as a Marine."

"You're going to do alright, kid." A sincere smile stretched across Jesse's face. "I can see you wearing a uniform."

Clayton and Scot returned to Wanda's home and told her of the circumstance.

"I guess two more days won't hurt." Miss Kitts stood and walked over to the door. "I can't believe it…just two more days. You boys…you boys…" Once more, she dabbed her eye with a Kleenex. "Thank you." Her voice cracked with emotion.

Clayton and Scot rode to Dad's store and shared the good news. Grandpa was also there.

"Proud of you both." Dad hugged his sons.

"Me too." Grandpa joined in the hug, squashing the kids in a sandwich grip.

"Okay, you guys have school tomorrow. Get home and prepare your clothes." Dad ruffled the hair of both boys. "Get your showers before your cousins get back."

"I'm heading out to pick them up now," added Grandpa. "They should be done with their chores."

"Can we go with Grandpa?"

"No, Scotty." Dad shook his head. "Morning is coming quick."

"Can me and Scot miss school on Thursday?" Clayton didn't dare hold his breath for the odds of that happening. Dad cocked his head to the side with a stern expression. "Sorry," added Clayton. "It was a stupid question."

"It wasn't stupid." Dad took hold of Clayton's shoulder. "I understand your desire, but Miss Kitts and Jesse deserve privacy. It's a monumental moment for them both. Understand?"

Clayton nodded.

***

When the cousins arrived back at the house, Clayton filled them in on the upcoming meeting.

"I would love to witness it." Jaylynn stood in front of the mirror and puckered her lips. "A girl loves a true love story."

Clayton turned to her. "There's no guarantee that the meeting will go well."

"Yeah," said Scot. "Miss Kitts kept switching back and forth from happy to angry."

"That's because there's love and then there's *love*." Jaylynn placed her open palm to her chest and wiggled her eyebrows.

"Huh?" Scot cocked his head to the side.

"Don't try to understand her, *son*." Johnny poked Scot's leg.

"Or any girl." Roger slapped his knee.

"That's right." Jimbo smacked his hands together.

"It's time to hit the sack!" Dad's voice boomed up the stairs.

Jaylynn made her way to the spare bedroom while the boys settled into their beds.

Clayton plopped his head on his pillow. He appreciated his cousins and how they had gone with him to the cemetery in the dark, especially Jaylynn and her spunk. Looking over to Scot, somehow, his little brother seemed taller, bigger, stronger, and Clayton smiled. Blowing out his cheeks, he stared up at the ceiling. The night was going to be a long one. How was he expected to sleep tonight or the next two nights for that matter? His eyes were wide-awake. The hairs on his head tingled from the electrical grid in his brain. Would the meeting between Jesse and Miss Kitts go well? What if the reunion went terrible because he meddled in the business of others? The answer would come in two days.

30

When the alarm sounded in the bedroom, Clayton leaped to his feet and got dressed. His eyes begged for more sleep, but today was the first day of school. After breakfast, Clayton and Scot took their school schedules from their mom. She had enrolled them yesterday. The boys said goodbye to their cousins and waited at the end of the driveway for the school bus. Mom drove the cousins to school in Fort Gay. Uncle Brian and Aunt Lucille would return home in time to pick them up from school.

***

The brothers exited the bus and eyed the brick two-story building. It looked modern. Groups of kids stepped from a long line of busses, pulling Clayton's attention to them. All seemed to know someone as they gathered and entered the school. Were he and his brother the only new kids? Clayton puffed out his cheeks and exhaled.

Beyond the busses stood the baseball diamond, dugout, homerun fence, well-groomed infield, and outfield along with lights for night games—a top-notch field for sure. Maybe he would give baseball a try? He turned his interest down Bulldog Lane, a road that led to the high school.

"You'll be going there next year, big brother." Scot elbowed Clayton's ribs. "Make way for me."

"Come on, Scotty. Let's get this over with."

***

During homeroom, an announcement came over the PA system. "All students report to the gym for an assembly."

Clayton found his brother and took a seat alongside him.

"Are you a sixth-grader?" a man asked.

"No, sir. I'm in the eighth grade." Clayton eyed the man who towered over him. He was middle-aged, muscular, wearing a white shirt and dark slacks.

"Then you don't belong in this section." The man's voice carried a heavy tone of authority. "Unless you want to go back two years," he added with a smile and a wink. Clayton shook his head. "I didn't think so, Mr. Clayton Hall."

The man knew his name! Did Mom have to show a photo to register him in school? Not likely. Clayton returned to his classmates.

A boy moved over to allow Clayton room to sit. "I see you met the warden."

"Do what?" Clayton felt his forehead scrunch up.

"The principal," the kid said. "Mr. Cecil. He runs a tight ship, but he's cool. I'm Denver Wade." He held out his hand.

Clayton eyed Denver. The kid looked like he might be a victim of bullying two or three times a day. His clothes needed ironing, but they did seem to be clean. He had reddish-brown hair, and its thickness challenged a comb because it was all over the place on his head. It looked thick enough to hide two school mascots, bulldogs, while the canines fought over a bone. Clayton smiled, shook hands, and introduced himself.

"That's my brother Scotty, third from the left in the blue shirt." Clayton pointed to the opposite side of the gym. "Mr. Cecil called me by name."

"He knows everyone."

"But this is my first day here."

"Really?" Denver's mouth dropped open.

Clayton looked over and locked eyes with Mr. Cecil. Clayton shuddered and turned his gaze to a podium that stood on the floor with a microphone. Above it, a big banner hung on the wall:

WELCOME TO LMS
BULLDOG COUNTRY!

The principal got to his feet, walked over to the podium, and tapped his fingers on the microphone. The minor explosions amplified through the speakers, and the students settled. Mr. Cecil gestured toward the girl's locker room. Cheerleaders ran onto the floor, followed by the football, baseball, soccer, and cross-country teams. Everyone rose to their feet, yelling and jumping up and down. After that, the principal calmed the crowd.

"I am Mr. Cecil, the principal here at LMS. If you need to speak with me, I have an open-door policy. I welcome you all, those of you who are returning and those who are new. As for the sixth-graders, I hope your three years here are great ones." He held up a little red book for everyone to see. "In my hand is the Louisa Middle School Code of Conduct," added Mr. Cecil. Several teachers stepped onto the floor and started handing out a copy to each student in the gym. "Open to page one and follow along with me."

Clayton paid little attention to the reading of the rules. He and Scot were familiar with regulations. They had them at home and had them at their old school. Instead, Clayton eyed the students. There had to be one or two bullies in the group. Would he and Scot need to prove themselves? Back in their old school, he and Scot had several friends, and it was tough leaving them behind. Sure, he and Scot would make new relationships, but what would they have to go through first? Dad had said that bullying had been around as long as humans. Dad also admitted that bullying was easier with today's technology.

Clayton fought the urge to look over to Mr. Cecil. His willpower lost the battle. The principal's eyes were there to meet Clayton's. Why? Was it because he was a new student, or did it have something to do with finding Jesse? Maybe it was nothing at all, nothing more than a coincidence. Clayton glimpsed over at Denver. When he turned his eyes back to Mr. Cecil, the principal had his gaze elsewhere. Whew!

Clayton and Denver continued getting to know each other. According to their schedules, they shared social studies during the last class of the day.

"I like history," said Denver.

"Me too," agreed Clayton. Denver seemed okay, someone he might befriend. How was Scotty doing with making pals? It wasn't easy leaving the old schools and friends behind. It was true that Louisa was a much smaller town than Columbus. The people in Louisa were protective of their own, but this also pleased him. Looking out for each other was a good thing.

"I'm most fascinated with the Civil War." Denver placed his palm on his knee and leaned in closer to Clayton. "Imagine brother fighting brother. Had to be tough."

Clayton bit his tongue. Now was not the time to tell his new friend about his meeting with the Confederate Major. It sounded as ridiculous as it did impossible. He wasn't sure he believed it himself. It required more than one day to develop trust in someone to reveal such a far-fetched event.

Denver leaned in closer. "Imagine going back and meeting a soldier from the Civil War. Wouldn't that be cool?"

Clayton's head snapped back. What was Denver not saying? Did Jaylynn say something in Fort Gay, and the news had already spread like wildfire? Louisa and Fort Gay were almost like one big city, separated only by the rivers.

"Wouldn't it be awesome if a ghost from the Civil War came in here riding a horse?" Denver slapped his knee. "I could see it now."

Clayton squirmed in his seat. Should he smile, laugh, or stay silent? He chose the latter.

When the assembly ended, Clayton dashed over to his brother. "How's it going?"

Scot frowned. "I miss summer vacation."

Clayton rubbed a hand through Scot's hair. "You'll be alright. See you after school."

The rest of the day passed slowly. Clayton kept picturing Jesse and Wanda and the upcoming meeting. He would give anything to witness it, but then again, maybe it was best he couldn't be there.

***

On their way home, Scotty talked on and on about his day at school. Clayton caught a word here and there and nodded his head as if he were listening. But he wasn't. His stomach carried an awful knot. Why had he gotten involved with a fifty-year-old love story? When would he learn to mind his own business?

The moment the boys entered the house, Mom asked how their first day was.

"I made new friends with a couple of the guys in homeroom." Scot sat his books on the kitchen table. "The teacher had everyone stand in front of the class and introduce ourselves. It seems everyone knows Grandpa."

"And how was your day, Clayton?"

"Did you show the principal my photo?"

"No. Why?" Mom cocked her head to the side.

"The principal knew my name without me telling him."

"Mine too," said Scot.

"That tells me that Mr. Cecil knows his job." Mom smiled.

Clayton shrugged, grabbed his backpack, and went to his bedroom. The moment Scotty climbed the stairs, Clayton cornered him. "Did you tell anyone about Jesse and Miss Kitts?"

"No."

"What about me seeing a ghost?"

"Why would I do that? No one would believe it if I did."

Clayton eyed his little brother. Scot was right. There was no benefit in telling either story. Clayton called Jaylynn, and she told him the same. She and her brothers had said nothing to their friends.

"Come down and eat, boys," boomed Dad's voice.

As Clayton reached the bottom step, Grandpa entered the kitchen from the garage.

"Big day tomorrow, eh?" Grandpa looked out over his glasses. "The whole town is talking."

"Who did you tell, Grandpa?" Clayton took a seat at the table.

"Not I." Grandpa took a sip of coffee. "Steve Cooper told me. I guess Jesse and Marty told him. You remember meeting Cooper, don't you?"

Of course, he did. How could Clayton forget Cooper, the man with the cane he met at the library? Clayton was sure Mr. Cooper couldn't shed a tear if his life depended on it. "So much for a fifty-year-old secret."

"Son, what you've done is bigger than an old secret," added Grandpa. "You brought it out to the open." Grandpa winked. "Everyone's wondering how it's going to turn out."

"What if it turns out bad? What if what I did was…" Clayton stared at his food.

"Well, son, should that happen, it'll not be your fault." Grandpa dropped a spoon into his empty coffee mug, and it clanged. "You brought the truth to an old woman, and to Jesse, you brought another chance. You can't do more than that."

Clayton forced a smile. Grandpa was trying to ease his worry, but the words didn't help. Clayton should have stayed out of it. Let life take its course.

"I'm proud of you, son," said Dad. "Regardless of how it turns out."

"Me too." Mom winked.

"Yeah." Scot tipped his cup like he was making a toast. "It was cool how you never gave up, like a Marine. Oorah!"

Clayton ate dinner and excused himself.

"A little early for bed, isn't it?" asked Mom. "You feeling okay?"

Clayton saw his mom's eyes linger on him for a few seconds, and then stare over to Dad in silence. Clayton nodded. Yeah, he felt as good as one could feel before discovering if his nose had destroyed an old woman's heart. "Goodnight."

31

Clayton woke and prepared for school. Had Jesse made it home safe from Chicago? Was the meeting with Wanda still on? The questions wouldn't leave his mind. Time after time, he sighed, trying to push the doubts out of his head and concentrate on the present, brush his teeth, get dressed, and don't forget his schoolbooks. The answers would come today.

***

Jesse connected the top button on his uniform coat and stared over at the photo on the end table. A million butterflies swarmed in his gut. Could he go through with this? Of course, he could. Clayton had promised to tell Wanda of his condition. But still...

Marty squeezed Jesse's shoulder. "You ready?"

Jesse glanced around his home. How many times had he sat at the table, drinking coffee, imagining Wanda sitting across from him? Every day, Jesse had pictured it, and more. As much as he loved Marty, it was Wanda he visualized at his side. He wouldn't blame her should she explode with anger. No one deserved a verbal lashing more than he.

Again, Marty squeezed Jesse's shoulder.

Jesse's gaze locked on Marty. For thirty years, Marty stood at Jesse's side, doing this, doing that, whatever Jesse needed or wanted. But today, Jesse stood alone. Sure, Marty would be nearby, but it was Jesse who had to...

Marty squeezed Jesse's shoulder a third time. "You ready?"

Jesse spun the wheelchair toward his bedroom door. "No. I'm not."

***

Concentrating in math class was impossible. The second hand on the clock over the door continued ticking. But each time Clayton looked, it seemed the hand moved slower and slower. Jesse and Miss Kitts were due to meet in one hour and eight minutes.

"Cops!" A girl sitting in front of Clayton stood and leaned against the window. The entire class bolted from their chairs.

"Two police cars," said a boy. "One from Fort Gay and one from Louisa."

"Sit down!" ordered the teacher. "Now!"

The kids grumbled as they returned to their seats.

A male voice came blaring over the loudspeaker. "Clayton and Scot Hall, please report to the office immediately."

"Uh-oh!" cried the students.

Clayton's head jerked up, and he gawked at the speaker on the wall near the ceiling. What's going on? Why were he and Scot being called to the office? The teacher motioned with a nod of her head. Clayton stood and took a step toward the front of the class.

"You better take your backpack," said a kid in the back row.

"Yeah, you may not be returning," replied another student. Loud laughter spread through the classroom.

This was crazy. His second day in a new school and already called to the office. Had something happened at home? He met Scot at the end of the hall.

"What's going on?" Scot held his elbows tightly against his sides. His hands trembled, and his face flushed pale.

"I don't know," admitted Clayton. "Let's go." Rounding the corner, he came to a sudden halt. Two male police officers stood near the office door. Their parents stepped out from behind the cops. "Mom! Dad!"

Mr. Cecil walked out of the office. There was no reading his face. No smile, no frown, just a blank expression with his eyes locked onto Clayton.

Clayton's jaw dropped. Was Jesse or Wanda hurt? Where was Grandpa? "What's going on, Dad? Did something happen to Grandpa?"

Dad stepped forward. The Louisa police officer moved out in front of Dad.

"We're taking a ride downtown, gentlemen." The Louisa officer glared with a stern face.

"Downtown?" Clayton's heart raced, and his knees buckled. On the cop shows he had seen on television, the word "downtown" was not a good word out the mouth of a cop.

Dad wrapped his arm around Clayton's shoulders. "I'll explain in the car."

The officers held open the door. As Clayton stepped outside, another announcement came over the PA system. The voice was too faint to make out the words. It was probably a message about staying out of jail.

The Halls loaded into Mom's van. The Louisa police officer pulled his car in front of Mom's vehicle while the Fort Gay cop fell in behind. Both activated their emergency lights. It was a three-car procession through town.

Mom twisted in her seat and faced Clayton. "Jesse called and asked for you to meet him at the home of Miss Kitts. He said that you started this ordeal, and you needed to be there."

"What can I do?" Clayton leaned out as far as the seatbelt would allow. Sure, being there to witness it would've been cool, but... "I feel sick."

Scot grinned. "Yeah, what if..."

Dad kept his eyes on the road. "I'm to park across the street a couple of houses down. We sit and watch. That's all."

The streets downtown were empty. Not a soul was walking or standing. And what vehicles were on the streets moved over and stopped to allow the police cars to pass. If not for those few vehicles, Louisa appeared deserted.

"Where is everyone?" Clayton stared out the window.

"Looks like a ghost town," added Scot.

At South Main Cross Street, both cop cars turned into the parking lot of a vacant building on the corner. Dad guided the van onto Wanda's street. Miss Kitts sat on the front porch dressed like she was going to church, brushing her hair, and gazing up the road.

Dad guided the van into the parking lot of the elementary school and made a U-turn. He parked on the street with a clear view of Wanda.

"She's nervous," said Mom. "The way she keeps brushing her hair."

"Fifty years is a long time," said Dad. "Here comes a van heading this way."

Clayton unbuckled his seatbelt and stretched over the console. "That's Marty." Was Clayton scared at all? His limbs were trembling, heart racing, the back of his neck pulsating, lungs begging for air, but he was energized more than afraid. This day had been long in the making. It was way overdue. Then he remembered what he had not done—inform Miss Kitts of Jesse's condition. Fear suddenly drowned his energy. Was the world of Miss Kitts about to crash and burn because he failed to step up and keep his promise to Jesse?

The van came to a stop in front of Wanda's home. Clayton waited for Marty to climb out and put down the ramp. But Marty didn't. He sat with his hands on the steering wheel, leaning toward the rearview mirror—no doubt speaking with Jesse. Don't back out now, Jesse. Please! Clayton begged.

"Look." Mom pointed at the digital clock on the dash. "Eleven, eleven. Make a wish, boys."

"Huh?" Scot said.

Clayton sat up straight, remembering he had seen the numbers on his alarm clock more than once the last few days.

"I did a research paper in college on that number," added Mom. "According to the angels, number eleven, eleven is a reminder of God's power, telling us that our guardian angel is nearby."

"It's just a number, Mom."

"True, Scotty, but we all need something to believe in." Mom patted Scot's hand. "We call it faith."

It made sense to Clayton. All had gone well at the cemetery, spirits, wendigos, a wolf, and bitten by a snake at Jesse's. Definitely, someone had been watching over him and the others. As far as faith, there was no stronger example of it than Wanda's.

"Will the wish come true?" asked Scot.

"Nothing is promised to us, son," said Mom.

Scot leaned over the console. "Then why bother?"

"There's always hope." Mom's eyes lit up.

Hope! That'd been the fuel Clayton had been running on. But now, hope, had taken a back seat. It was time for action, to step up. Otherwise, Jesse might never get out of the van. But Dad had said they were to do nothing but sit and watch. Really?

"Why are they sitting there?" asked Scot.

"As I said, fifty years is a long time," repeated Dad.

"Shouldn't they be eager to see each other?" Scot pressed his forehead against the side glass.

"They are," said Mom, "and then some."

"Today's August Eighth," whispered Clayton. "Fifty-one years to the day." He continued to observe Miss Kitts. Her hands gripped the arms of the chair. "I'm getting out." Clayton swung open the side door and jumped out, ignoring his mom and dad's orders for him to wait. He sprinted over to Marty's van and peered in the side window. Jesse sat in the wheelchair staring out the windshield. Clayton rapped his knuckles on the glass. "Jesse. Are you getting out?" The Marine ignored him. Clayton moved to the passenger side window and mouthed the words, "what's going on?" Marty shrugged and turned his palms upward. Clayton climbed the stairs and took a seat alongside Miss Kitts, alternating his gaze between the van and the woman.

"Does Jesse expect me to wait another fifty years?"

Clayton didn't reply. She was talking more to herself than she was to him.

"I know why Jesse isn't getting out." Miss Kitts twiddled her fingers. "Look at me, son."

Clayton turned toward her.

"I'm not much to look at nowadays."

Before Clayton could comment, Marty climbed out, opened the side door, and dropped the ramp.

Miss Kitts yelped and sat back in the chair.

Marty stepped inside the van and guided Jesse down the ramp.

Miss Kitts stood, pressed her fingertips to her temple, and closed her eyes. A moment later, she lowered her fingers to her lips. Upon opening her eyes, they carried a glazed look. She took a couple of steps and then stopped, balancing herself on the railing as if she might fall at any second. After taking a deep breath, Miss Kitts descended the steps and met Jesse halfway down the sidewalk. "Jesse…is it really you?"

"Who else were you expecting? The President?" Jesse chuckled.

"But-but-but…" Her gaze dropped to where his legs should have been.

"You didn't know?" Jesse spun in the chair and faced Clayton. His dark eyes were smoldering.

Clayton opened his mouth to speak, but an apology wouldn't be enough. He had let the Marine down and held back a vital fact from Miss Kitts.

Wanda shook her head. "No. I had no idea."

"Take me home, Marty!" snapped Jesse.

Wanda bent down and smacked Jesse's face. It was a resounding smack. "That's not for what you think."

Clayton flinched and stepped back. His worst fear had come to life. Miss Kitts had fire in her eyes and ice in her voice. Was she about to turn on him next?

Jesse repeatedly blinked in silence. His bottom lip trembled.

"That was for believing it made a difference to me about your legs." Wanda straightened. A hint of a smile played at the corners of her mouth. "But I guess that makes us even."

Jesse looked from Wanda to her ankles and back to her.

"You didn't picture me as an old woman," said Wanda, the smile now on full display.

"I still don't." Jesse grinned so wide it nearly cracked his face.

Miss Kitts leaned over and hugged Jesse, and then planted a kiss on his lips. A moment later, she straightened and pulled a necklace up over her head. Clayton recognized Jesse's dog tags and Wanda's class ring. Miss Kitts placed the chain around Jesse's neck. "I've missed you."

Clayton smiled at his parents. Mom was on her cell phone. Dad raised a thumb. As Scot jumped out of the van, Aunt Lucille and Uncle Brian drove up with Jaylynn and the triplets.

A lone trumpet sounded from up the street, drawing Clayton's attention. Fifteen seconds later, snare drums joined in. It was one of his favorite songs— the Marines' Hymn, the Halls of Montezuma. An ensemble of students from Louisa and Fort Gay filed down the street, led by Joetta Hatfield, Mayor of Fort Gay, and Harold Slone, Mayor of Louisa. School band members from both towns followed with cheerleaders leading the way. A massive crowd of townsfolk flanked the bands. Behind the kids marched military men and women in uniform, some carried flags.

"Mercy," whispered Wanda.

"Whose idea was this?" Jesse looked from Marty to Clayton and back to Marty.

Mr. Cecil, the school principal, patted Clayton on the back. "This is amazing."

Frostie snuck up from behind and embraced Jesse with his big burly arms. "Welcome home, brother." He kissed Jesse on the cheek.

Jesse sniffled and pulled his brother in for an extended hug.

Choking back a sudden burst of emotions, Clayton turned in response to someone tapping him on the shoulder. Mr. Cooper stood alongside him, balancing himself on his cane. The man's hand trembled, and his eyes flooded his face with tears.

"You did it, son. I can't believe it, but you did it." Mr. Cooper saluted Clayton.

Clayton sucked in his cheeks to keep his smile from going all the way around his head. Mr. Cooper indeed was capable of crying. It was as if a dam had broken in the man's skull.

Marty whispered in Wanda's ear. Her face lit up, and she giggled. She took hold of the handgrips on Jesse's wheelchair and headed for the main thoroughfare. The band and citizens fell in behind.

At the intersection of Madison Street, Mr. Green greeted Clayton with a hug.

"Mr. Green! How did you—"

"Your grandfather called me a couple of days ago." Mr. Green nodded as Grandpa came out of the crowd and stood alongside Clayton. "I wouldn't have missed this for anything," added Mr. Green.

"Wow!" Scot pumped a fist to the air. The triplets shared fist bumps.

"Yahoo!" shrieked Jaylynn.

Tears streamed down Clayton's face. "Now, I know the taste of happy tears, Grandpa."

"I see," replied Grandpa grinning. "You sure do." He handed Clayton a hankie. Once Clayton had dried his eyes, Grandpa dried his.

Marty leaned over Jesse. "Remember the Medal of Honor that you ignored?" Jesse nodded once. "The offer to go to Washington has been taken off the table." Marty bent over and hugged his brother-in-arms.

Screeching tires pulled everyone's attention in the direction of the bridge. Several black SUVs came to a halt. Men dressed in suits and ties emerged from the vehicles, each wearing an earpiece. The men blocked off the street at Vinson Avenue and Madison Street. They formed a barricade shaped in a horseshoe near the entrance of the bridge.

Whop, Whop, Whop came the sound of helicopter blades.

The crowd gazed upward. A green and white helicopter descended toward the ground. Papers, leaves, confetti, and anything that wasn't tied down flew every which way. Painted on the side of the aircraft was an American flag along with the words UNITED STATES OF AMERICA.

"The President has come to you, Sergeant," added Marty. "That bird is—"

"Marine One," said Wanda. "For my number one Marine!" She kissed Jesse on the lips.

Marine One landed in the middle of the street near the American Legion and Veterans of Foreign Wars. More police cars arrived from the Louisa police department and the Lawrence County Sheriff's Office.

"Wow," said Denver Wade, the boy from the school assembly. He stood alongside Clayton. "This is what I call watching history being made."

"How'd you get here?" Clayton asked.

"The entire school is here. We rode buses." He slapped his palms together. "Thanks for getting us out of school for a day."

Clayton signaled for his brother and cousins to follow him. Together, the kids maneuvered their way through the crowd to where they had a clear view of Marine One. The door opened, and the stairs extended out to the ground. The President stepped out, followed by several men and women. Marines dressed in uniform stood nearby saluting the President.

Clayton looked over to Jesse. Marty reached out to take control of the wheelchair from Miss Kitts only to stop as if he had decided against it. Instead, Marty leaned close to Wanda and whispered in her ear. Wanda's face lit up, and she pushed the wheelchair over to the President. Jesse exchanged salutes with the Commander in Chief.

The school bands broke into playing Hail to the Chief.

"Well, cousin," said Jaylynn. "What's next?"

Clayton squinted. "Huh?"

"I know where there's an abandoned coal mine." Jaylynn wiggled her eyebrows.

"I say we check out the old Lock House on the river in Fort Gay," said Roger. "It's got to be haunted."

"Maybe we'll find a killer clown?" said Jimbo, grinning.

Scot rolled his eyes.

"*Son*, hopefully, the clown won't be naked." Johnny looked over to Roger.

"Shut up," Roger mumbled.

Clayton pulled his little brother in for a hug. He wasn't sure what was next. An abandoned coal mine was tempting. But there was also a part of him that still yearned for answers, answers that required him to venture back to the graveyard. And the wolf, if that's what it was, tugged at his need to know more. Had he and Cagey come to an understanding?

For now, Clayton was content. How long would he be satisfied? He had no idea. The town thrived with friendly people. Even the ghosts, if they had been real or not, brought him and the others no harm. But history indeed surrounded Louisa and supported its core. He was going to love this city. Louisa was home.

ACKNOWLEDGEMENTS

I want to thank my skilled editors who helped make this book a reality: Dennis Doty and Kelly Sohner. Also to Kari Holloway for formatting. I owe a debt of gratitude to a talented cover artist, fellow author John F. Green. I offer a sincere thank you to those who allowed me to write them into the story as characters: Joetta Hatfield, Mayor of Fort Gay, West Virginia, Joe Cecil, Principal Louisa Middle School, Karen Gauze, owner of Dee's Drive-In. I owe my deepest debt of appreciation to my family and friends, far too many to name. Lastly, but most importantly, to my son Scot, for teaching me that sometimes death has nothing to do with dying.

ABOUT THE AUTHOR

Eddie lives in Columbus, Ohio, with his five dogs: four Maltipoos and one Chihuahua. He began writing stories in the fifth grade at the age of ten. He is the father of six sons and one daughter. All are grown. Raising seven kids required made-up bedtime stories. Some, he hopes to bring to life in upcoming books.

Eddie has held several occupations over the years, from a jock at two radio stations, WFGH in Fort Gay, West Virginia, and WUCO in Marysville, Ohio, to being a ventriloquist performing in nightclubs and a cruise ship, as well as being a police officer and a city transit operator.

For more information: www.CrazyFiction.com

Did you enjoy Ghosts of the Big Sandy River?

Online reviews are crucial for indie authors like me. They help bring credibility and make more books discoverable by new readers. Regardless of where you purchased your book, if you could take a few moments and give an honest review at the following website, I'd be very grateful.

Thank you and thanks for reading!
Eddie

www.ingramcontent.com/pod-product-compliance
Lightning Source LLC
Chambersburg PA
CBHW031723170626
46808CB00005B/1860